# THE RETURN
# OF THE DOG TEAM

## WILLIAM W. JOHNSTONE
### With Fred Austin

**PINNACLE BOOKS**
Kensington Publishing Corp.
http://www.kensingtonbooks.com

PINNACLE BOOKS are published by

Kensington Publishing Corp.
850 Third Avenue
New York, NY 10022

All Kensington Titles, Imprints, and Distributed Lines are available at special quantity discounts for bulk purchases for sales pro-
motions, premiums, fund-raising, and educational or institutional
use. Special book excerpts or customized printings can also be
created to fit specific needs. For details, write or phone the
office of the Kensington special sales manager: Kensington
Publishing Corp., 850 Third Avenue, New York, NY 10022,
attn: Special Sales Department, Phone: 1-800-221-2647.

Pinnacle and the P logo Reg. U.S. Pat. & TM Off.

ISBN: 0-7860-1687-6

First Pinnacle Books Printing: September 2005

10 9 8 7 6 5 4 3 2 1

Printed in the United States of America

Dear Readers,

In 1979, I wrote a little book entitled *The Last of the Dog Team*, about a young man named Terry Kovak, a patriotic young American man from small-town Georgia who becomes the most deadly assassin the U.S. military has ever produced. Kovak's killing skills take him from the jungles of Vietnam to the bloody revolutions in South America to the killing fields of Africa.

When *The Last of the Dog Team* was first published in 1980, the world was a much different place. Hardly anyone had ever heard of Saddam Hussein. Iran was just one more Middle Eastern wasteland. Radical Islam was two decades away from being the menace to Western society that it has become. And that mass-murdering son of a bitch Osama Bin Laden was barely out of diapers and doubtless more interested in marrying one of his forty-eight wives than he was in parking a couple of passenger jets on the top floors of the World Trade Center. Our enemies were many in 1980, but they seem pretty tame compared to some of the red hots the United States is faced with today, like that crazy Kim Jong Il in North Korea or the nuke-seeking mad mullahs of Iran.

Needless to say, with the horrific and tragic events of September 11, 2001, the world is a much, much more dangerous place. Americans and American interests overseas, which were once considered untouchable by the dirtbags of the world, are now hard targets. But what the Bin Ladens and Al Qaeda started, Uncle Sam and the good people of America are going to finish.

With this in mind—and at the urging of my wonderful readers who wanted a sequel—I herewith present *The Return of the Dog Team*. But be warned. I've never flinched from portraying bloodshed in my work and I'm not about to start now. So keep this in mind: anyone who knows my work knows that I'm not about killing people. I'm about killing the *right* people.

Respectfully yours,

William W. Johnstone

# One

Kilroy and Vang Bulo were driving east on the Baghdad to Azif highway in East Central Iraq. They were west of Azif, on a ridge overlooking the town. A Coalition truck convoy had been several miles ahead of them. It consisted of a half dozen or so trucks carrying construction supplies and building materials. It was going through the center of town when a bomb went off.

The bomber's timing was off by a few seconds, and so all of the convoy escaped the blast but the last truck in line. It got smeared.

Its fellows knew better than to stop and try to help. There was no help for the straggler. It was gone. Besides, the would-be rescuers would only have ridden into an ambush. The rest of the convoy speeded up and raced out of Azif, east along the highway toward Greentown.

Kilroy pulled over to the side of the road and drove off it, sheltering behind a farmhouse wall. "Bullets, bombs, beheadings—that's Iraq today," Kilroy said, adding, "My kind of place."

Vang Bulo made no reply. None was needed for so patently obvious a statement of fact. Kilroy was made for the boiling pot that was contemporary Iraq. So was Vang Bulo. They were killers, both of them. But not any ordinary, everyday killers. They were Dog Team assassins—a killer elite.

They were in a dark tan SUV. Even idling, the engine had a heavy sound that spoke of plenty of automotive muscle. The windows were rolled up, and the air conditioner was blasting. It was midafternoon of a November day. The rainy season had begun, though it was dry now. Dry and hot.

Kilroy said, "Let's let things settle out before making our run."

Vang Bulo said, "All right."

Kilroy sat behind the wheel, Vang Bulo occupied the passenger seat. Kilroy, an American in his early forties, was raw boned and rangy, with a long, narrow face and eagle-beaked nose. Vang Bulo was a Ugandan, a big black guy, huge, hulking, bald, with a soccer ball–shaped head.

Both men wore sunglasses and civilian clothes, khakis, and hiking boots. They were outfitted with flak jackets and sidearms. Assault weapons and grenades lay near at hand, squirreled away in various places in the vehicle's front compartment. Plenty more weapons lay stowed in the rear, a mini-arsenal's worth.

Those who go forth in Iraq today had better go well armed. Especially a pair of infidel outlanders such as Kilroy and Vang Bulo.

This part of the country was better watered than most of Iraq, brightening the tableland's browns, tans, and grays with welcome flashes of green: a line of palm trees, a weedy field, a trickling stream. The overcast sky was hazy, yellow-white. Hot.

The town of Azif lay in a shallow, saddle-shaped hollow several miles long that dipped between a pair of low, gently rounded ridges running north-south. The SUV stood just below the inside crest of the west ridge.

Not all the wall they sheltered behind was intact. Parts of it had been chewed up, allowing the two men to see through the gaps to the town below, while affording them and their vehicle some cover. Up on the ridge where they were, the landscape was empty of all but a few scattered ruins, some boulders, and trees. No people. There were plenty of people down in town, out on the streets, but their attention was focused near at hand and not on the remote slopes beyond the city limits.

The center of town lay north of the highway. A commercial area of several square city blocks was clustered with two- and three-story concrete buildings that had been built mostly during the reign of Saddam Hussein. Saddam was a Sunni, and Azif was a Sunni stronghold.

The two great branches of Islam are Sunni and Shia. They stand in about the same relationship to each other today as the Catholic and Protestant faiths held toward their opposite numbers during the Hundred Years' War. Most Arabs are Sunni. Most Iranians are Shiites.

Modern-day Iraq was created after World War I by the British—by Winston Churchill, in fact. It is a Frankenstein monster stitched together from three separate and mutually antagonistic groups: the

Kurds in the north; the Sunni Arabs in midcountry; and the Shiites in the south.

The Sunnis make up less than twenty percent of the population, yet have dominated the country (and their countrymen) for the last thirty years—three hundred, if you count back to the Ottoman Empire. The Shiites make up over sixty percent of the population. Now, in any democratic election, the majority Shiites would wield the lion's share of power, a reversal that the once-dominant Sunnis can only regret. The Kurds in the north had a big hurting put on them by Saddam Hussein. They hate the Sunnis, but are willing to form alliances with the Iraqi Shiites.

Next door to Iraq is Iran, a Shiite state ruled by the ayatollahs in the holy city of Qom. Iraq and Iran had a hot war during the 1980s, featuring World War I–style trench warfare and megacasualties on both sides, poison gas attacks, minefields cleared by squads of boy martyrs, and various other horrors.

Sunni Azif was located about thirty miles east of the border with Iran and was of strategic importance in the region. So was nearby Quusaah, a Shiite town located several miles northeast of Azif.

Iraqi democracy's rough rise found the minority Sunnis mounting the most violent insurgent attacks against the American-led coalition. The Shiites hated the Americans, too, but were willing for now to lay back and let the Americans knock off the even more hated Sunnis.

Such a tangle of hostilities can sometimes yield strange alliances. A sinister combine of radical Sunni militiamen, criminal gangs, and even more shadowy

Iranian elements had come into being in the Azif border zone and was making itself objectionable in various underground ways. The Dog Team's Top Dog had sent Kilroy and Vang Bulo to nip it in the bud. Exterminate it, root and branch.

Beyond the handful of city blocks' worth of commercial district lay Old Town, the real center of Azif. It looked like a mound of yellowed sugar cubes. Many of its buildings had been continuously occupied since first being built several hundred years before.

The heart of Old Town was the Red Dome Mosque. Its pointed dome was actually more reddish brown than red. It had three minaret towers and dominated the town's skyline. The mosque's spiritual leader, fiery radical Sunni fundamentalist preacher Imam Hamdi, dominated the region's politics.

The district's slums seethed with thousands of men, women, and children who would have liked nothing better than to see the Shiite-dominated interim government, and especially its American enablers and advisors, boiled in oil. Gangs of violent young males trembled in eager anticipation of the day when the Imam would give them the word to rise up in jihad, or holy war, against the occupying infidels.

Until then, there was still plenty of hell for them to raise against the hated invaders: kidnappings, assassinations, bombings, and other fun and games. Such as this most recent bombing.

A column of smoke rose into the sky. The smoke

was oily black, greasy. It climbed up and up, forming a spindly black funnel. It came from the bombed-out truck that lay on its side in the middle of the road. The gas tank had gone up, and the vehicle had burned quickly, becoming a charred, gutted hulk.

The fire had peaked but was still burning. It must have still been pretty hot, because the crowd ringing it was keeping their distance. Scores of people were massed on the roadway around the blazing wreck. From the ridgetop vantage point, they were blurred, antlike figures. The swarm was restless, agitated, its members streaming back and forth in constant motion around the blast site.

"Party time," Kilroy said, indicating the crowd at the bomb site. "They haven't had this much fun since the last time they blew up the U.S. embassy."

"There's no U.S. embassy in Azif," Vang Bulo pointed out.

"Uncle Sam will have to build one, then, so they can blow it up."

"They seem to be doing all right at blowing things up without it."

It was warm inside the SUV, close, even with the air conditioner running. Vang Bulo's face was misted with sweat. He took off his visorlike sunglasses. He was slightly pop eyed, with yellowed eyeballs. He squeezed his eyes shut, rubbing them with his thumb and forefinger.

Kilroy continued to watch the mob swarm around the wreckage. "Probably Waleed Tewfiq's militiamen. They're the ones who shot up that mail truck last week, the bastards." He and the other exchanged glances. Officially they were employed by a private contractor to secure the safety of the mail and ensure that it got delivered to U.S. bases. That was their cover. It was a good front for a Dog Team assassin duo.

The fact that Red Dome militiamen had indeed shot up a mail truck recently gave the Dogs a plausible reason for operating in the area.

Above the roadway, on a number of buildings fronting the highway, figures appeared on the rooftops.

Kilroy said, "Spotters."

The spotters waved their arms over their heads and shouted to attract the attention of the mob below. Once they had it, they began gesturing and pointing toward the east.

A new ferment stirred the crowd. They stopped surging toward the blast site and began moving away from it, arrowing away in all directions. Scattering. The swarm broke up into smaller groups, and those groups into individual figures, all putting distance between themselves and the wreck.

A speck appeared in midair above the eastern ridge, making a beeline west toward town. It cut the distance rapidly, a fast-closing blur that resolved itself into an aircraft: a helicopter.

An A-130 Spectre gunship. A formidable machine.

It neared Azif, slowing, then hovering high above the roadway blast site. It hung in the air to one side of the smoke column, tearing it up with the propwash from its rotors. Its massive shadow crawled across the ground.

The gunship had enough firepower to level the whole town. The area below was now empty of all but a handful of people, most of the crowd having scattered before the copter's arrival. Only the most hard-core fanatics remained, shaking their fists at the aircraft. Nearby, others huddled in doorways or crowded, hunched, in alley mouths, craning around the corners of buildings, heads tilted back, looking up.

The propwash broke up more of the smoke column, forcing it back down toward the ground, hazing the streets below. Obscuring the visibility. Buildings faded to vague outlines in the haze. Haze brought concealment, anonymity. Emboldening the local red hots. A couple of rooftop spotters opened fire on the gunship.

Small-arms fire went pop-pop-pop. Muzzle flashes speared through the blue-gray haze. The aircraft returned fire with a few bursts of light machine-gun fire, merely swatting at a few flies. It was the lightest and least they had, to minimize collaterals and avoid bringing down the buildings. Clouds of dust were kicked up by the rounds ripping into the flat concrete rooftops.

The sniping stopped. No telling if the shooters had been taken down or not.

Vang Bulo nodded with satisfaction. "That cleared the streets of the last diehards."

Kilroy said, "Good. With those idiots out of the way, all we have to do is wait until the gunship leaves. Otherwise, they might shoot our ass. Friendly fire kills you just as dead."

Suddenly, a line of fire jetted from somewhere deep in Old Town. It arched up and over the rooftops, trailing smoke, closing on the gunship. Kilroy puckered his lips as if to whistle, but no sound came out. He said, "Rocket attack!"

The gunship banked steeply, narrowly avoiding the

rocket, which streamed on past it. The sharp, sudden maneuver put added strain on the engines and rotors, increasing the volume of its angry hornet buzzing.

The rocket continued onward, arching south, plummeting to earth on the open, empty flat about a quarter mile south of town. It struck with a boom.

The men in the SUV peered toward the rocket's point of origin. Kilroy said, "Looks like it came from the mosque."

Vang Bulo nodded. "I'm sure it did. Look there, you can see that the rocket's trail points straight down to one of the minarets."

Slowly, ominously, the gunship turned in place, pointing its nose toward the mosque with the brick-red dome. There was deadly intent in its slow, deliberate movements. But the gunship never made the fatal strike. It hung in place, holding its fire. The pause stretched past the point where action was still an option.

Kilroy sighed, a touch deflated. "No action today. Game called on account of politics."

Vang Bulo agreed. "A bad mistake, not hitting the mosque. Imam Hamdi is a fanatic, and Waleed Tewfiq is a cutthroat with a nose for other people's weaknesses. The surest way to encourage them to attack is to let them get away with something."

Kilroy shrugged. His attitude said, What're you going to do? That's the way it is. "You know it, I know it, the guys in the chopper up there know it, and I suspect that even CENTCOM might know it by now. The only ones who don't get it are the politicians in Washington—but they're calling the shots," he said.

Vang Bulo said, "Not all of them."

They knew what that meant. The Dog Team was strictly an Army operation, an above-top-secret one at that, from whose chain of command civilian politicians and administrators were excluded.

Kilroy indicated the gunship. "I can tell you what's going on up there right now," he said. "Base told them not to return fire on the mosque. The chopper crew is repeating their request for permission to do so. Base is telling them no. Too much risk of collateral damage. Of course, if they get their tail shot off, that's all right."

Abruptly, the gunship stood down, turning until it pointed east. It quit the scene, flying back to base.

"It's called 'winning hearts and minds,' I guess," Kilroy said, shaking his head. "Depressing."

Vang Bulo tsk-tsked.

Kilroy shook off his mood like a wet dog shaking off water. "Time to move, before the gunship is so far away that the locals come back out again."

His hands busy on the controls, he put the SUV in drive, rolling out from behind the wall toward the road. The vehicle lurched and jounced. Weapons and gear had previously been secured to prevent their bouncing around loose.

The SUV clambered heavily on to the blacktop road, rocking on its springs. Tires bit deep once planted on hard pavement. Kilroy pointed the vehicle downhill and stepped on the gas. The SUV swooped along the downgrade, plunging toward town. It moved along at a nice clip, not racing exactly, but not dawdling, either, picking up momentum during the descent.

Kilroy gripped the wheel in both hands, leaning forward. "NASCAR's got nothing on this!"

Wrecks began to appear on both sides of the road. Wrecks of other bombed, burned-out vehicles, some sieved with bulletholes. They dotted the roadside like boulders. The closer the road got to town, the more wrecks.

The road wasn't in such great shape, either. It was mottled with bad patches that were pocked by bullet holes and cracked by bombs. The SUV's tires thrummed over them. Like the wrecks, the bad patches increased as Azif neared.

The vehicle closed in on the blast site, as yet unnoticed by the locals, who were beginning to emerge from doorways and from behind cover to once more take to the streets. Their attention was on the gunship dwindling in the southeast.

The truck in the middle of the road had mostly burned itself out now. A thin blue-gray haze that looked like big-city smog blurred the scene.

Some rooftop spotters fired off rounds in the general direction of the now-distant gunship. Figures emerged from the sidelines into the open. They stood facing the direction in which the aircraft had flown. Their backs were to the western branch of the highway, so they didn't notice the onrushing SUV until it was almost upon them. Their shouts and shots had served to drown out the sound of its approach.

The vehicle slowed, weaving around some potentially axle-busting potholes cratering the pavement. It swerved to avoid a wagon wheel that lay in the middle of the road like some absurd relic of old Wild West days.

It was a donkey cart wheel. Two-wheeled wooden donkey carts were in wide use throughout Iraq, not only in the outlying rural areas, but even in the cities, including Baghdad. That made them a popular choice as bomb-delivery vehicles.

That was what happened here. A donkey cart loaded with explosives had stood at the crossroads, waiting for the target—the convoy—to arrive. But for some reason or another, the cart had been delayed until all but the last truck in line had already driven to safety.

The bomber had probably used a cell phone to detonate the IED, or improvised explosive device. That was military jargon for a bomb. The Red Dome Mosque militia was partial to cell-phone detonators. They'd picked up the trick from Al Qaeda bombmasters who were working with the Sunni insurgency. For balance, the Shiite insurgents were getting their lessons in advanced terrorism from experts sent by Tehran.

The blast had punched the side of the truck, splitting it open at the seams. The cab had accordioned, pulping its occupants. The gas tank had ruptured, blown, and burned. Tires had melted into pools of molten rubber.

The SUV closed in on the crossroads. It was about thirty yards away when the militiamen first noticed it. Most of those out on the roadway were militiamen, and even those who weren't were armed. They were grouped in a loose arc around the wreck, standing between the SUV and the open road east out of town.

They turned around, leveling their weapons, trying to get them into play. Kilroy didn't give them any time to do that. He stepped on the gas. The SUV picked up speed, bulleting toward them. Contact was imminent, a matter of split seconds.

The militiamen broke and scattered to avoid the oncoming vehicle. Their shouts of surprise and outrage were clearly audible to the pair in the SUV, even through the bulletproof glass and over the noise of the engine. For a moment, the scene seemed frozen into a snapshot. Militiamen goggled, their mouths gaping. Kilroy was able to make out individual faces.

Among them was a man in a yellow turban. He wore round glasses and a beard, and was short and stocky. He ran to the side, short stumpy legs working as he dashed to safety. Kilroy had the crazy feeling he'd seen him before but couldn't place him. Besides, things were moving too fast.

Ahead, a youth in a red and white–checked kaffiyeh head scarf raised a rifle to his shoulder and pointed it at Kilroy in the driver's seat. He was slight and thin faced, with hollow eyes, sunken cheeks, and a wispy beard.

It was too late for the youth to shoot. He had time only to throw down the rifle and dive to the right of the oncoming vehicle, throwing himself into a ditch. The SUV's right front bumper brushed against the tail of his coat before he was clear.

The militiamen had cleared the way, but the road ahead was littered with debris, including some tub-sized scraps of twisted metal that glowed a dull red. Kilroy swerved to avoid them. Tires squealed. SUVs run toward top-heaviness and have a tendency to tip on too-tight curves. This vehicle was heavier than most, and with special fittings. Kilroy held his breath as all four wheels stayed on the asphalt.

The road was open. The SUV accelerated. Some militiamen fired at its fleeing form. A jackhammer pounding stitched the vehicle's rear, hot rounds foiled by the vehicle's armor plating. The SUV had been customized for Iraqi motoring. Armor plate and bulletproof glass, with the chassis and frame specially reinforced to bear the load. Heavy-duty springs and shocks. Hidden gunports in the sides and rear. Solid tires, puncture proof, bullet immune. The engine was a turbocharged beast, a massive mill of high-velocity horsepower.

Kilroy punched the accelerator, and the SUV zoomed forward. More militiamen were firing at it, but their rounds ranged far wide of the target. Bursts sounded, none hitting, sleeting harmlessly through the air.

A tree stood south of the roadside, a stunted one whose branches formed a gnarly, spiky canopy. Snagged in the middle of it was a donkey's severed head and neck.

"A waste of a perfectly good jackass," Kilroy said. "I get the same feeling myself sometimes."

The SUV barreled east, toward Greentown, a fortified Coalition compound several miles farther down the road.

Kilroy, uneasy, said, "Did you see that guy in the yellow turban? I think that was Waleed Tewfiq—"

"The militia chief himself? I doubt it," Vang Bulo said.

"A yellow turban is supposed to be one of his trademarks."

"There are lot of yellow turbans around."

"I only caught a glimpse, but it sure looked like him."

"Too bad you didn't run him down."

"I would've, if I'd recognized him in time," Kilroy said. He seemed downcast.

Vang Bulo tried to accent the positive. "There's always another time."

Kilroy said, "The next time I see him, I'll shoot his ass."

# Two

Kilroy and Vang Bulo stayed east on the highway, passing Greentown and continuing on to Border Base Foxtrot. A line of brown foothills stretched north-south along the eastern horizon, marking the Iraq/Iran border. The terrain marked the difference between the two countries. The land on the Iraq side was mostly flat. The foothills signaled the advent of the more rugged, hilly Iranian landscape.

The highway continued eastbound, edging the foothills, terminating at a gap that provided a natural corridor between the regions. The gap had been dynamited during the run-up to the Gulf War between the two countries, filling the pass with countless tons of rubble and sealing it off from incursions by either side.

The main pass was destroyed, but the hills were threaded with a number of smaller valleys, clefts, and gorges providing access to either side. The area had been a haunt of smugglers and bandits since the days of the Babylonian Empire.

The locale where Border Base Foxtrot was sited

had been an Iraqi army outpost under Saddam Hussein. It was close enough to the border to keep an eye on it, but far enough to be out of range of sniper, mortar, or rocket fire from the hills.

The Coalition used the base for the same reason Saddam had: to monitor both sides of the border. Iran's ambition to possess atomic weapons had ratcheted up the tension between itself and the West. Iran had a large pool of sympathizers among the Iraqi Shiites.

Foxtrot was a border station, tasked to watch both sides of the border and suppress the movement of weapons and fighters across it. Should Iran ever decide to make an incursion into Iraq at this key corridor, the base would be a frontline bulwark against the onslaught.

The base sat on a low rise several hundred yards south of the highway. A gravel road connected highway and base. The ground surrounding the base was open and flat, with little cover and few places for ambushers to lurk. This fact helped minimize mortar and rocket attacks from insurgents, hazards from which few coalition bases were exempt.

The outpost was well fortified behind concentric rings of ever-stiffer defenses. It was bounded by alternating layers of barbed wire and metal chainlink fences. The inner redoubt was ringed by high, concrete slab antiblast barriers designed to withstand car and truck suicide bombers. Watchtowers equipped with heavy-duty machine guns covering all angles of approach stood at all four corners of the site.

Foxtrot housed several combat infantry and light cavalry units and a helicopter base, all ready to respond swiftly to action on the border or in Azif and Quusaah. It was a lot to cover, and the facility was overstretched, but they did the job with what they had. They were results oriented.

The tan SUV carrying Kilroy and Vang Bulo arrived at the base in late afternoon. It had to pass through a series of checkpoints.

It halted at the main gate, which was manned by a squad of military police. A senior MP came around to the driver's side of the SUV.

Kilroy lowered the window. Heat came pouring in. He presented his and Vang Bulo's IDs, authorization papers, and clearances. They were heavily credentialed, with all kinds of top-priority clearances and total-access passes.

The MP gave them a close inspection, then radioed base security for verification. Security certified that the newcomers were okay. The MP returned the documents. The gates opened, and he waved the SUV through.

Indicating it to another MP, he said, "There go a couple of heavyweights."

"I'll say! I don't know about the driver, but that black guy weighed three hundred pounds if he's an ounce," the other said.

The senior MP gestured impatiently. "What I mean is that those two have some major juice for a pair of civilians. Those clearances were authorized by the top brass in country."

The other was unimpressed. "That don't mean much. There are lots of civilians with plenty of clout walking around in Iraq today. Private security contractors, bureaucrats, businessmen, reconstruction effort officials—"

"Those two didn't look like bureaucrats," the first said. "They looked like action men."

"They came to the right place."

The SUV proceeded through a series of checkpoints before entering the base proper. A wide open central area was ringed by an armory, a motor pool, administrative and staff headquarters buildings, barracks, a mess hall, and a training area. Some of the buildings were solid masonry construction left over from the Saddam era. They gave the base a more solid, permanent feel, as compared to other bases, where the structures were mostly tents put up by the Coalition.

The scene had that air of purposeful activity typical of a combat zone outpost. And although the Iraq war had been officially declared won and over several years ago, make no mistake—Iraq was still a combat zone. This time, the name of the game was counterinsurgency warfare.

The SUV pulled over to the side, out of the way of ongoing operations. Kilroy and Vang Bulo got out. Kilroy held a clipboard under one arm. Vang Bulo got into the driver's seat after first adjusting it to give himself some legroom. He drove the machine to the motor pool to give it a once-over to make sure that the Azif militiamen's bullets hadn't done any damage.

Kilroy started across the parade ground on foot, angling toward the intelligence office. The sun was low in the west, a dull red-orange ball whose upper half was hidden by gray clouds streaking the horizon. It looked like it felt: hot, sullen. Long shadows slanted across the landscape.

The intelligence office was housed in a canvas tent. The senior officer on duty was Captain Bricker. His face was long, narrow and squared off at the hairline and jawline. He was well named, thought Kilroy, since his face was shaped like a brick standing on its short end.

Bricker wore thick, square-rimmed glasses. His desk looked like an oversized card table, and he sat on a metal folding chair. Power cords and cables snaked across the floor, bundled at junction boxes and USB multiport hub connectors. Electricity was supplied by a portable generator outside the tent.

Kilroy reported on what he'd seen in Azif. It was not required of him. Bricker was nowhere in Kilroy's chain of command and had no jurisdiction over him. He was outranked by Kilroy, too, although he didn't know that, since the information was sealed away deep in the Army's most above-top-secret recesses.

All Bricker knew was that Kilroy had some major-league military connections and that he was not only authorized but required to assist him in any way possible, should Kilroy make such a request. That was all he needed to know. Bricker hadn't become an intelligence officer by not knowing when not to ask questions.

Kilroy gave a quick, brief verbal report of what he'd seen in Azif, minimizing his and Vang Bulo's mad dash through town. He thought it was important, or at least useful, to pass along the information that he'd seen a man in a yellow turban who could have been Red Dome Mosque militia leader Waleed Tewfiq in the locale of the roadside bombing.

Bricker showed real interest. "Waleed's a major pain in the ass, and it's been getting worse every day."

He opened a folder, laying it out on his desk. It contained a handful of glossy black-and-white photographs. He pushed one across the table to Kilroy, who picked it up and examined it. It was a head and shoulders shot showing a round-faced bearded man with glasses and a dark-colored turban. He was squinting and scowling.

Kilroy said, "I only got a glimpse, but that looks like him. On the other hand, you see a lot of guys who look like that running around in Azif."

"It probably was him," Bricker said. "He turns up at a lot of terror scenes. He's careful to avoid being directly linked to them, though."

Kilroy nodded. "I just thought I'd pass the information along, give you a heads-up."

"And we appreciate it, Mr. Kilroy."

Kilroy returned the photo to the other. Bricker slipped it back in the file, closed the folder, and rose.

"I'll notify the appropriate persons that Waleed was observed at the scene," Bricker said. "Not that it'll do much good. He'll be long gone. Probably hiding out at the mosque. He's safe there. Still, who knows? He might be hanging around at the bomb site, trying to whip up a crowd against our guys."

Kilroy pushed back his chair and stood up. "One more thing. I didn't stick around to take too close a look, but it seemed like the militiamen were sporting a lot of firepower. Those weapons looked new, too."

Bricker nodded, tilting his head so that reflected light shone off his glasses, making them opaque. "The Iranians are shipping them across the border.

Times past, they only sold guns to their Iraqi Shiite counterparts, but no more. In the last few months, they've been selling them to the Sunnis, too."

"Imam Hamdi at the Red Dome Mosque is no friend of Iran—or the Shia," Kilroy pointed out.

Bricker said, "Neither is Waleed Tewfiq. They hate the Shiites, and vice versa. But both sides are willing to overlook their age-old animosities and work together when it comes to killing us. Tehran would like to see an armed Sunni uprising against the Coalition. That way, Iran wins no matter what. The more slaughter on both sides, the better for them—and the Shiite government they figure will ultimately take power in Iraq."

Kilroy said casually, "I've heard things are pretty hairy up in the hills on the border. Lots of shootouts and ambushes between gunrunning gangs." He'd more than heard it, he knew it for a fact, because for the last two weeks he and Vang Bulo had been making night raids into the hills, stirring up trouble. He'd made the remark to see if he could fish up any new information.

Bricker was tight around the mouth. "The border is forbidden territory for us—the Coalition, that is. Our troops are not allowed to cross the border. Or even get too close to it, for fear that they might get fired on from the hills and create an international incident."

He made a pushing gesture, as if warding something away, like a cat pushing away a bowl of food it finds unappealing. He went on, "There's been some vicious firefights up there recently. Several gunrunners have been robbed and killed. Some kind of a turf war between smuggling gangs, we think."

Kilroy said, "Maybe the militiamen got tired of paying for weapons and decided to just take them."

Bricker shook his head. "Nobody kills the goose that lays the golden eggs. Besides, Waleed is tight with Hassani Akkad."

"Akkad? The local Al Capone?"

"He's that and more," Bricker said. "Leader of the biggest criminal gang in the province. Gunrunning, kidnapping, smuggling, murder, you name it and he deals in it. Akkad's connected on both sides of the border. He's the middleman between the Iranian gunrunners and the militiamen. We'd sure like to get our hands on him."

Kilroy said, "If I hear tell of him, I'll let you know."

"If you hear tell of him, run. He's a bad man to mess with," Bricker said.

Kilroy looked suitably impressed. "Need me for anything else?"

The other shook his head no, then reconsidered and looked up. "Not unless you've got something else to tell me."

"That's all for today, Captain."

Bricker paused, then said, "You'd be well advised to stay clear of the border area. It's a hot zone there now. The migratory Bedouin tribals who graze their herds on both sides of the border have all cleared out. A man could get his head shot off just for sticking it up and taking a look around."

"You could say the same about Azif or Quusaah. Or Baghdad."

"Quite true, Mr. Kilroy."

"I'm careful about where I stick my head. It's not much, but I'd like to keep it all in one piece."

Kilroy picked up his clipboard, said so long, and

went out. He wondered how much Bricker knew or suspected. The intelligence officer was a bright guy. Bright enough to stay out of things that were above his pay grade. He had to know that Kilroy was more than merely an expediter for Mecury Transport Systems, his official cover. The high-powered clearances and authorizations carried by Kilroy gave him unlimited entrée to virtually all civil and military sites in Iraq.

But Bricker knew nothing of the Dog Team or Kilroy's role in it. Or did he? Dog Team data were disseminated solely on a need-to-know basis. For all Kilroy knew, Bricker could be a clandestine Dog Team operative under deep cover, so deep that Kilroy's handlers thought it unnecessary to inform him of same. Which was only good sense: you can't betray what you don't know.

Kilroy didn't think Bricker was on the Dogs. He didn't radiate that aura of the carnivore typical of action men. But he could be on the team—there was always that possibility. It was part of the wheels-within-wheels nature of clandestine service. You tended to see wheels even when there weren't any. A hazard of the profession.

Kilroy dismissed the subject from his mind and moved on to the next errand, one that was directly related to and helped confirm his cover identity as a mail-and-parcel delivery troubleshooter for Mercury Transport. He went to the base post office/message center, which was housed in a Quonset-shaped tent. Sgt. Teed was on duty, baggy-eyed and bassett-hound-faced. He knew Kilroy from past dealings related to the mails. The beautiful part of the cover story was that so many noncombat jobs had been farmed out to private civilian contractors, it made perfect sense for someone like Kilroy to be untangling the knotted mail-delivery system.

Teed noted that recent deliveries had been spotty. He spoke, not confrontationally, but with the air of a man stating a fact.

Kilroy said, "It's backed up at the distribution center farther west. Azif's become a real bottleneck, so we're sending our shipments along alternate routes. In a few days the slowdown should be cleared up, and the mail back to its normal schedule."

"Good," the noncom said. "Troops sure count on that mail from back home. Especially out here, isolated from everything else. Not everybody uses e-mail. There's no substitute for that handwritten note from someone back home. When the mail is stalled or stopped, morale sure takes a nosedive."

Kilroy went to work. His clipboard carried a sheaf of papers: manifests, parcel post numbers, receipted package tags, mail sorting serial numbers. He and Teed went down various lists item by item, comparing notes, checking and double-checking. Kilroy had to perform all the duties of a mail-delivery expediter to maintain a credible cover. He took out a pocket notepad and began making some entries.

The noncom said, "No fancy Palm computers for you?"

"They don't last long out here. Sand gets into them," Kilroy said.

"Don't I know it."

"Besides, I never had a notepad crash on me."

Kilroy generated his quota of paperwork and made ready to move on. He said, "Where's the mail truck that got shot up?"

Teed shrugged. "Motor pool, I guess."

Kilroy finalized his paperwork and exited. The sun was lower in the sky so that the upper half of the orange-red globe showed above a horizontal band of slate gray clouds.

The base was busy, humming. Helicopters landed and took off from the landing pad. Lines of Humvee patrol vehicles returned to base while other patrols departed. Chow time was near, and food smells wafted out of the mess hall.

Kilroy's stomach rumbled, reminding him that he was a long time between meals. Ignoring his hunger, he crossed to the motor pool, which was made up of a separate compound in and to one side of the base. It was bordered by an eight-foot-high chain-link fence topped with rolls of concertina barbed wire. The main gates opened on the bare earth of a gravel-strewn, oil-stained yard. Grouped around it were vehicles of all types: trucks, forklifts, Humvees, even some civilian cars and SUVs.

A prefab steel building served as a multibayed garage. In front of it stood several sets of fuel pumps for gas and diesel fuel. Groups of fatigue-clad troops were clustered around different spots in the yard, carrying out various automotive-related tasks and chores.

The tan SUV stood in one of the garage bays. The hood was open, and Vang Bulo stood with tools in hand, leaning over the engine. In another bay, at the opposite end of the shop, a couple of Special Forces guys and some mechanics were installing some customized armor plating, gun ports, and mountings on a Humvee.

Vang Bulo's back was to Kilroy, and so he was unaware of his approach. He had his head deep in engine innards. Kilroy was going to hail him but thought better of it; the big Ugandan looked busy, and Kilroy didn't want to disrupt his concentration.

Besides, he had other business to transact. Mercury Transport business. Officially, Vang Bulo was carried on the Mercury employee rolls as an assistant. In reality, it meant that he was exempt from having to fill out all but the most minimal paperwork relating to the cover job.

Kilroy went around to a side shed adjacent to the garage. It was a small hut, barely able to fit a table and the man who sat behind it in a chair. A couple of filing cabinets lined the walls, further shrinking the space.

Kilroy stayed in the open doorway facing Sgt. Cowdery, the man in charge of the motor pool. Cowdery was jowly, with a paunch. His clean-shaven face was flushed red under a sheen of sweat. A lock of oily black hair emerged from below his cap, falling on his forehead. Sweat pasted it in place. Pale eyes, almost colorless, contrasted with his florid red complexion.

He was sitting in a chair with his face shoved close to the grille of a portable desk fan. It was a revolving fan, so he kept shifting around in his chair, trying to keep his face aligned with the airstream.

When he couldn't ignore Kilroy any longer, he sank bank in his chair, the springs groaning under him. Kilroy flashed his photo ID at the other, holding it in front of Cowdery's face so he could see it. He didn't want Cowdery putting his sweaty fingers on it. Cowdery flicked his eyes at it, giving it barely a glance. He nodded, signaling Kilroy to continue.

Kilroy identified himself as the Mercury man and said, "A mail truck was shot up the other day. I'm here to make arrangements for its disposition."

"It's disposed of," Cowdery said.

"You got rid of it?"

"Nope. It's out back. What I mean, it's a total wreck. Lucky the driver was able to get it this far. Lucky for him, that is. You don't want to be stuck out alone on the highway with a dead machine. It was shot up pretty bad and leaking coolant and oil like crazy, but somehow it limped in to base. The engine's all fused up now. A mass of metal."

Kilroy said, "Guess I'll have it towed or hauled out on a flatbed."

Cowdery started to shrug his shoulders but gave up the attempt for lack of energy or interest. "Why bother?"

Kilroy smiled thinly. "Mercury Transport's just like the Army. They've got a system, and that's how things are done. If the rules say that the vehicle was to be brought back to its issuing depot in Baghdad, then that's how it has to be done. Red tape, you know."

"I know," Cowdery said, nodding so vigorously that the drop of sweat fell off the tip of his nose. "If I spent half as much time working on engines as I do filling out forms, well, there'd be plenty more mechanized stock rolling, believe you me."

"Where's the truck?"

"In back of the garage," Cowdery said, jerking a thumb in its direction.

"I can find it," Kilroy said quickly. "Don't bother to get up."

Cowdery had made no indication of rising from

his chair, but Kilroy had tossed that in as a little zinger. If Cowdery took offense, he gave no notice of it. He gripped the table edge with both hands and leaned forward, shoving his face toward the desk fan, looking like a dog sticking its head out of a car window to catch the breeze.

Kilroy circled around to the rear of the garage. A number of wrecks were heaped back there. One of them was the mail truck. Actually, it was more of a panel van than truck. It was shot up pretty bad. If it hadn't been armored, it wouldn't have made it. Neither would the driver. He'd been wounded, but not critically, and had already been airlifted back to a hospital in the Green Zone.

Cowdery was right: the van was a total loss. It was good for little more than scrap and would cost more to haul it away than to leave it here. But that was procedure. He hadn't been kidding when he'd said that Mercury Transport had a bureaucratic system. And it wasn't his place to interfere with that system where it didn't directly affect his real job, the one for which his role as cargo expediter was just cover. His job as Dog Team assassin.

He went back to the shed and told Cowdery that he'd arrange for the wreck to be hauled away. The noncom didn't much care. His mission was to keep vehicles running, not look after those that were already defunct. Especially ones that weren't Army.

Kilroy crossed the yard to the garage where Vang Bulo was working on the SUV. He said, "She going to live?"

"Affirmative," Vang Bulo said. "The armor plating was barely dented. It held up. It can take plenty more. I had her up on the rack just in case, to check to make sure there was no damage from stray slugs."

"And—?"

"There wasn't."

"So she's ready for action."

"That's right."

"Good. Tonight we'll make a special delivery," Kilroy said.

Vang Bulo said, "I'm looking forward to it."

"Let's head over to the mess hall and get some chow."

"You go on ahead. I've still got some tweaking I want to do on the engine."

Kilroy exited the garage. The Special Forces guys had finished what they were doing on the Humvee and had gone outside. Somewhere, somebody had found a wooden door and painted a human-sized outline on one side of it. It was propped up against a couple of fifty-gallon drums, and the Special Forces guys were throwing knives at it.

Kilroy paused to take a look. There were three of them. Throwing knives accurately is a difficult skill to master. Kilroy had tried his hand at it more than once, but the skill had eluded him.

It was the same for two of the Special Forces guys. They had trouble getting the knives to stick in the wood, never mind about actually hitting the target. The knives stuck in about half the time they threw. The other half, the blades bounced off, clattering.

The third was a wizard with the blade, though. He was a big guy, in his early twenties, built like a pro football linebacker. Big, but he could move. His name tag read: IRELAND.

You could tell by his form that he had the art

down cold. Each time he threw, the blade landed square in a vital spot of the outlined human target: between the eyes, in the heart, or in the belly.

While Kilroy was watching, Ireland flung a blade that landed dead square in the middle of the figure's throat. The thin, black blade struck with a twang and hung there quivering.

Kilroy said, "Bravo."

The Special Forces trio turned to look at him. Their expressions weren't unfriendly, but they weren't exactly warm, either. They were guarded, waiting to see what would come next. The stranger wore civilian clothes, and civilians were always an unknown quantity. Was he just being friendly, or was he some kind of asshole with an agenda or something to prove?

Kilroy indicated the dagger in the target. "You have talent."

"Thanks," Ireland said. "Want to try your hand?"

"Not me," Kilroy demurred. "The only knife I'm handy with is a knife and fork, and I'm going to try my hand with them in the mess hall. But I appreciate talent when I see it."

He nodded pleasantly and moved on, crossing the yard to the main gates.

The Special Forces trio watched him go. They were all noncoms. Sgt. Webb Tillotson was the senior man. He was forty, sandy haired, clean shaven, neat, compactly muscled. A communications expert.

Sgt. Hector Garza was in his mid-thirties, a bull of a man with fierce black brows and mustache, a weapons specialist.

Sgt. Steve Ireland's Green Beret was more newly minted. He was six feet two, broad shouldered, athletic. He'd played college ball and been named an All-American. When he was a boy back on his family's ranch in Arizona, a hand named Latigo had taught him how to throw a knife. He'd spent hundreds of hours practicing, throwing knives into targets chalked on the side of an outbuilding. But that was long ago and far away. Or at least it felt that way to him. Here in Iraq, all else in the outside world seemed long ago and far away.

The three were members of the same team: Operational Detachments Alpha 586. ODA 586, as such Special Forces units are called.

The team had recently been brought in to the base to carry out a near-future mission in the border area. A mission whose nature was as yet unknown to them. But they knew it would be something hairy. That was why they'd been called in.

Webb Tillotson's narrowed eyes followed Kilroy's dwindling form. "I've seen him before."

Garza said, "That's Kilroy."

Tillotson looked at him, surprised. "You know him?"

"Not personally, but he's around. He's like a postal inspector or something."

"Or something." Tillotson laughed, but his eyes were thoughtful as they looked in the direction Kilroy had gone.

Garza said, "What does that mean?"

"I've seen him before," Tillotson said again. "Under unforgettable circumstances. And they didn't include working for the post office."

Steve Ireland, interested, said, "How so?"

Tillotson said, "About ten years ago, I was serving in the Balkans, on a peacekeeping mission around

Srebenica. It was a real shithole. Ethnic cleansing, massacres, mass rapes, you name it. Warlords, crime bosses, and what seemed like every cutthroat in the region were all fighting and double-crossing each other. With the usual innocent civilians caught in the middle and getting whipsawed by all sides.

"One day, Kilroy arrives from out of nowhere on the scene. Only his name wasn't Kilroy then. I forget what it was, but it's not important, since it was fake. Kilroy's probably not his name, either. He was in civvies then, like now, but you could smell military coming off from him from a mile away.

"He ran around with a couple of local wild men. Real maniacs, outlaw types, looking like Balkan mountain men who hadn't been down out of the hills in years, and maybe they hadn't. Stone killers. The word came down from the top—and I do mean the top—that Kilroy was to be allowed to come and go as he pleased. Which was a good way to get dead in that place at that time."

Garza, doubtful, said, "If it was the same guy."

"It's him. He's not the type you forget. Anyway, right around that time, Vukan Maledar, the Serb death squad leader, got knocked off. Assassinated, shot with a high-powered rifle. It was a hell of a shot—caught him going into church on the occasion of his first-born son's christening. The town—hell, the whole region—was in an uproar, but the shooter escaped. That night, Kilroy, or whatever the hell he was calling himself, was driven to an airfield and flown out at night. The plane was in place for that one purpose, to take him away."

Steve Ireland said, "Your point being that Kilroy was the shooter?"

"Maledar was giving everybody a hard time, not least of all including our troops. He was a real road-block to progress," Tillotson said. "Kilroy cleared that road. He's a shooter, a big-game hunter."

Garza was unconvinced. "You know this? Or is it just some war story you heard?"

"A buddy of mine was in the car that took Kilroy to the airfield," Tillotson said, "and that's a fact."

There was a silence.

"Interesting," Steve Ireland said at last. "What's he doing here? Think he's connected to our mission?"

Tillotson said, "I could answer that better if I knew what our mission is."

Garza said, "Don't be in such a hurry. We'll find out soon enough, and when we do, it's sure to be a ballbreaker."

"One thing's for sure," Tillotson said. "With Kilroy here, something's cooking. Something big."

"I still think he's with the postal service," Garza said.

Tillotson said, "Dead letter office, maybe."

# Three

On the night after the supply truck was blown up in Azif, Fadleel the smuggler and chieftain and about ten or so of his kinsmen were moving a load of contraband weapons across the border from Iran into Iraq. The transfer point was a *wadi*, a dry watercourse, in the rugged hills east of the Azif highway terminus.

Fadleel was heavyset, with graying hair and a beard. He was heavily armed, with a Kalashnikov assault rifle and a pair of 9-mm pistols worn low on his hips, gunslinger style. They had to be worn low. His big belly ensured that. Even so, his stomach slopped over the top of the gunbelts.

He was part of a clan of Iranian border hoppers that had been specializing in smuggling for generations. Their business was moving contraband back and forth across the border: gold, drugs, women, whatever was in demand. These days it was weapons.

His men were all related to him, being nephews or cousins at one or two removes. They were bound to him by the sacred ties of blood and family obligation. That's how business was done throughout the region.

Fadleel and company were holding a midnight rendezvous with their Iraqi counterparts, members of Hassani Akkad's criminal gang.

The *wadi*'s winding path through the hills connected both sides of the border. It was one of many such routes that honeycombed the district, making it a smuggler's paradise.

The meeting place was a wide spot in the *wadi*. It was a lonely site, a sand- and dirt-floored gully snaking through a maze of rocky ridges. An overcast sky screened out the stars and moon.

Two pickup trucks stood side by side on the *wadi* floor, their beds filled with crates of weapons. A handful of men, gunrunners, stood around the trucks, smoking cigarettes, talking in low voices, waiting for the transaction to be concluded. Fadleel's men, all well armed. Vigilant.

What looked like a wasteland wasn't. There was usually plenty of human presence here, for those who knew where to look for it. Farmhouses were planted deep among the rocky ridges. The district was a corridor for nomadic Bedouin tribes that grazed their flocks of sheep and goats on both sides of the border. There wasn't much pasturage, but there was enough to sustain them. When a grazing area was played out, the tribes moved on to the next one. One often saw their campfires, heard the barking of their dogs.

But not tonight. The border zone had gotten hot in the last two weeks. There had been shootings and ambushes. A phantom third force had moved in. Several gun shipments had been hijacked, the gunrunners slain, and their contraband stolen. Both sellers and buyers had been hit.

Who was responsible? The Bedouins knew better than to target the brigands. Attacking the long-established smuggling trade brought swift and sure retribution. The nomads might nevertheless be tempted by a target of opportunity once in a while, but this latest assault was a sustained effort.

Whoever the marauders were, they would pray for death, Fadleel vowed. Once he'd caught up with them.

Smugglers always thrive and prosper through collusion with the local authorities. In this case, Fadleel was acting as an agent, not of the local authorities, but of the supreme authority of the mullahs of the holy city of Qom and the lesser but still potent civil powers in Tehran. They wanted weapons to flow across the border into East Central Iraq. They wanted the weapons pipeline up and running. They were even providing the weapons. Tremendous profits were there for the gunrunners.

"Let the Sunni dogs use them to bite the Crusaders with. When the time comes—and it will, soon—we Shia will shoot them down like the curs they are. But for now, let them use their fangs against the infidel and their lackeys."

So had said Captain Saq, head man of the Iranian border patrol guards in this district, explaining the rationale for trading with the enemy to Fadleel. Not that Fadleel needed convincing. He'd trade with anyone who could meet his price. Even the Americans—though his price to the unbelievers would be slightly astronomical, in the unlikely event that he'd ever be approached by the occupiers. Or was it so unlikely? Shadowy insurgent warfare made for strange alliances.

Captain Sayed Saq was the key contact man in this area. He got the weapons from Tehran, supplying them to Fadleel and his cohorts and splitting the profits with them. Of course, he took the lion's share, but that still left plenty to be shared among the smugglers.

Fadleel was scrupulous in accounting for every dinar to his military senior partner. He was afraid of Saq and not afraid to show it. Saq liked it that way.

The district smuggling clans had an up-and-down relationship with officialdom. Sometimes they were allowed to operate freely, so long as they made their payoffs. Other times, when politics were involved, the regime would make efforts to suppress the trade. At such times, Saq and his border squad could be supremely suppressive.

For now, though, he and Fadleel were conducting a joint operation. Earlier that day, Saq had summoned the smuggling chief for a final preparatory meeting.

Saq was a vigorous, athletic individual, a superb horseman who'd once been on the Iranian equestrian Olympics team. He was vain about his appearance. He'd once shot a man who'd sought to flatter him by comparing his looks to that of the international film star Omar Sharif, famed for playing Dr. Zhivago. Saq professed to be indignant that he, a Muslim believer, had been compared to the actor, a Christian Arab. In truth, he was flattered, but he'd shot the flatterer anyway, not fatally. Saq was prideful of his dark wavy hair, moist chestnut-brown eyes, and chiseled features.

He was all business with Fadleel, though. His face set in a perpetual fierce scowl, he said, "Hamdi and Waleed's Red Dome militiamen are putting pressure on the Americans. The more weapons they have, the more pressure. Tehran doesn't want to see a letup of that pressure—no loosening of the thumbscrews by even a single turn. So the weapons flow must continue uninterrupted."

Fadleel said, "But who is attacking our shipments?"

"That's what I am asking you."

"It is a mystery. If I knew, I would wipe them and their posterity from the face of the earth," Fadleel said solemnly.

Saq said, "Find out."

Fadleel ventured a suggestion. "Might it not be Akkad?"

"Ridiculous! He would lose greatly should the operation collapse. Besides, some of his men have been killed, too," Saq said.

"He would not be the first to spend a few men to gain much wealth."

Saq shook his head, his manner dismissive, scornful. "It's not him. For certain reasons of state that need not concern you, I know for sure that his loyalty is unimpeachable."

Fadleel knew that Iraqi crime boss Akkad and Iranian border guard Saq were involved in more matters than were known to him, Fadleel. Deep matters that would be worth one's life should one be caught looking into them. He shrugged.

"One of Akkad's men, then, going into business for himself," he said.

Saq nodded. "It's possible."

"Or the militiamen. Why buy guns when they can just take them?"

Saq said, "No. That would be the surest way to dry up the supply. The imam would never risk that."

"Perhaps he already has enough weapons," Fadleel countered.

"One can never have enough weapons, least of all Hamdi and Waleed, with their vaunting ambition. The swine," Saq added.

He went on, silkily, "Might not the raiders be from our side of the border?"

Fadleel looked shocked at the idea. "Who would dare go against you?"

"That is true, that is true," Saq agreed, with no sense of irony or self-consciousness whatsoever.

"Rest assured, whoever they are, we will find them and destroy them."

Saq held up a cautionary finger. "Until then, there can be no mishap, no interruptions."

Fadleel tried to project resolution. "Tonight, I will personally oversee the transfer."

"That is good," Saq said. "And some of my men will go with you to protect both our interests."

Fadleel was uneasy at the idea of Saq's armed patrolmen being present when a large amount of currency would be exchanged, but he kept his face blank and his misgivings to himself. He said easily, "No need to trouble yourself or your troops. My men are equal to the task."

"I never doubted it," Saq said, showing off a dazzling, white-toothed smile. His teeth were all capped, like a movie star. "Still, my men will accompany you," he added, a tone of finality sealing the fact that it was a done deal.

Fadleel said, "As you wish."

"As I command," Saq corrected. "Lieutenant Nasruddin will accompany you. My men can watch your men, and your men can watch my men, and they can both watch Akkad's men."

"It is well."

So ended the meeting.

But it was not well, not really, not at midnight in the *wadi* when the weapons transfer between Fadleel's gunrunners and Akkad's brigands was taking place. Not when Fadleel was so acutely conscious of being under the guns of Captain Saq's men.

Lieutenant Nasruddin commanded a crew of three Iranian border-patrol guards. They were the crew of a 4X4 light armored scout car that stood on a rise east of the wide place in the *wadi* and commanded a clear field of fire over it.

The four-wheeled vehicle was low slung, lightweight, and minimally armored, more of a Fast Attack Vehicle than anything else. Part dune buggy, part armored car. Well armed, too. A rear gun turret was equipped with a minicannon and heavy machine gun.

Lt. Nasruddin was thirty, thin, and wiry, with a shiny, blue-black mustache and goatee. His eyes were narrow, close set. He sat in the open-topped front passenger seat. It was a hot night, and it was cooler and more comfortable to leave the protective roofing plates open.

A bored, gum-chewing driver sat beside him in the front compartment. The windshield and side windows were made of bulletproof glass.

The raised gun turret was protected by metal shielding but was also partially open. The scout car could have been better zipped up behind its full array of armor plating, but that would turn the machine into an oven. Besides, the vehicle design sacrificed armor for speed, mobility, and fuel economy.

A gunner sat in the cockpit, manning the guns. He was bareheaded, his helmet resting beside him on the curved, padded seat.

A fourth trooper stood on the ground near the passenger side, holding an assault rifle at port arms. This man was Sgt. Maroof, Nasruddin's personal bodyguard and executioner.

Akkad's men had come in two vehicles, a utility truck and a pickup truck. There were seven or eight of them. Half of them helped unload the weapons crates from the gunrunners' trucks and load them into the gang's trucks. The others stood watch, armed, alert, ready. The same proportion of loaders to gun-toters held among the smugglers.

The recent round of shootings and ambushes had left all the players keyed up, on edge, the gang members perhaps more so, because they were so obviously outgunned by the Iranian border patrol contingent.

Fadleel was down on the *wadi* floor, flanked by his enforcer, Khargis, a bull of a man with curly black hair topping a thick-featured, lumpy, black-bearded face. They stood by themselves off to one side of the trucks, out of the way from where the work was being done.

Khargis muttered into his beard, "I don't like having that pig Nasruddin at our backs."

Fadleel said, "What can he do?"

"Kill us and take all the money and the guns."

Fadleel's humorless laugh echoed hollowly. "He does what Saq tells him to do."

Khargis frowned, glowering, eyes shifting from side to side. "Who trusts Saq?"

"Tehran."

"Who trusts them?"

"Enough," Fadleel said, meaning that the discussion was at an end. He didn't trust Tehran either, but why go there? Whatever happened, happened. It was Fate.

The night was dark, but the *wadi* was lit by the soft glow of the parking lights from the different vehicles. Beyond the zone of light in the wide part of the *wadi*, the gully's rock walls were black against the charcoal gray of the overcast sky. About half the contraband had been transferred from the gunrunners' trucks to the buyers' vehicles.

Fadleel and Khargis met with Jafar Akkad, Hassani's younger brother. Jafar was oxlike, sly eyed. He handed Fadleel a briefcase filled with cash.

"We pay in good, old-fashioned American dollars," Jafar said.

Fadleel appreciated the irony, smiling with his lips. "If the dollar sinks any lower, we'll insist on being paid in euros or Saudi riyals."

"How about Iraqi Interim Government money?"

Fadleel chuckled politely. Khargis said, "That currency will soon be as worthless as money with Saddam Hussein's picture on it. Good only for wiping your ass with."

It was an insult for an Iranian to speak derisively of an Iraqi leader, even (or especially) a deposed despot of the Saddam variety. Jafar's face stiffened, but he chose to let the remark pass. A pillar of the

Akkad crime family never lets personal feelings interfere with profit. So Jafar told himself.

He indicated the scout car. "Do you fear us so much?"

Khargis stepped forward. "I fear only Allah!"

Jafar's expression remained blandly unimpressed. His eyes and lips turned up at the corners. "Perhaps it's there to watch you as much as us," he said.

Fadleel made little warding motions with his fingertips, as if shooing away the thought. "Some well-meaning friends merely wish to assure that we can continue our trade without fear of interlopers. A defensive measure, nothing more."

Jafar said, "So?"

Fadleel took the briefcase into the light from the trucks and began counting the money packs, brick by brick.

Jafar said, "It's all there."

"Of that I have no doubt," Fadleel said, with complete insincerity. "I trust you implicitly. But it is not a matter of trust. I must answer to others who do not know you as well as I, and to them I must account for every last penny. Do I protest that your men open every crate to inspect what was inside them?"

"This is how business is done," Jafar said offhandedly.

"My point exactly."

Fadleel had the ability to keep up a conversation while simultaneously counting cash and never losing track of the amount. "There are many fine new rifles and thousands of rounds of ammunition. There are grenades and plastic explosives enough for you to open the gates of hell in Azif."

"This is well and good," Jafar said, "but we'd like to move on to something bigger."

"Who wouldn't?"

"Tank- and armor-piercing shells. Artillery. Katyusha rockets. Stinger missiles to bring down crusader aircraft."

Fadleel said, "If and when such hard-to-find hardware should become available, we will let you know. For now, I'm sure you'll make good use of what we have to offer."

"Indeed," said Jafar.

Fadleel finished counting the money. He closed the briefcase lid and locked it. "It's all there. Not that I ever doubted it, of course."

Jafar's smile was openly mocking. "Of course."

The deal was done.


Lt. Nasruddin was chain-smoking cigarettes. A half a pack's worth of butts littered the ground beside where he sat in the scout car. He didn't offer any smokes to his men.

He was something of a dandy, with a eyebrow mustache and a custom-tailored khaki uniform. He watched the transfer, not bothering to hide his boredom.

His second-in-command, Sgt. Maroof, was a bodybuilder with a powerful physique. Bulging biceps swelled out of the shirtsleeves of his khaki shirt. He had an inky walrus mustache and held a short, stubby machine gun with a folding metal frame stock.

He stood beside the scout car, leaning an elbow on the top of the passenger side door. Lt. Nasruddin frowned at the familiarity, but Maroof was oblivious, having eyes only for the transaction taking place down on the flat.

"The money's in that suitcase, eh?" he breathed, sounding like a pervert panting his way through an obscene phone call. His eyes were small, hot. "Look at that pig Fadleel with all that money."

Resting a beefy forearm on the top of the door, he loomed over Nasruddin. The lieutenant touched the tip of his lit cigarette to Maroof's hairy forearm, burning him.

Maroof swore, jumping back. The smell of scorched hair and singed flesh hung in the air. "Ow! What did you do that for?"

"Covetousness is a sin," Nasruddin said calmly. The cigarette he'd ground into the other's arm had gone out. He flicked it away and took out another cigarette, lighting it with an expensive solid gold lighter. The yellow flame burned with a hissing sound.

Maroof rubbed his arm where it had been burned. He was careful to keep his face blank and his resentment to himself, but his dark eyes were sultry in a stiff face.

Nasruddin turned his attention to the transaction in the *wadi*. It was almost done; the last of the crates were being loaded into the Akkad gang's trucks. He was happy to stay where he was, sitting in the scout car and smoking. He was in no mood for anything so strenuous as going down the *wadi* to look over Fadleel's shoulder and verify the money count. It wasn't worth scuffing the finish on his coal black, spit-shined combat boots (and not his spit, either). The money would either all be there, or it wouldn't.

"If Fadleel has sticky fingers, his hands will be cut off," Nasruddin said to himself.

Maroof edged away, drifting into the darkness.

"Where are you going?" Nasruddin demanded

Maroof said, "Road call."

"Oh." Even Nasruddin couldn't crab about that. When you gotta go, you gotta go. He didn't think of it in those terms, exactly, but the sentiment was the same.

The big man moved off to one side of the knoll, by a heap of waist-high boulders. Nasruddin and the others looked elsewhere.

Maroof faced the rocks, his back to the scout car. He needed his hands free. He looked around for a place to set his machine gun. He placed it on the flat top of a boulder to his right. He unbuttoned his pants and urinated into the weeds. He murmured, "Ahh . . ."

He finished, buttoning up. When he looked up, his machine gun was gone. The look of bewilderment on his face was almost comical, but not to him.

He assumed it had slid off the top of the rock and fallen down the other side. Funny he hadn't heard it fall, though. Good thing it hadn't gone off; the lieutenant would have chewed him up alive if that had happened. It wouldn't have been too good to have a gun go off with all these excitable and heavily armed smugglers and gang members about, either.

He'd better secure that gun, though, and quick. Resting a hand on the rock, he leaned over it, peering into the darkness on the other side.

Behind the rock was a mass of inky blackness and

what looked like another boulder. But it wasn't inert stone; it was moving, alive.

For an instant, Maroof was stupefied. Was this some *djinn* or ghoul, some evil spirit of the night?

It was a man, crouched down and hiding behind the rock. A black man. It was Vang Bulo, although Maroof didn't know that. Vang Bulo, who'd crept up to the knoll stealthily unobserved. He wore loose-fitting dark clothing and held a knife in one hand.

He reached up with his free hand, grabbing Maroof's shirtfront and pulling him down. The knife thrust up to meet him, burying itself deep in his belly. The Ugandan gave the knife a twist. The shock paralyzed Maroof, rendering him unable to cry out.

Vang Bulo pulled him the rest of the way, headfirst over the rocks and down to the ground, cradling him in his massive arms to stifle any noise. He lay Maroof flat on his back as carefully as a mother laying an infant in its cradle.

He cut Maroof's throat, a deep slash of the knife that severed the windpipe. It was done with neatness and dispatch, with a minimum of noise or fuss.

On the *wadi* floor, the last crate had been loaded in the gang's trucks. The gang members piled into them. Engines started, raucous in the studied silence of the place. The utility truck drove away, disappearing into the westward branch of the *wadi*. It was followed by the pickup truck, whose riders kept their weapons pointed toward the gunrunners.

At the same time, a small commotion erupted in

the rear of the scout car. The sound was muffled by the engine noise of the Akkad gang's trucks.

The gunner in the turret bowed, slamming into the machine gun and its stand, collapsing on the cramped, circular metal plate floor. He lay motionless, not even twitching.

The impact of his fall rocked the scout car on its springs. Nasruddin and the driver were jarred in their seats. They turned around, peering into the obscurity at the rear of the vehicle.

Behind the back of the scout car stood a man pointing a gun at them. Kilroy.

He wore black garments: a knit cap, a sweatshirt, and pants. His face was daubed with camouflage black—war paint. He held a pistol at arm's length. Screwed to the muzzle was a tubelike suppressor. A silencer. It was several inches longer than the barrel to which it was attached.

Nasruddin barely had time to register what was happening, but it was long enough for him to realize that the slayer was an American.

Kilroy squeezed the trigger, drilling Nasruddin through the forehead. The pistol's little apologetic cough that sounded through the suppressor was drowned by the sound of the departing militiamen. There was no muzzle flare. Nasruddin whiplashed in his seat, a thin plume of blood jetting from the hole in his head.

The driver cringed, throwing his arms up in front of his face as Kilroy's pistol swung toward him. He opened his mouth to cry out but before he could, Kilroy fired. The silenced pistol made a sound like a man with a bad chest cold clearing his throat. The driver made more noise, flopping around in his seat, banging against the steering wheel and column. Kilroy put another round into him, finishing him off.

Nasruddin, the gunner, and the driver all lay dead in the scout car. It had all taken place within the span of a handful of heartbeats. That's how long it had taken Kilroy to actually deliver the fatal shots. It had taken some considerably greater length of time for him to get in position to do so.

Earlier at dusk, Kilroy and Vang Bulo had gotten into the armored SUV, exited Border Base Foxtrot, and driven east, into the foothills on the Iraq side of the border. Several hours later, they left their vehicle safely hidden in a concealed nook in another *wadi,* one of the many that honeycombed these hills in an intricate, interlinked network.

They made their way on foot for several miles, arriving at the place where the gun deal was scheduled to go down. Kilroy knew all the details as to time, locale, and disposition of hostile forces. He had an informant, a highly placed one, in Hassani Akkad's gang. He and Vang Bulo arrived some time before Fadleel's advance men, who scouted the area while the duo lay in their places of concealment, watching them. The scouts never even came close to where they were. Then Fadleel and the gunrunners and the armored car had arrived, and presently some of Akkad's gang in two trucks.

All were unaware of the presence of the uninvited. Kilroy and Vang Bulo moved into position on the armored car. Kilroy circled around to the back of it, crouched almost double, scrambling for cover from rock to rock. And there weren't that many rocks. He'd had to lowcrawl for the last ten yards of the final approach to the scout car.

It was no fun, a slow, painstaking, demanding process. Dust got in his nose, and he was afraid he was going to sneeze. Somehow he stifled the impulse. He'd had a bad moment when Maroof had stalked away from the scout car toward the sidelines. He lay flat on his belly on an open piece of ground a few body lengths away from the rear of the vehicle. But he'd been unnoticed as Maroof made his way over to the heap of stones, just happening to wander into the area where Vang Bulo was hiding. Not so unlikely, really. The boulders provided the best cover on the knoll.

Kilroy had planned to take out all four men in one swoop. He never questioned his ability to kill all four before they could raise so much as an outcry, never mind actually defending themselves.

As it was, Maroof had been a bonus. Vang Bulo had peeked out from behind a rock and given Kilroy the high sign that the noncom had been neutralized. That left three for Kilroy.

The trucks below started their engines, triggering Kilroy's onslaught. He rose, closing in on the scout car, the silenced pistol held out in front of him. His first shot had taken the gunner in the back of the neck just below the base of the skull, severing the spinal cord and negating all reflex nerve activity while causing instant death.

The extermination action was carried out like a gangland-style hit And why not? Mob hitmen could be extraordinarily efficient. Besides, it made it look like the killings had been carried out by crime gang shooters, pointing the finger at Akkad's people.

Now it was done, with no one in the *wadi* any the wiser.

Below, Akkad gang's trucks were gone, leaving a pale ribbon of dust to mark their wake. The thin dust curtain faded into nothingness.

The gunrunners stood grouped around their two vehicles, all eight of them, all but Fadleel and Khargis, who stood apart from the others. The two started toward the knoll where the scout car stood. Nasruddin had to get his cut; or rather, Captain Saq's cut. The lion's share.

Fadleel and Khargis were used to the muted light of the trucks. Away from the glow, their eyes were slow to adjust to the dark. The scout car was a dim, bulky block outlined against the top of the knoll.

Fadleel carried the briefcase. Speaking softly, he said, "You should not have made that remark about Saddam Hussein, Khargis. Some of Akkad's kin were Saddam Fedayeen."

"Their kin, yes, but not Hassani or Jafar. They're too busy with their infamies to court martyrdom. They should burn in eternal hellfire along with the tyrant Saddam," said Khargis. "Besides, I have no fear of those Sunni dogs."

Fadleel's sigh was that of a long-suffering man. "It's a matter not of fear but of diplomacy. This is business. Why provoke one of those hotheads into violence that could undo us all?"

They were about midway to the knoll when the scout car's headlights came on. They were bright, dazzling. Fadleel raised his free hand and held it in front of his face, shielding his eyes from the glare. In the light, he and Khargis cast long, giant shadows across the *wadi* floor. Khargis growled. Ever suspicious, he was already unlimbering his AK-47 assault rifle for action. Behind him, the other gunrunners stirred, some shouting, all reaching for their weapons.

Kilroy stood in the turret atop the rear of the scout car, manning the machine gun. Vang Bulo sat in the driver's seat, hands on the wheel.

The scout car was empty of corpses, the dead having been dragged out and placed on the ground nearby, where they lay sprawled in grotesque attitudes of violent death.

Khargis leveled his weapon, bringing the muzzle up in line with the scout car.

Kilroy fired first, squeezing off a heavy machine gun burst that stitched Khargis across the middle. A quick burst—brrrip!—and it was done. Khargis crumpled.

Fadleel was outraged. He couldn't believe that he was about to fall victim to a fatal double-cross—he, who had engineered so many similar fatal reversals for others. The injustice of it!

Kilroy chopped him with a stuttering burst. A line of fire ripped through the briefcase, popping it open, the high-powered rounds shredding wadded blocks of bills into confetti.

With smooth, swift ease, Kilroy swung the machine gun muzzle toward the gunrunners milling around the trucks. He depressed the firing studs, pumping lead at them.

They threw up their arms, whirling and dancing in the storm of steel that sieved them. Yellow flares speared from the machine gun's muzzle. It ground out rounds like a mill—a murder mill. Gunsmoke clouded the scout car. The headlights' beams probed through the haze.

Kilroy sprayed the other gunrunners with

machine-gun fire. Rounds ripped through truck metal with pinging sounds like a cowbell being struck. Most of the men at the trucks were cut down in the initial fusillade. Some lasted several seconds longer, then fell.

One ran for cover. A burst cut off one of his legs. He fell down. He lay on the ground, writhing and screaming. Another burst danced across his prone form, silencing and stilling him.

Kilroy eased off the trigger. There wasn't anybody left to kill. He put some more rounds into their prone forms to make sure. Cordite fumes were thick in his lungs. He realized he was panting, like he'd just run a race. It was hard to catch his breath with the fumes choking him. Gunsmoke billowed up out of the *wadi*. Beyond the protection of rock walls, the ghostly gray haze was broken apart by the winds.

Kilroy was pleased to note that the scout car and machine gun were well maintained and in good operating condition. Captain Saq's border guards were an elite unit, and he was a demanding taskmaster. Of course, if they'd really been an elite unit, Nasruddin and his men couldn't have been taken so easily. But at least the hardware was well maintained. The machine gun had seemed fully operable and in good working order during the hasty but thorough inspection he'd given it before pressing it into service for the mass liquidation of the gunrunners.

Still, one could never solely rely on somebody else's weapon. Kilroy and Vang Bulo had kept their own assault rifles and some grenades near at hand, too, as a backup. But they hadn't been needed.

This way fit the frame better. Fadleel's people and the other smuggling clans in the area would all think that Captain Saq had set the scout car to slaughter the gunrunners. Saq and his higher-ups would think that the scout car crew had been slain by Akkad's gang, thereby sowing mutual distrust, hatred, and fear among the various interested parties.

Kilroy picked up his own rifle, a Kalash. It fit the cover story that he was trying to lay down here. Besides, it was a superior weapon.

He hopped down to the ground, landing lightly, eyeing the massacre scene. The gunrunners lay strewn on the *wadi* floor, their bodies contorted in twisted postures. The killing ground was littered with fallen leaves of paper that was money.

Nearer was the body of Lt. Nasruddin. He lay flat on his back. His eyes were open, bulging, and staring. The hole in his forehead looked like a third eye. Kilroy turned out his pockets and patted him down, searching him. He found Nasruddin's identification papers and took them. Such documents had value. He did the same with the driver and gunner.

When he was done, he climbed into the front passenger seat of the scout car. Bloodstains splashed the compartment, but there was no place here for squeamishness. He ignored them.

The machine's diesel engine had an electric starter. Vang Bulo tripped it. There was a slight hesitation, then with a cracking sound like a logjam breaking, the motor turned over. It blapped, stuttered, then varoomed into full, roaring action. The engine idled heavily, its vibrations agitating the entire vehicle.

Vang Bulo worked the twin stick shifts and clutch pedals, throwing them into gear. The scout car lurched forward, its headlight beams hanging level for an instant, then pointing down. It rolled down the slope of the knoll, leveling on the *wadi* floor. It swung wide to avoid the bodies strewn around the bullet-riddled trucks.

"A nice clean sweep," Kilroy said. "Too bad we couldn't bag Akkad's gang at the same time."

Vang Bulo said, "That would ruin the buildup."

They were both shouting over the engine noise. Kilroy said, "With any luck, this should flush out Colonel Munghal to handle things personally. Especially with that big delivery coming up."

"Right."

"This scout car will come in handy, too. I have a use for it later on."

"Of that I've no doubt."

The scout car advanced, nosing into the westward branch of the *wadi*, the one taken earlier by the gang members. Leaving the carnage behind. Making for Iraq. Toward future carnage.

One thing about the downfall of Saddam Hussein: it sure had enlivened the nightlife of such places as Azif. When Saddam was in power, prospects for nightlife were simple. There wasn't any. Saddam didn't like people running around unsupervised after dark—or in the daytime, either—but it was worse at night because the darkness made it likelier that somebody might get away with an anti-Saddam action, such as weeping over the fate of an executed family member or friend. Such mourning in itself was regarded as an act of treason, since the bereaved was lamenting the fate of one who'd com-

mitted the unforgivable crime of falling afoul of
the Great Man himself. In Saddam's day, night was
for citizens to seal themselves up in their homes and
hope that daylight would come without some of
the dictator's secret police breaking down their
doors and taking them away.

That was then. But Saddam's downfall had also lib-
erated Iraqi after-dark activities in town and country.
Which is not to say that the citizenry had suddenly
developed a passion for such nocturnal activities as
taking in a show, nightclubbing, or barhopping.
There were less of those kinds of activities now than
there had been before the overthrow, because at least
then the members of Saddam's inner circle were free
to drink, drug, and carouse to their heart's content,
as long as they remained in favor with the regime.

But there was a soaring increase in some of the
more traditional and time-honored pastimes of
those who do in darkness what they dare not do in
daylight. There was more crime, subversion, and
wholesale killings of all sorts: personal, familial,
tribal, religious, and political.

Azif was a case in point. The typical nocturnal cycle
went something like this: in early evening, the police
halted their patrols, returning to the station houses
and barricading themselves behind locked doors in
hopes that they wouldn't be attacked, raided, or
blown up before dawn.

The streets were given up to Red Dome Mosque
militia patrols. Some drove around in cars and trucks,
prowling the streets and alleys, looking for foes to
tangle with or citizens to crack down on. They
avoided the Shiite district on the far side of town. The
Shia minority had their own militia and defense

organizations, well-armed bands that were supported and supplied by their coreligionists in the Shiite-ruled town of Quusaah. They were able to defend themselves and their neighborhood; consequently, the Red Dome militiamen stayed away. Otherwise, Imam Hamdi's followers had free run of Azif.

An important role was played in the town's domestic affairs by the imam's Purity League patrols. Technically, their name was the Society for Suppression of Vice—the morality police. Their mission was to root out what they called violations of Islamic law. In practice, this meant the intolerant anti-Westernism preached night and day in the Red Dome Mosque.

These zealots enforced the dress code that forbade women and girls to go about with their heads uncovered or wearing revealing clothing. Violators were subject to fines and whippings. Repeat offenders were subject to more serious penalties. And that was during the day. Any females found going abroad unescorted at night were regarded as prostitutes and were run out of town following a thorough beating.

The one liquor store in Azif had been one of the first casualties. The owner and several family members were shot, and the store burned. Its stocks of alcohol made a splendid and spectacular bonfire to delight the hearts of the believers.

Red Dome Militia purity patrols roamed the streets during the first half of the night, searching for violators so they could beat holy hell out of them. Those caught drinking or even smelling of alcohol on their breath were flogged right on the streets where they were taken, for all to see.

By midnight, though, the purity police usually called a halt to their activities, leaving the streets to those with more lethal intentions. That was the hour that the Red Dome death squads came out. Their kill lists were long and varied: Imam Hamdi's rival clerics from other mosques, local strongmen who refused to bow down to militia boss Waleed Tewfiq, Iraqi interim government officials, collaborators with Coalition forces, police chiefs, political foes, dissidents, grumblers, those of suspect loyalties—the lists went on and on. Red Dome disciples never doubted that all would come right in the end if only they killed enough people.

Another power in Azif was crime boss Hassani Akkad. Nighttime was the right time for Akkad's small army of thugs, thieves, gamblers, gunmen, extortionists, kidnappers, and killers to carry out the dark deeds of their criminal enterprises. There had been some embarrassing confrontations when crookdom bumped up against militiamen as they made their respective nightly rounds. Neither side was eager to force a showdown with the other, especially during this vital Sunni time of struggle against a Shiite-majority government.

To defuse the situation, Hassani Akkad and Waleed Tewfiq had entered into a kind of nonaggression and mutual-assistance pact. Akkad's ability, through his Iranian contacts, to supply the militia with virtually limitless stores of weapons and ammunition at bargain prices was a major incentive to forging the new alliance. It was this alliance that had come under the gunsights of the Dog Team.

\* \* \*

One place that night prowlers of all persuasions shunned was the Graveyard of Martyrs. That made it useful for Kilroy's purposes. Three o'clock in the morning found him in the graveyard awaiting a planned meeting.

The graveyard was located about a half a mile south of town, on a lonely, forsaken flat. The site was old and undistinguished, and the landscape had a dreary quality. Marshy lowlands, no good for farming, grew mostly spiky thornbushes, bramble patches, and rank, weedy fields.

The Graveyard of Martyrs had achieved its status during the Iraq war, when several companies of Saddam loyalists had dug in there in an attempt to withstand the advancing coalition forces coming up from the south. The defenders initially mounted a stiff resistance with artillery, mortar, and machine-gun fire, stalling the enemy advance. However, their defense was foredoomed from the start. It held for just as long as it took for the coalition to call in air support. Jets had bombed the site; AC-10 Warthog aircraft cleaned up with nose cannons and Gatling guns. What few survivors there were cleared out at the first lull in the shooting. Later, after the war, the dead there were buried in mass graves.

The site had been bordered by a chest-high stone wall. Parts of it had survived the bombing, but not many. Of those, none stood unbroken for a span of more than three or four yards. Some sections of wall slanted out of the ground at acute angles.

Within, the ground was torn up, cratered, and knobbed as though pummeled by giant fists. Grave markers stuck out at odd angles from plowed-up ridges and mounds. Sinkholes existed where rows of graves had been. The ground was weedy. Small, stagnant, scummy pools of water lay in the bottom of bomb craters. Bats flew overhead, circling above the graveyard.

In the southeast quadrant of the site were several stone mausoleums dating back to the late nineteenth century. Most of them had been blown to bits, but a few had survived relatively intact. One of them had been half buried by a mound of bulldozed earth. It provided Kilroy with a good vantage point. By standing on top of it and looking northwest, he commanded a view of the graveyard, the flat beyond, and a handful of buildings at the southern edge of Azif.

Not that he was actually standing on it. He didn't want to be outlined against the bare backdrop of the empty sky. He crouched down, his form blending in with the humped masses of bulldozed earth.

At this hour, Azif was mostly dark, with few lights. Every now and then, sporadic bursts of shooting could be heard coming from the town. They seemed random, unselective. A crackle of gunfire would sound, blazing up and just as swiftly falling silent. There would be a lull. Then inevitably, some new burst of fire would break out in a different quarter, only to repeat the pattern.

Every now and then, a set or two of vehicle headlights could be seen driving in and around town, flashing into and out of sight in the open spaces of traffic squares. None of them came within half a mile of the graveyard, though.

The wind blew, rattling the spidery limbs of bare, dead trees. There was the sound of running water, a trickle of which spilled through a nearby ditch. A small fan of smudged yellow light showed distantly in the southern sky where the moon shone through a rent in the clouds.

Moonlight picked out the approach of Kilroy's contact crossing a field north of the graveyard and closing in on it. The figure flitted through a gap in the wall, entering the site. Kilroy no longer perched atop the tomb mound. He'd eased down from his observation post, dropping silently into the graveyard.

The graveyard scene was quite different when one experienced it directly instead of merely looking down at it from on high. The top of the tomb mound showed the depressions and ridges all laid out below. When one was in them, the big picture vanished, replaced by the tighter, more immediate view of the near surroundings. You could be in a crater, and there could be a gang of cutthroats lurking in the next one, and you wouldn't even know it unless they made some betraying noises.

Kilroy was armed with an M4 machine gun. It was short and snouty with heavy firepower, well fitted to tight, close spots like the graveyard. He'd long since gotten his night vision, but even so, it was tough going. Moonlight threw exposed areas into bold relief, but shadowed places were coal black. Shadows were welcome to those who wanted to hide in them.

Kilroy stepped into the open, coming face to face with his contact. He held his weapon with the muzzle pointing down at the ground. He stood on one side of a crater facing north, while the other stood on the north side of the crater facing south. The crater was eight feet deep and fifteen feet across at its widest part.

A hunter needs to know where the game is. The

Dog Team apparatus had sources in the unlikeliest places. A chance had led to acquiring an important asset deep in the enemy camp. A high-level person in the Akkad crime clan had been turned and was supplying invaluable information and intelligence on the inner workings of that secretive, murderous organization.

Now that vital informant stood on the far side of a crater in the Graveyard of Martyrs, meeting with Kilroy. Moonlight shone down on and into his face, revealing his identity: Jafar Akkad.

Jafar Akkad, roly-poly younger brother of Hassani Akkad, leader of the crime clan. In Azif's criminal society, Jafar was known as "The Whale," though no one ever called him that to his face. Because he was fat faced and seemingly jolly, he was better liked than his notoriously ill-tempered older sibling. Hassani may have ordered the executions, but Jafar was the one who saw that they were carried out. He accompanied the murder squads on their rounds just for fun. Every now and then, he liked to go out and cut a throat or blow somebody's brains out, just to keep his hand in. People excused his violence, blaming it on Hassani. Their attitude was that Jafar was just carrying out orders, an obedient and dutiful younger brother.

He looked fat—was fat—but he moved pretty well. Kilroy had barely heard him making his way in the dark to the meeting place.

Jafar had no use for Americans, but he had even less use for Hassani. He'd long since tired of the role of dutiful kid brother. Hassani was a permanent bar to his ambitions. With Hassani gone, Jafar could move into the top slot.

Jafar had made a tentative approach in that direction, but the assassin he'd hired had fallen short of taking down Hassani. The hireling had been killed in the attempt, leaving Jafar secure in the belief that his authorship of the plot was safe from detection. He began working up another plot.

The failed killer had had links to American intelligence agents, keeping them well informed about Jafar's machinations. The Americans, like Jafar, could only heave a sigh of relief that the assassin had been killed before he could be made to speak of his dealings with them.

In due course, Jafar was confronted with the knowledge that the Americans had in their possession damning facts and evidence of his plan to murder his brother. It was a carrot-and-stick approach to recruitment. The stick was the threat to reveal Jafar's treachery to Hassani. The carrot was the admission that they were not unsympathetic to his ultimate aim of eliminating and replacing his brother.

Here was the basis for a working arrangement. One hand would wash the other. Jafar would supply the Americans with inside information about Hassani's criminal operations, his kidnapping rings, and his alliances with militia leader Waleed Tewfiq and the Iranians. In return, they would provide the solution to his Hassani problem and rig it in a way that no suspicion would attach to Jafar.

It was Jafar who'd supplied the information about tonight's midnight meeting between the gunrunners and Akkad gang members, just as he'd previously mentioned several other smaller, similar contraband operations that had been hijacked by Kilroy and Vang Bulo.

Now, by prearrangement, Jafar and Kilroy met in the graveyard. No doubt that Jafar had come alone. He didn't dare risk having any of the gang, not even his own loyalists, discover his dealings with one of the hated Americans—especially a first-class bastard such as Kilroy.

Jafar was more right than he dared dream possible. Kilroy was a first-class bastard. He was the illegitimate son of the long-dead Terry Kovak, one of the top guns in the subterranean history of the Dog Team.

Jafar looked around at his surroundings, his expression bleak. "A fine place you pick for a meeting!"

Kilroy said, "What's the matter—afraid of ghosts?"

"Of unexploded artillery shells. There are said to be many of them in this battlefield of a graveyard. That is why it is so studiously avoided," Jafar said with a wintry smile.

They spoke in Arabic. Kilroy could communicate in several languages. Nothing fancy, but enough to get his basic points across. Arabic was a language in which he'd become fairly fluent over the last decade, having carried out numerous assignments in the Middle East during that time.

Jafar said, "I have done what you wanted. When will you do what I want?"

"Soon," Kilroy said.

"Soon," Jafar echoed, not without bitterness. "Always soon. I grow weary of this soon. When does soon become now?"

"Soon," Kilroy said. "When Hassani moves The Package. When will that be?"

"Any day now. Tomorrow night, or the night after that. No later," Jafar said. "The Iranians are putting pressure on him to deliver."

Kilroy said, "After tonight, there'll be more pressure."

Jafar paused. "It went well, then."

"For me, it did. Not for the Iranians."

"What does it matter? They were dogs."

"There's dogs, and then there's dogs," Kilroy said, smirking, thinking, *Dog Team dogs, sucker.*

Jafar frowned, irked. "I fail to take your meaning."

"Let it pass. When Hassani moves The Package, I want to know."

"No more than I. I chafe, I ache with the need to be relieved of the pestilential presence of my overbearing brother. Each day of delay becomes ever more intolerable to me."

Kilroy showed a wolfish grin. Jafar bridled, said, "You find something amusing in this exchange?"

Kilroy avoided the question. "You hate hard, Jafar. I respect that. Because I'm the same way."

The other got huffy. "You flatter yourself, my friend."

"It's not flattery, and I'm not your friend."

"How true. On that note of agreement, let us part then."

"You know how to contact me. When the time comes, see that you do," Kilroy said. "Otherwise, I'll come after you."

"Ha ha," Jafar said, "I laugh at your threats."

"It's not just my neck on the line. It's yours, too. Betray me, and your betrayal will be made known to

Hassani. This is a one-way trip, and the train has already left the station. There's no turning back now. Hassani dies, or you die."

"When he comes out, you'll know. See that you don't make a botch of it."

"If that's all that's worrying you, you can start trying out for size Hassani's chair now," Kilroy said.

Jafar permitted himself a small self-satisfied smile. "Time enough for that after the funeral."

Kilroy said, "The next time we meet, you'll be the head of the Akkad family."

The oily smile slipped away. "There will be no next time. Such meetings are dangerous. In the future, should the occasion arise, we will communicate at several removes," Jafar said.

Kilroy said, "Okay."

There was nothing more to be said. The meeting was over. Jafar readied himself to withdraw.

"You can tell your friend to come out now," he said.

Kilroy played dumb. "What friend is that?"

"The one hiding behind the mound in back of you."

"You're imagining things."

Jafar bobbed his head in a mock bow. He took a few steps backward, into the shadows. He stepped behind a mound and was lost to sight.

Kilroy faded back, too. No sense in standing out in the open, making a target of himself. He slipped into a gap between two humps of earth, plowed up ridges. Something touched his shoulder.

He started, looking over his shoulder to see what had him. A skeletal white hand, long torn from its grave, jutted outward from the top of a dirt pile, reaching for him. Kilroy stepped away from it, thinking, *Not yet, bony boy. You don't have me yet.*

Several minutes passed. Down on the flat beyond the north graveyard wall, an engine started up. A car drove away, bumping along a dirt road, guided only by its parking lights. It made for Azif in a roundabout way, swinging a wide circle out before curving back in toward the city.

Kilroy and Vang Bulo came out in the open, the latter holding a machine gun and emerging from behind the very mound which Jafar had indicated as the hiding place for a lurking accomplice.

Vang Bulo said, "He's pretty good. He knew I was there, and I swear I didn't make a sound."

"He's sneaky," Kilroy said. "He figured that if he were in my place, he'd have a backup there, and that I'd do the same thing."

"He came alone, though. I checked."

"He's motivated. He wants Hassani dead, bad."

"That's brotherly love for you, eh?"

Kilroy said, "I wouldn't know. I'm an only child myself."

Vang Bulo said, "You trust him?"

"Only where it comes to killing his brother. But that's enough. Like I said, he's motivated. Besides," Kilroy added, "I've got something better than trust working for me: technology. I don't have to take his word about where The Package is. Thanks to the locator implant, I can see for myself. If Jafar says The Package is at X and the locator shows him at Y, I'll know he's lying.

"Like the saying goes: Trust but verify."

The two began making their way toward the south side of the graveyard. Kilroy said in an aside, "He thinks that there are unexploded shells in the cemetery."

Vang Bulo's steps did not falter. "I didn't see any."

"It's the ones you don't see that you have to look out for."

Both men became more careful about where they placed their steps. They passed the mound with the half-buried stone tomb and followed a winding path down a long slope that leveled out on weedy, open fields. The SUV was hidden in a stand of trees in a hollow. They went to it and drove away, going to Greentown.

The scout car had been hidden earlier in a safe place where no one else would find it and where it would be ready when they needed it.

When would that be? Soon.

# Four

There was nothing green about Greentown. It took its name from the Green Zone, the citadel at the heart of Baghdad where the executive Iraqi government and the Coalition authority were housed. The Green Zone was supposed to be a safe area, but in Iraq today, nowhere is safe from attacks by sniper, mortar, or rocket fire.

Greentown was located south of the highway between Azif and Border Base Foxtrot and was closer to town than to the base. It was a depot and warehouse complex that had been built along an east-west rail line that stretched nearly from the border to Baghdad. Azif was a stop on that line.

In the last decade of Saddam Hussein's rule, the transportation system, like much of the rest of the infrastructure, had gone to rot and ruin. The depot complex had fallen into disuse and was long abandoned when victorious Coalition forces chose the site as a linchpin of the provincial reconstruction effort.

At the time, there had been big plans for rebuilding and renewing Azif and the surrounding area. U.S. planners believed a Sunni stronghold so near to the Iranian border had vital strategic and tactical value. That had been early on, when optimism about the long-term American presence in Iraq had been at its height. The theory was that Azif would continue to be a bulwark of anti-Iranian resistance, which it did. But it was even more a center of rabid anti-Western resistance, with Coalition forces the focus of Iraqi ire.

Greentown was where the provincial reconstruction effort had set up headquarters in anticipation of a lengthy stay. The previously existing complex had been pressed into use by the NGOs, the nongovernmental organizations hired to rebuild and renew Azif. There were civilian administrators, inspectors, regulators, and interpreters. There were contractors, construction gangs, welders, riveters, heavy equipment operators. Other contractors provided food, drinking water, and housing facilities.

The complex was divided into an administrative area, a living area, and a work area. The administrative area was set up in one of the old warehouses. Another section of the compound housed the construction effort, including the heavy-duty equipment, yellow-painted earthmoving machines, bulldozers, backhoes, cranes, derricks, and flatbed and dump trucks. The living area consisted mainly of some prefab barracks buildings and a cluster of mobile homes. The compound was ringed with bombproof concrete slabs and layers of barbed wire and chain-link, barbed wire–topped fences.

A prime target for insurgents, terrorists, and crooks, the site was guarded by both a private security firm and a large detachment of Coalition troops.

The train line was unable to recover under Coalition hands. Sections of track were buried under dirt and sand. Rails were rusting, bent, or just plain gone. It was easier to bring supplies up from Basra in the south by truck convoy. Easier, but not safer. Insurgents just loved to target those convoys.

Military personnel generally lived in the barracks, while civilian permanent party contract employees were largely housed in the mobile-home area. Others were boarded in the Visitors' Quarters building, a civilian-operated four-story building with rounded edges and a flat roof. Its shape reminded Kilroy of a metal Band-Aid box, a resemblance heightened by an unfortunate paint job the color of a flesh-colored bandage.

But the place was relatively clean and convenient, and Kilroy and Vang Bulo had taken rooms. It was a convenient place to rest for a while between missions while they were operating in the area.

Dull predawn grayness showed in the sky when Kilroy and Vang Bulo came straggling in to the Visitors' Quarters lobby and dragged themselves to their rooms. They each had a single room on the third floor. The rooms were small, basic cubicles.

Kilroy let himself into his room, switching on the overhead light. There was a cot, a night table with a lamp, a gray metal double-doored clothes locker, a square-topped table and a straight-backed, armless chair.

Kilroy peeled off his clothes and crawled between the sheets, hitting the sack. He was dog tired. He was asleep as soon as his head hit the pillow.

When he awoke, the room was filled with heat and light. It was day. He swung his legs over the side of the bed, placing his feet on the floor and sitting up. The thought came to him that he ought to use the locator to check on the status of The Package.

He stifled the thought, putting it firmly from his mind. It could wait until after he'd showered. The world wasn't going to go to hell in the time it would take him to take a shower. And if it did, let it.

He donned a bathrobe and a pair of flip-flops, grabbed his shaving bag by its loop handle, and went down the hall to the shower room. The shaving kit was hefty, weighty. He set it down on a nearby shelf within reach of the shower stall. He kept the plastic curtain open a crack so he could keep an eye on the kit while he was showering.

Showered and shaved, he returned to his room. He put the shaving kit on the bed and opened it. The leather bag held a can of shaving cream, soap, a razor, and some deodorant. It also held a snub-nosed .38 revolver and a device resembling a video game console.

He took out the device. It was about the size and shape of a paperback book. The face was divided into an inset screen and a set of buttons that included directional arrows and a numerical keypad.

He switched on the power. A pinhead-sized light glowed green. The machine hummed faintly. The screen lit up. The handset was loaded with a video game, a military-themed tank combat game.

He sat down on the bed with legs crossed, back propped up against the wall. He fiddled with the game, playing it for five minutes. As always, it took hold of his competitive instincts, and he played to win, grinning when he destroyed an enemy tank and frowning when his tank was hit. It took no small amount of willpower to switch mental gears and decouple his attention from the game.

Kilroy input a six-digit number on the keypad and entered it. The handset throbbed with a rush of added power. The hum deepened. The tank combat game screen graphics vanished, replaced by a grid-square map of an urban area. The sector depicted was a scale map of Azif's Old Town district, centering on the Red Dome Mosque and its surroundings.

He pressed some more keys, zooming in on the image and magnifying it. Streets radiated out from the mosque in a starburst pattern. A trapezoidal shape that was a building stood at a corner of an intersection. Inside the trapezoidal shape was a green dot that blinked on and off.

The dot represented a transponder that continuously emitted signals on a preset frequency. The transponder had been implanted in what Kilroy liked to think of as The Package. The handheld device was a locator disguised as a video game. Its purpose was to keep track of The Package through the transponding implant.

The readout confirmed that The Package had not yet been moved. The locator and implant rig were his way of keeping Jafar honest. If Jafar's reports coincided with the locator's findings, well and good. If not, Kilroy would still be able to identify the whereabouts of the package.

The device was hardened against tampering. Its locator function could only be accessed with the correct numerical code, which was updated every few days. Any attempt at unauthorized interference would activate a destruct mechanism that would turn the interior hardware into a mass of melted slag in less than thirty seconds.

Kilroy switched off the power and set the device aside.

He got dressed, donning a T-shirt, baggy pants, boots, and a utility vest. He slipped the locator in the inside breast pocket of the vest. The gun went into an oversized cargo pocket on his right pant leg.

He pulled on an Atlanta Braves baseball cap. He was from Georgia, not from Atlanta, but from the rural town of Bishop. He'd enlisted in the Army as soon as he was legally of age to do. His father of record had been only too happy to see him go. He had no love for this bastard son of an Army killer that an adulterous wife had foisted off on him. Kilroy reciprocated the other's dislike. He shook the dust of Bishop off his shoes and never looked back. He'd only visited the place a couple of times since in the last two decades, one of them to attend his mother's funeral. He had nothing against the town, but he had nothing for it, either. He hadn't been back since his mother's death and he had no plans to do so. He never stopped being a big Braves fan, though.

He exited, going down the hall to Vang Bulo's room. It was empty. He found the big man in the lobby, sitting in an armchair near one of the front windows, reading a copy of the *World Business Weekly* newspaper. He wore a sporty, oversized jogging suit and a pair of size fourteen sneakers.

Vang Bulo folded the newspaper, set it down on a side table, and rose. Kilroy crossed to him. He said, "Let's get some breakfast."

Vang Bulo said, "It's lunchtime."

"Let's get some lunch, then. I really didn't want to eat breakfast anyhow."

They went through the front doors and outside. They paused, standing in the watery shade cast by a projecting overhang.

Kilroy immediately broke a head-to-toe sweat. "Whew . . . Hot!"

"Yes, it's hot," Vang Bulo said fiercely. "Of course it's hot. It's always hot here. Confoundedly hot."

Kilroy showed mild surprise. "I thought you were used to the heat. Uganda's hot."

"Ah, but that's a moist heat. It lets your skin breathe and keeps your moving parts oiled," Vang Bulo said. "This dry heat sucks the moisture out of you and dries you up like a toad in a hole. The dust clogs my pores, gets into my nose and throat."

"You do sound kind of stuffed up, like you've got a head cold or something."

"How I long for the rainy season."

"It's a little delayed this year," Kilroy said. He eyed the landscape to the south and the sky above it. "Looks like it's going to be delayed a little longer."

The sky was a dirty gray-white color, marbled with brown streaks of windblown dust. The sun was a tawny, lion-colored disk. A wind was blowing in from the south. A hot wind, hot as a blast from a pizza oven.

Kilroy said, "This could turn into a sandstorm without half trying."

Vang Bulo said, "Is that good or bad for us? Operationally speaking, that is."

Kilroy answered by changing the subject. "Let's head over to the mess hall." The other nodded. They started forward, descending a short flight of stone steps, then crossing an open area toward the mess hall.

Kilroy said, "There's a rumor that the Visitors' Quarters are wired. That the rooms and lobby are bugged. Maybe by some intelligence agency of ours, maybe by the security apparatus of the big contractors—maybe both. Or neither. I don't know if it's true or not. I never found a listening device in my room. But I didn't look too hard, either. I figured if there was a bug, I didn't want to alert the monitors that I was on to them. If there were monitors.

"But what the hell, more likely than not, it is bugged. That's what I'd do. You could pick up a lot of valuable information overhearing some of the steals and deals that are cooked up by the guests in that building. If the inside of the building is wired, it would make sense to wire the outside, too."

Vang Bulo frowned. "By that logic, you could assume that every building in the compound is bugged."

"It's possible," Kilroy agreed. "But it's unlikely that they could wire the compound out here in the open. I mean, if somebody really wanted to listen in they could eavesdrop with a parabolic microphone. But if we were under that kind of heavy surveillance coverage, we wouldn't have to guess. We'd know."

Vang Bulo returned to the interrupted topic of the weather. "How does the storm affect us? If there is a storm."

"Depends. It would be good cover for Hassani to make his move. But if it's too heavy, he won't move. He'll sit tight and wait for it to stop. The same goes for the Iranians at the other end of the pipeline," Kilroy said.

The compound was a scene of lively, buzzing activity. A line of flatbed trucks rolled past, bearing bulldozers, backhoes, lengths of pipe, I-beams, bags of cement, and other supplies. The trucks made for the main gate, en route to construction projects in progress out in the field. The convoy was under heavy military escort.

Kilroy and Vang Bulo paused to let it pass. Vang Bulo said, "They've had to stop all work in Old Town because of the militia. The only projects still functioning are in the market district and government buildings. Even there, they sometimes lose two or three men a day to insurgent sniping."

Kilroy nodded. "The reconstruction effort needs reconstruction."

The convoy passed, and the duo continued on, halting outside the mess hall. Kilroy eyed the sky and the scene to the south.

He said, "Looks like it could develop into a storm, but it's early yet. It'll take twenty-four to thirty-six hours to get rolling."

They went into the mess hall. It was filled with good food smells. It was run by a private contractor and was open to civilian and military personnel. It was set up cafeteria style. Kilroy and Vang Bulo got on line.

The big man said appreciatively, "The chow here is pretty good."

Kilroy said, "It must be, the way you're filling your tray."

They both loaded up on food and beverages, paid at the register, and went to a table in the rear. Vang

Bulo sat facing the front entrance, Kilroy sat facing the rear. Between them, they had the whole space covered, so no one could sneak up on them. Not that they expected anything to happen here, not really. The odds favored that the noonday meal would pass without incident. But there were no guarantees. Iraq was a hot zone. Azif and environs were red hot. Things happened.

Midway through the meal, Vang Bulo paused with his fork suspended in midair, staring at something over Kilroy's shoulder.

He said, "Hey, it's your buddy."

Kilroy kept on eating, not bothering to turn around to see who was approaching. The Ugandan's demeanor indicated that the newcomer posed no threat. "Who?"

Vang Bulo said, "Company man."

That could only be Albin Prester, a slippery character and longtime acquaintance of Kilroy's. Kilroy shrugged.

"He's got a woman with him. She's good looking, too," Vang Bulo said.

Kilroy glanced over his shoulder to see them. Mainly the woman. He'd seen Prester before. Women were scarce in these parts, especially good-looking ones.

Albin Prester and a short, shapely blonde finished paying at the cash register and came down the long central aisle, making for the rear of the mess hall. They were toting plastic carryall sacks filled with plastic water and juice bottles, sandwiches, and fruit.

Prester was big, rumpled, shambling. His thinning,

wavy bronze hair needed a trim and a combing, and his watery blue eyes could have used an eyewash to take the red out of them. He had a wedge-shaped nose with a wide, flat bridge. His ruddy complexion was shot through with the blue-veined traces of the habitual drinker. Heavyset, paunchy, he wore a safari jacket open over a lime green sport shirt, tan twill pants, and hiking boots.

The woman beside him was young, alert, vital. Unmistakably American. She couldn't have been more than an inch or two taller than five feet, the top of her blond head barely level with Prester's shoulders. At first glance, her figure had an almost girlish slimness, but she had womanly curves where it counted. Dirty blond hair was worn pulled back in a ponytail. Her eyes were hazel, her full-lipped mouth pink and wide. She wore a khaki top and pants.

Kilroy gave her a quick, scanning glance. Well, not so quick and not so little as a glance, either. More of an eyeful. He realized he was staring. He wasn't alone. So were most of the men in the room.

Prester caught sight of Kilroy and steered toward him, the woman in tow. They stood to one side of the table. Prester, beaming, smacked his thin lips.

"Joseph, we've got to stop meeting like this," he said.

Kilroy nodded, smiling pleasantly. The woman said, "Albin, who're your friends?" Her voice had a sharp nasal twang in it. Kilroy would have said she came from somewhere in the midwest.

"I'll handle the introductions," Prester said. "Debbie Lynn Hawley, meet Mr. Joseph Kilroy and Mr. Vang Bulo.

"Gentlemen, this is Debbie Lynn Hawley. Dr.

Debbie Lynn Hawley. The doctorate is in physics—
is that intimidating enough for you? It certainly is for
me. She's been engaged as an energy futures con-
sultant by the Transworld Capital Fund. I've been
showing her around the province, this little Garden
of Eden."

Debbie Lynn smiled brightly, acknowledging the
introductions. She said, "Gentlemen, please don't
get up."

That left Kilroy and Vang Bulo more than slightly
abashed, since neither one had thought to rise on
being introduced, as good manners demanded.
Kilroy guessed that they were no gentlemen. He wondered if they hadn't spent too much time away from
polite society.

On the principle of better late than never, Vang Bulo
pushed back his chair and rose, Kilroy following a beat
later.

Vang Bulo said, "How do you do?" and shook her
hand.

Kilroy said, "Glad to know you." He shook her
hand, too. She had a strong, firm grip. No wedding
or engagement ring, Kilroy noticed. Her hand was
smooth and warm. It was nice to hold. Kilroy would
have liked to go on holding it, but he reluctantly released it from his grip.

Prester said, "Be nice to her, Joseph. Not only is
she smart and attractive, but she controls fabulous
sums of money. She tells Transworld where to invest
in energy in the region."

Debbie Lynn said lightly, "That's why you attach
yourself to me, isn't it, Press?"

"Absolutely," Prester said.

Debbie Lynn said, "What's your line of work, Mr. Kilroy?"

"Call me Joe."

"Please call me Debbie Lynn."

"Glad to, Debbie Lynn."

"What did you say your line of work is, Joe?"

Prester said, "He didn't. Joseph doesn't give out much."

Kilroy said, "I'm an expediter for Mercury Transport. I help keep the mails going."

She said, "You're with the Post Office?"

"The Postal Service is part of the U.S. government. Here in Iraq, Washington likes to contract out as much work as it can to private industry. Mercury pays me to make sure that mail from the States gets to where it's going, to the troops and civilian employees. Any kind of mail: postal service or private delivery or shipping firms. When traffic gets bottlenecked, I clear up the jam and get things working smoothly again."

Prester said, "So now you know—he expedites." He pointedly checked his watch. "We'd better be going, Debbie Lynn, if we want to keep to our site inspection schedule. It looks like there's a storm blowing up, and it could hamper our movements in the next few days."

Debbie Lynn nodded agreement. "Nice meeting you, Kilroy, Mr. Vang Bulo."

Kilroy would have liked to shake hands good-bye with her, just to have an excuse to hold her hand again, but he decided not to take advantage of the acquaintance. Yet.

He said, "Watch yourself out there. Take good care of her, Prester."

Prester laughed. "I'm counting on her to protect me! Not to worry, Joseph, we'll be shepherded around the countryside by some of the finest bodyguards that Transworld's money can buy."

He and Debbie Lynn started toward the side exit door. Kilroy called after her, "See you around, Debbie Lynn."

She said, "You never can tell."

They crossed to the exit. Kilroy eyed her, admiring the rear view. Debbie Lynn had a juicy, rounded rump that pleasingly filled out the seat of her khaki pants.

"She looks as good going away as she does coming," he said.

Vang Bulo set down his knife and fork, mopping around his mouth with a napkin. "Albin Prester—he can't be as much of an ass as he seems to be, can he?"

"Nobody could," Kilroy said.

"CIA?"

"He sure seems like a Company man. He does everything but walk around wearing a button that says, 'Ask me about Central Intelligence.'"

"What about the blonde? What do you make of her?"

"Nothing yet, but give me time. I just met her," Kilroy said, leering.

Vang Bulo made a wry face. "Never mind the salacious fantasies. Is she CIA, too?"

"Remains to be seen. But don't worry. Kilroy is on the case. I'll investigate in depth. If you get my meaning, heh-heh."

"The sad part is that I'm sure you mean it," Vang Bulo said.

\* \* \*

They finished eating, went out, and loaded up the SUV. Kilroy started toward the driver's seat, but Vang Bulo was ahead of him.

"You drove yesterday. My turn to drive today," Vang Bulo said.

Kilroy said, "What difference does it make whose turn it is?"

"It makes a difference to me. Why should you have all the fun?"

Kilroy made a disgusted face. "Oh, all right, if that's the way you feel. Here's the keys. You drive." He stalked around to the passenger side and got in.

Vang Bulo started the vehicle and drove it to the main gate and out, taking the highway west, then circling north around the outskirts of Azif before heading east on a course parallel to the main highway but several miles above it. The route was north of Azif and south of Quusaah. It was a diversionary maneuver designed to shake any tails they might have had.

The SUV wandered down a few side roads and dirt trails, passing vast fields gridded by irrigation ditches and canals. Empty land. The border foothills loomed ahead.

The Iranian scout car was stashed away in a secure locale, a concrete pillbox fortification that was built into the side of a rocky hill. It had been abandoned and forgotten since the Iran-Iraq war until some Army map analysts had rediscovered it. By some subterranean channel, all files relating to the blockhouse had vanished from official Army data banks and been transferred solely to the Dog Team's computers. The data had never been shared with any other military or civilian agencies.

The concrete block structure was about the size of a firehouse. Most of it was buried underground. Its long axis lay north-south. It was dug into the east side of a hill. On the north, short side, a ramp dipped below the surface of the earth, downtilting to what looked like a solid wall. A close examination would reveal a razorline crack in the shape of a massive square-sided block.

Some months ago, a team of anonymous Dog Team technicians had come this way, cleaning out and overhauling the bunker blockhouse. They did their work for a day and a night and then moved on. One of the improvements they'd made was the installment of a new locking mechanism.

Now Vang Bulo piloted the SUV to the head of the underground ramp. Kilroy got out and descended the ramp. He took out a device similar in size and shape to a keychain flashlight. It was a kind of remote-controlled electronic key.

He pointed it at the seemingly solid wall at the foot of the ramp and pressed the switch, triggering an invisible electronic beam that activated an exterior sensor that connected to an interior, automatic locking mechanism.

A click sounded, like the pendulum ticking of an old-fashioned grandfather clock in an empty house at night. The hairline crack in the wall widened. The door was made of steel-reinforced concrete twelve inches thick. It was mounted on a sophisticated counterweight swivel system. When the automechanism was electronically unlocked, the door was free to rotate on the axis of an internal circular gatepost. So precisely balanced was it that Kilroy was able to open it with one hand.

The door was rigged with a fail-safe device. Should anyone try to force it open, it would detonate a cache of explosives that would destroy everything inside the bunker and bring the walls down.

A gritty scraping sound accompanied the inward opening of the door. Light slanted into the rectangularly shaped bunker. The air was stale, musty but breathable. Air shafts and ventilating tubes connected to hidden surface vents.

Squatting on the bunker's stone floor was the scout car. On the inner wall to one side of the doorway was a round metal fixture inset with on-off switches. Kilroy switched them on, filling the vault with electric light.

The SUV had to be gotten out of sight to avoid the suspicion its presence might provoke in any chance passersby who came this way. This was an empty land, and dangerous for those who traversed it, the haunt of nomads, smugglers, fugitives, and brigands. The recent violence in the hills had cleared the land of their presence. But there was no point in leaving the SUV out in the open where it might be seen.

Topside, Vang Bulo reversed the SUV, backing down the ramp and into the bunker. The vault had room for two such vehicles, no more. The SUV stood facing out for a quick getaway.

Kilroy and Vang Bulo went to work on the scout car, giving it a tune-up. The Ugandan was a mechanical whiz and did most of the real work, with Kilroy mostly handing him the proper wrench or pitching in when some extra muscle was needed. When it came to overhauling the armaments, though, Kilroy came into his own, making sure the minicannon and heavy machine gun were in fine working order.

The overhaul was hard, dirty work that ate up the afternoon and went on into evening. They finished at dusk. They didn't want to wait to leave but they had to, at least until it was dark.

Finally the SUV rolled up the ramp to the surface. The stone door was once more set flush with the wall and the remote locking mechanism was triggered, to the accompaniment of a ponderous metallic click.

The SUV crept across vast, sprawling fields, arrowing southwest. It drove with the lights out, in the dark. The sky was murky with airborne dust, dulling the stars. The rising moon looked like it was shining through a burlap screen.

The vehicle cut into the highway and headed west toward Greentown. Hot winds gusted from the south, slamming broadside into the SUV. A storm was rising.

# Five

Debbie Lynn Hawley was a screamer, as Kilroy found out later that night when he went with her to her room in the Visitors' Quarters.

The building had a modest day room on the ground floor. Some of the guests liked to hang out there after hours. There was a Ping-Pong table and a bumper pool table with one cue and half the balls missing. A soda machine stood against the wall, under a dial clock. At the rear of the space was a kitchenette, complete with an ice chest, sink, and paper cups.

Alcoholic beverages were officially discouraged in the compound, "for fear of offending our Iraqi hosts," as the line went. Alcohol was forbidden to the believers, according to Islamic law. It was one of the factors that made serving in Iraq the most beat duty for any American G.I. since the worst days of the Korean War. And even then, in Korea there had been booze and women. In Iraq, booze was forbidden. As for women, Iraqi women, well, forget it. If an Iraqi woman made a date to meet a U.S. soldier in a nice secluded place, it was almost always to lure him into a death trap. As for Western women, a handful of them worked for the Coalition, but a guy had to rate pretty high to get a second look from them.

In Greentown alcohol wasn't even officially available. Getting around that was no problem, of course. Every base had its purveyors of beer, wine, and the hard stuff. It was tolerated. Even the most tight-assed company commander occasionally had need of alcohol, if only to entertain visiting dignitaries such as Pentagon disbursement officials, U.S. civilian contractor executives, Iraqi government administrators, and similar vest-pocket potentates. Drinkers were expected to be discreet, which in practice meant anything short of busting up the furniture.

Returning from the field to Greentown, Kilroy went to his room in the Visitors' Quarters. He was hot, tired, and dirty from hours spent working in the underground bunker. His muscles ached. A long, hot shower soaked some of the stiffness out of them. So did a couple of shots of Wild Turkey from a bottle he had stashed in his room. He dressed and met Vang Bulo, and they went to the mess hall. It was after the dinner hour, but there were still some guys on duty in the kitchen. They were able to scare up some sandwiches and snacks, which the duo wolfed down.

They went outside and took stock. A locator reading indicated that The Package remained in the same place in Azif it had occupied earlier this day. A number of methods lay open to Jafar to communicate with them if he wanted to, including special one-use-only cell phones, text messaging, and third-party messengers and go-betweens. None of them had been set in motion.

Kilroy said, "My guess is that Hassani won't jump tonight. Too soon after last night's little shindig. He'll want to get all his ducks in a row when he makes the delivery, and that means waiting for the storm. It won't reach its height until at least tomorrow."

No action tonight. Of course, they were never really off duty. If Hassani Akkad pulled a fast one and went tonight, they'd get in harness and get after him. Tonight they would be on standby, sticking close to Greentown.

Vang Bulo decided to catch the last feature at the compound's movie theater. He didn't know what was playing and didn't care. He was a big movie fan. The louder, brighter, and stupider the films were, the better he liked them. Hollywood product was so far removed from anything even remotely approaching reality that it allowed him to escape into a candy-colored fantasyland. It didn't matter if he missed the beginning of the picture or came in at the middle and fell asleep before the end. In fact, it was better that way, since he didn't have to follow the inane plotlines.

Kilroy said, "I'm going back to my room. I'd rather sleep in a bed than a cramped movie seat. More comfortable."

They went their separate ways, Kilroy to the Visitors' Quarters building, Vang Bulo to the movies. Kilroy entered the lobby. Voices and movement came from the back of the building. Kilroy decided that he wasn't ready for sleep just yet. He strolled past the front desk and into the day room.

The lights were low, unobtrusive. There was enough to see by without being blinded by the glare. After the harsh contrasts of the Iraqi landscape, the pattern of shadows alternating with soft lights was soothing to the eye. The green and white marbled linoleum floor, waxed and buffed, reflected overhead lights with a smooth, burnished glow.

A cone of muted yellow light fell on a handful of small, square folding tables near the soda machine. A handful of people were scattered at the tables. One table held a couple of civilian construction contractors. Another, a group of administrators.

A third held Prester and Debbie Lynn Hawley. Prester motioned for Kilroy to come over. He and Debbie Lynn were drinking out of paper cups. Between them stood a clear plastic bottle of a name brand of bottled water.

Kilroy went up to the table. Prester, red faced, seemed to radiate heat. His eyes were glittery and glazed at the same time. His shirt was unbuttoned down to midchest.

He hailed Kilroy. "How goes it in the postal inspection line?"

"The good news is that the mail is getting through," Kilroy said. "The bad news is that the post offices keep getting blown up."

Debbie Lynn frowned, giving her a look of serious concentration. "Again? Damn! I'm waiting on some important letters from back home."

"I was just kidding," Kilroy said. "There weren't any post offices blown up today. Not in these parts, anyhow."

Prester said sardonically, "Have you checked

lately?" He gestured toward the table. "Sit down and join us, Joseph. Make it a threesome."

Debbie Lynn gave Prester a look that said, *There he goes again.* She raised her eyebrows and rolled her eyes.

"I don't know nothing about no threesomes," Kilroy said doubtfully, "but I'll take a load off." He pulled out a chair and sat down beside the woman.

Prester said, "Just some good-natured ribbing, my dear."

She said, "Press's joshing. He likes to make fun of me for being a prude."

"Not at all, not at all," Prester said. His face contorted in a grotesque combination of a squint and a leer that was supposed to be a knowing wink. He tried to affect the manner of a man of the world, cynical and amused, but he just looked owlish.

"In fact, I happen to admire your good sense in never having slept with me throughout the time of our acquaintance," he said.

Debbie Lynn said, "It was for your own good. I didn't want to leave you more of a wreck than you are now."

"It's true. I am a wreck." Prester's mouth turned down at the corners. "You should leave me abandoned by the side of the road, Debbie Lynn, along with the rest of the burnt-out wrecks littering the landscape."

"You're getting maudlin, Press."

Kilroy said, "I don't know, maybe he's right." He indicated the water bottle. "You must be slipping, Prester, sticking to plain old $H_2O$-type water. That's a lot lower octane than your usual variety."

"That's what you think," Debbie Lynn said. "That's not water, it's vodka."

Kilroy said, "Mind if I fix myself one?"

Nobody minded. In fact, Prester was insistent that he join them for a drink or ten. Kilroy went to work. He went to the kitchenette, filling a paper cup with ice. The vending machine yielded a can of orange soda. He returned to the table, filling the cup halfway with vodka. It was a twenty-ounce cup. He filled the rest with orange soda.

Prester grimaced, shuddering. "Gah! How can you drink that swill? Look at the label and you'll see it says *orange drink*. Not orange juice, mind you. Orange *drink*. Lord knows what kind of artificial crap they put in it. Whatever they use to give it that radioactive glow-in-the-dark neon color, it can't be found in nature. It must come out of a chemical vat."

"That's okay. What's in that water bottle is sure to sterilize it," Kilroy said. "Straight-up vodka's a little raw for me. I need something to cut it with."

"Suit yourself. It only leaves more for me," said Prester.

Kilroy glanced across at Debbie Lynn, at the ripe swell of her high, firm breasts where they thrust out against her khaki blouse. The collar was unbuttoned and open down past her collarbone, affording a glimpse of the tender flesh at the top of her breasts.

She said coolly, "Looking for something?"

Unabashed, he said, "I was just admiring the creases in your khakis."

"Is that right?"

Kilroy nodded. "I was wondering how you got them so sharp and clean edged."

"I have them starched at the post laundry."

"The khakis."

"Yes, of course. What else? My bosom?"

Prester took another swallow of his drink. "I'm getting pretty starched myself. Which is not surprising, really, since vodka is nothing but distilled potato juice."

"Not always. Sometimes it's made from wheat," Kilroy pointed out.

Prester nodded, intoxication exaggerating his bobbing head movements. "Quite right, Joseph. You have me there."

They sat and drank and made small talk. Prester did most of the talking. That suited Kilroy, allowing him to concentrate on Debbie Lynn. Her face was heart shaped and fine featured, the features so cleanly chiseled that they just missed being sharp. Her nose was slightly snub, with a sprinkling of freckles across it. Her hazel eyes occasionally glinted yellow when the light struck them a certain way. She had a kewpie-doll mouth. The corners of her lips were slightly upcurved so that she looked like she was smiling to herself. She had an elfin quality. Kilroy wouldn't have been surprised if her ears were pointed. He was surprised that they weren't.

Prester looked debauched, overripe. His face was flushed bright red. His forehead was shiny with sweat. His eyebrows were pointed in the centers, Mephistophelian style. Several lank strands of hair hung down over his forehead, constantly vibrating with his movements.

Kilroy drained his cup, made a face, and turned to Prester. "You were right. That orange pop has a nasty taste. I'll take the next one straight."

Prester looked canny. "Now you're getting smart."

"Getting stinko," Debbie Lynn said tartly. "Your heads will smart tomorrow morning with a hangover."

Prester put a hand to his forehead. "Come to think of it, my head already hurts. Good thing I'm too drunk to feel it."

He stood up, rising from his chair in a series of abrupt straightening maneuvers, like a fire truck ladder unfolding in sections. His hands rested on the table's edge; his head hung down below his shoulders. His face was very red. It looked boiled. So did he. He was swaying slightly.

Kilroy dubiously eyed the table. It seemed unsturdy, like it might collapse if Prester put too much weight on it. Ever mindful of what really counted, Kilroy reached out to steady and secure the water bottle.

Prester wagged a chiding finger. "Stealing my liquor? That won't do, my man. Won't do at all."

Kilroy said, "I just wanted to make sure it didn't get knocked over."

"It won't It'll be in safe hands minc."

Kilroy shrugged goodhumoredly. "Suit yourself. It's your bottle."

"I'm not greedy," Prester said, pouring some more vodka into Kilroy's cup, filling it almost to the brim. For all his seeming drunkenness, his hand was steady, and he spilled not a drop.

Kilroy said, "Whoa, that's plenty."

"That's all you get, and it could be a long night ahead, eh, what?" This last bit was said in a grotesque parody of a British accent.

He moved to refill Debbie Lynn's cup but she

put her hand over the top of it, thwarting him. "I'm fine, thanks," she said.

He faced the two of them. "I'm sure you two will find some way to occupy yourselves without me and my bottle. And now, I bid you all a fond adieu."

Debbie Lynn said, "We'll meet by the desk at six A.M. That way we can have breakfast before leaving to make our morning rounds."

Prester shuddered. "The thought of food at that hour—or now, come to think of it—makes me ill."

"There'll be plenty of black coffee, too."

Prester said good night, took his bottle, and went away. He crossed the floor, his center of gravity located in his spreading paunch and heavy hips. He entered the lobby, rounding the front desk and disappearing from view.

Debbie Lynn watched him go and shook her head. "Come morning, though, he'll be fresh as a daisy, and I'll be the one with the hangover."

Kilroy said, "He's older than you. He's had a lot more time to practice his drinking."

"He doesn't need any practice; he's a master at it."

The vodka mingled with melted ice to make a nice slurry mix. Each swallow added to the pleasantly tingling feeling of numbness that began at the back of Kilroy's neck and soon spread over his cranium and all points in between, bruising his brain. He felt pretty good.

He and Debbie Lynn were chatting about something. Time passed. Kilroy's elbows were on the table and he was leaning forward, head thrust across the table toward her so that their faces were only inches apart. He was aware that they'd been getting chummier and more intimate for some time. He'd forgotten what they were talking about. It was okay because she was talking, and if he listened long enough he'd pick up the thread of the chatter well enough to fake it.

His elbow brushed against something on the table and set it in motion. It was his paper cup, which lay on its side. Luckily it was all but empty, except for what looked like a teaspoonful of liquid that sloshed around in the bottom of the cup.

He realized that he was a little bit drunkee. He also realized that something was rubbing against his thigh—Debbie Lynn's leg. She studied him for a moment. "I hope you're not too drunk."

"I'm never too drunk," he said indignantly. Then, after a beat: "Too drunk to what?"

"To take me to my room," she said.

"Hell, I was counting on you to take me back to my room."

They got up and left. Kilroy thought he was walking pretty good, considering the way the floor kept tilting, with a seesaw motion.

Climbing the stairs was a chore, but not without benefits. It allowed him to circle Debbie Lynn's slim waist with his arm. He could feel the warmth of her flesh through her clothes. As she climbed, the khaki pants were pulled tight against her shapely buttocks, whose ripely rounded curves Kilroy admired as he followed her up the stairway.

It was a long climb. He lost track of what floor they were on. The thirteenth, at least. Which was funny, since it was only a four-story building.

Then they were in a hall, at a door. He was leaning on Debbie Lynn while she fitted her key into the lock and opened it. They went in, the light from the hall shining through the open doorway into the room.

Kilroy and Debbie Lynn went into a clinch. She was about a head shorter than he. She was a nice little armful. Her lips were soft, her breath sweet, and her mouth warm and wet.

One thing led to another, and before too long they were on the bed, naked.

Debbie Lynn had a beautiful little body. Tight. Pear-shaped breasts and pointy pink nipples. A wicked little shape, a provocative ass, pert and dimpled. She was surprisingly wiry and athletic, in top condition. Beneath her satin skin lay powerful, compact musculature. When her folded legs wrapped around his hips, they hugged him with a viselike grip. She was built and conditioned like a gymnast or dancer.

Trouble was, she was a screamer. Kilroy found that out when he started hitting his stride putting it to her. She was vocal about her pleasure. They were making plenty of noise without it. The cot sounded like it was shaking itself apart.

Debbie Lynn sounded like she was getting killed. A couple of times, between hard breathing, he urged her, "Shh, shh."

She was on her knees with her rear raised up and her head pressed down against the mattress. He knelt behind her, putting it to her doggy style.

That was a good one. Well, who better? If he wasn't qualified for it, who was? The thought amused him, and he almost laughed out loud.

Debbie Lynn bit down on a corner of a pillow and stuffed it in her mouth, stifling her outcries.

Later, the two slept in each other's arms, damp

sheets tangled around them. Kilroy hovered in a feverish, half-drunken state before fatigue took over and he fell into a deep sleep.

He felt like his head had barely struck the pillow, and now it was daylight. Not sunrise, but the pale pearly glow of predawn. Curtained windows were oblongs of grayness against the fuzzy dark bulk of shadowed walls.

Kilroy lay there in the dimness, on his side, curled against Debbie Lynn's curvy body. Her breathing was deep and even, but somehow he sensed she was awake, too. He was right. She stirred restlessly, as if in her sleep, pressing her warm smooth rear against his groin. His reaction was immediate. He rolled her on her back and got on top of her as she opened to him.

Soon they were thrashing and writhing. She started wailing again. Her mouth was close to his ear, and she sounded louder than ever. Before it got too far gone and woke up everybody on the floor, if not in the damned building, he clapped a hand over her mouth to silence her.

That put her over the edge and she started spasming beneath him. She tried to bite his hand but he held it clamped over her mouth so she couldn't sink her teeth into it. Her nostrils widened and she bucked under him, coming.

At four A.M., she rolled out of bed, hopped up, and began doing a routine of stretching and aerobic exercises. Where did she get the energy?

Kilroy dragged himself out of bed and pulled some clothes on. He kissed her good-bye and went out into the hall, looking for his room. He had to find out what floor he was on first.

He stumbled into his room and hit the sack. Before falling asleep, Kilroy had the thought that he'd been wrong earlier in the mess hall, when he'd observed that Debbie Lynn looked just as good leaving as she did coming.

Hell, she looked a lot better when she was coming.

# Six

The next night, Hassani Akkad came out. With The Package.

The storm was high. It had blown in from the south, from as far south as the Gulf, masses of superheated air that barreled north for several hundred miles, hurling along a mountain range's worth of windborne sand and dust. Like a sandstorm, only dirtier.

Searing hot winds scoured topsoil from the land, peeling it down layer by layer. A brown fog, cutting down visibility, cloaked the scene in murk. The wind howled.

No one ventured out of doors tonight without good reason. All but the most confirmed malefactors and evildoers were inclined to stay safely dug in their holes, waiting out the storm.

Only the most motivated came out. Such persons were no doubt to be found in the Red Crescent ambulance that crept out of the border foothills, heading deeper west into Iraq.

Like the Red Cross, the Red Crescent provides

emergency medical service and humanitarian relief in distressed areas. Presumably the ambulance was returning from some errand of mercy in the Iraqi borderlands.

It pushed west along a dirt road, a back road snaking its way through some bumpy and irregular open land. Bold red crescent emblems were blazoned on the roof and sides. It looked like a hearse, except that it was painted red and white and had a roof-mounted light rack. Headlights were twin cones of amber light, poking into the mass of cottony brown dust clouds.

Its progress was slow and crablike, as if it were crawling through rushing streamers of muck and ooze along a dirty river bottom. Hillocks and ridges occasionally arose to blunt the wind and force the vehicle to detour around them. At a point about six miles or so west of the border, the road tilted upward, climbing a gentle slope and coming out on a flat.

Now that the ambulance was out of the relative shelter of the lowlands basin and in the open, it was subjected to the full force of the wind and given a buffeting. There was less cover here, the ground was more open. The way was easier. The ambulance's speed edged up, reaching about ten to twelve miles per hour. It slowed as it neared a canal, meeting it at right angles. A bridge spanned the gap between banks. The canal was little more than an overgrown ditch, about twenty feet across and between four and five feet deep. It was not filled with water but with dirt. It had been dry for a long time, long enough for its floor to be dotted with bushes, brambles, and reeds that had taken root there.

The bridge was a low, wood plank one. Nothing

marked its presence, no warning signs, reflectors, or flashing lights. You were supposed to know it was there. If you didn't, then you didn't belong there.

The ambulance driver knew it was there. He slowed to a few miles per hour for the approach, nosing the ambulance on to the bridge. It was a stout-planked bridge, strong and sturdy, and it neither groaned nor sagged under the vehicle's weight.

The ambulance had reached the midpoint of the crossing when a pair of dull, muffled crumping noises sounded from beneath the bridge.

It was the sound of two minibombs exploding. Two small squares of puttylike explosive material had been molded to joints where the bridge's main horizontal support beams met the vertical upright posts in midspan. Miniaturized radio-controlled detonators were fixed to the explosive wads and triggered remotely.

The microblasts were set to collapse the bridge with minimal damage to the vehicle. The bridge imploded, pitching the ambulance down into the ditch about five feet below. Neither the driver nor the cab passenger were wearing seatbelts. The driver pitched forward over the top of the steering wheel, hitting the windshield with his head. The windshield starred, frosted, and then went opaque white, but it held and didn't shatter.

The way the ambulance hit the ground caused the front passenger side door to pop open. The passenger was pitched out of the cab and thrown to the bottom of the ditch, where he lay unmoving.

The ambulance front crumpled. The engine stalled. The vehicle came down hard, rocking from side to side, teetering on two wheels. For an instant, it threatened to topple over on its side before righting itself.

The blast and crash generated a cloud of dust and smoke. Storm winds dispersed it quickly enough.

The ambulance had a crushed front and battered sides. It was unsprung and squatted heavily on its frame. One headlamp was broken and dark, but the other still shone, its cyclops eye beaming at a tilted angle toward the opposite side of the ditch. The lens was cracked, and it vented splintered shards of light. The stalled engine kept it from burning.

Steam clouds rose out from under the crumpled hood, stinking of coolant. A pool of oil grew under the vehicle.

The man who'd been thrown from the cab stirred. Groaned. His limbs thrashed feebly, like he was swimming on dry land. He was dazed, stunned. Half conscious. A slash across his forehead was dripping lines of blood down across his face. His eyes were glazed, unfocused. Still, he had enough left to be crawling away from the wreck rather than toward it. Away from the light, into the darkness.

Other survivors were heard from. Thrashing movement and feeble choked cries came from the rear compartment of the ambulance. Someone was inside, trying to get out. The rear door handle rattled. The survivor found the strength to fling open the door. He crouched, framed in the open doorway, clinging to the edges of it with both hands.

He was known as Kamal the Turk. His name wasn't Kamal and he wasn't a Turk; he was an Iraqi who looked like what his fellow Iraqis thought a Turk looked like. In Hassani Akkad's circle, almost no one gave their right name anyway. The Turk was a long-time member of the gang, of Hassani's inner circle.

He was battered and dazed, having taken quite a pounding inside the compartment when the vehicle had crashed into the ditch. He clung to the sides of the hatchway, head lolling, body reeling. Hauling himself forward, he stepped down to the ground. His legs weren't working properly, and he fell, crying out in pain.

The Turk crying aloud in pain? That scared the man in the ditch, prompting him to increase his efforts to crawl away. But he was semiconscious at best and didn't have much strength to draw on to drag himself away.

New cries sounded from inside the ambulance. They were weaker and more feeble than those made by the Turk.

Kamal labored, trying to gather himself into a sitting position. He had hard, thuggish features, but he was hurting, and now he didn't look so tough. His big strangler's hands were impressive, though. He managed to get them around the ambulance's rear bumper and use it to haul himself up to his feet. He braced himself by half leaning, half sitting on the vehicle.

Behind him, inside the compartment, a voice tried to call his name. The speaker suffered a coughing fit, subsiding finally with a groan. Then in faint, quavery tones, the voice called, "Kamal, Kamal!"

Kamal turned his head, looking dully over his shoulder. He could see little inside the compartment space beside thick, murky gloom. But he recognized the voice. He said, "Sirdar."

"Yes." Sirdar's voice was low, urgent. "Help me, Kamal . . . My leg. I think it's broken."

"What of Ali Mahmud? He was in there with you."

"Help me, Kamal—"

"Ali Mahmud?"

"Dead," said Sirdar. "Never mind about him. He's beyond help. Help me."

"Are you sure he's dead?" Kamal lacked the strength, or he would have checked for himself.

Sirdar said, "No man can live with his head hanging off his neck like Ali Mahmud's is doing." Sirdar was peevish. "Help me get out, I can't do it by myself."

Kamal blacked out for an instant, coming to as he pitched forward. That scared him, and he found the strength to scrabble for a handhold on the doorway.

Sirdar tried to pull himself out but failed. He writhed around in the compartment, suddenly shrieking with pain. "My leg! I tell you it's broken!" He choked off a sob.

Kamal buried his face in his hands and rubbed it. After a pause, he looked up. A figure stood facing him, about eight feet away. He hadn't been there an instant before. He stood to one side of Kamal, a huge black man in goggles who held an assault rifle pointed at him. The goggles were there to protect his eyes from the sandstorm. The rifle was there for what rifles are for.

Kamal was not so dazed that he didn't realize he was a dead man. Cursing, he grabbed for the gun holstered at his side. A single shot ripped through him. It made a loud, flat cracking sound like a piece of deadwood being snapped in two.

Vang Bulo stepped forward, moving toward the

back of the ambulance. The wind from the dust storm was stiff, but even so the scent of cordite was thick and heavy in the nostrils for a minute before being blown away. He poked the rifle barrel into the compartment.

Sirdar gasped, recoiling. "No—Don't!" Vang Bulo did. The shot filled the compartment with light, noise, and smoke. One hand held the rifle by the stock; the other held a pocket flashlight. He held it to the side, away from his body, so as not to draw fire.

He shone the pencil-thin beam into the compartment, shining it on Sirdar and then on Ali Mahmud. The corpses' heavily shadowed features took on a hobgoblin quality. Ali Mahmud's head hung down on one side of his neck, like a too-heavy flower whose weight has snapped the stalk that bears it.

Vang Bulo went around the side of the ambulance, approaching the driver's side, prepared to give the coup de grace. But the driver was already dead.

The man in the ditch had not been idle during this time. The sound of shots spurred him on to greater efforts. He crawled forward on his belly. He was already in the shadows. It was possible the enemy hadn't seen him yet. He felt around in his pockets, but his gun was gone. He'd lost it sometime during the crash.

He lowcrawled forward, proceeding no more than a half dozen paces before a pair of combat boots filled his field of vision. They came upon him so suddenly that he almost bumped his head into them. His gaze rose, following the boots upward to the baggy camo pants worn by their owner. Right around then the gun muzzle came into view, too, the bore of a

Kalash rifle barrel that was being held pointed downward at his upturned face.

The newcomer said, "Hassani Akkad." It was not a question but a statement of fact, like a presiding judge reading the accused's name from the bench before delivering sentence.

That was his name, the name of the man in the ditch: Hassani Akkad. The voice of the speaker was that of a foreign devil. Before Hassani Akkad could react, one of the booted feet became a blur of motion that delivered a smart snap kick to the point of his chin. He fell facedown into the dirt, limp, unconscious.

Hassani Akkad had come out earlier tonight and brought The Package with him. Kilroy had been periodically monitoring the locator for hours, anticipating such a development. The Package was human cargo, an abductee with a microminiatured transmitter implanted in a chip hidden in his flesh. When he was finally moved, his movements showed on the locator.

At about the same time, Jafar Akkad had contacted Kilroy by a onetime-use-only cell phone. Jafar was excited. You could tell from the throaty, husky quality of his voice that he was getting all choked up, anticipating the end of his beloved brother.

The Package was being taken from Azif to a farmhouse. The farmhouse was a safe house located near the border. It had been used before, in other kidnappings where the victims were transferred to the Iranians. Jafar supplied names and locations. He was thorough and precise—he didn't want Hassani to escape.

The Package would be transported by ambulance, a dodge the kidnappers had used before. The authorities were less likely to interfere with an ambulance than with most other vehicles. Whenever Hassani Akkad needed one, he sent some of his gang members out to steal one from the Red Crescent or the emergency ward of the nearest hospital.

It was unusual for Hassani to personally accompany this shipment of human goods. Unlike Jafar, the elder brother had no liking for going out in the field on action operations. He'd long since had his fill of that. But he made a point of personally escorting this abductee to the handlers on the border.

The Package must be very important to Hassani. Not even Jafar knew why, though he suspected that it had something to do with Hassani's high-level Iranian contacts, border patrol headman Captain Saq and secret police powerbroker Colonel Munghal.

Early in the evening, the ambulance had arrived at the place where the abductee was being held. His name was Ali al-Magid. To the gang members who guarded him, he seemed perfectly ordinary, almost drearily so. Nor was he rich. But he was valuable to Hassani and to the Iranians, too.

Ali al-Magid had been unconscious, drugged, as he had been throughout much of his captivity. It made him more easily handled. When the massive dosage finally wore off and he came to, he would find himself possessed of no small narcotics habit. But that would only furnish the Iranians with a handle by which to control him.

Hassani Akkad had set off with some of his most trusted men. He rode in front with the driver. Ali al-Magid, still unconscious, was strapped to a stretcher and loaded into the back of the ambulance. Riding in the compartment with him were Ali Mahmoud, Sirdar, and Kamal the Turk. Ali Mahmoud was the muscle, and Kamal was a shooter. Sirdar was a hospital orderly with some medical experience. He could monitor al-Magid's vital signs and make sure that he did not slip too deeply, perhaps fatally, under the influence of the drugs.

The alleys and warrens of the Red Dome neighborhood had been empty, abandoned due to the storm. The ambulance had crawled through streets made treacherous by sifting sands. It had exited Azif, traveling eastward on some of the lesser, rougher roads running parallel to the border highway.

It drove out to the farmhouse, nestled at the base of the foothills' western slope. The crew of handlers at the farmhouse were all trusted Akkad crime family veterans. They would make the final transfer, delivering the captive across the border to the Iranians.

Hassani Akkad had seen no need for his presence for that particular transaction. Captain Saq had been unhappy with him of late, suspicious that he'd been involved with the recent unrest on the border that had culminated in the massacre of the gunrunners, the murder of four border patrol guards, and the disappearance of an armored scout car. Hassani was furious and frustrated by this development, especially since he hadn't been involved in the attacks. It galled him to be suspected of something he hadn't done, gaining him all of the notoriety with none of the plunder. He wished he had done it.

The ambulance had not lingered but left the

farmhouse almost immediately after Ali al-Magid had been delivered. Captain Saq was not beyond making a quick thrust across the border with his troops to corral Hassani for a little questioning. Azif, with its double guard of the Akkad organization and the Red Dome militia, had never looked more inviting to the gang chief.

The ambulance headed west, following a backroads route that would inevitably take it to the plank bridge and the canal. Jafar had taken great pains to describe it so Kilroy would be sure not to miss it.

While the ambulance was at the farmhouse, Kilroy and Vang Bulo had rigged the minibombs on the bridge. Then waited for its arrival to spring the ambush.

Kilroy had had enough advance notice so that if he'd wanted to, he could have outraced the ambulance and ambushed it on the way to the farmhouse before it delivered Ali al-Magid to the handlers. But that wouldn't have suited his master plan.

# Seven

Now the trap had been sprung, and Hassani Akkad bagged. Kilroy looked down at Hassani stretched out facedown in the dirt, out cold.

Vang Bulo clambered over the top of the front of the ambulance. He eyed the man on the ground. "Hassani?"

Kilroy said, "Yes."

"Dead?"

"Just knocked out. I think. Unless I kicked him too hard and broke his neck."

Kilroy toed the body, working a foot under it and flipping Hassani over on his back. He was limp, unresponsive. His face and front were coated with dirt. The dirt had made a kind of paste on his chin where it dribbled with a trickle of blood from a split lip. His mouth gaped open and he breathed thickly, heavily.

"He'll live," Kilroy said. "For a while. Not that we needed him alive for what comes next, but it makes it more fun that way."

The ditch was partially sheltered from the sandstorm, avoiding its full force by being below ground level. Being in the lee of the ambulance also provided some protection from windblown dirt and chaff. The wind was hot and dry. Vang Bulo stood, crouching, ducking the top of his head below the walls of the trench.

Kilroy didn't bother to ask if the others in the ambulance had been taken care of. There was no need. Vang Bulo would have done what he had to do. He was a pro.

Kilroy went down on one knee beside Hassani and began searching him, turning out his pockets and squeezing the folds of his clothes. The gang chief had two pistols: one in his jacket pocket and another, smaller weapon, a flat little mini-automatic tucked in his waistband at the small of his back. He was also armed with a switchblade knife, a spring-operated stiletto. His cell phone might yield potentially valuable intelligence on his contacts, but the possibility of its being equipped with a locating device made it too dangerous to be taken along. Kilroy crushed it under the heel of his boot.

Hassani's pockets bulged with a couple of fat billfolds. Kilroy relieved him of them. Each wad of cash was in a different currency: dollars, euros, and Iraqi money. The Iraqi wad was the thickest and had the least value. His pockets also yielded a leather pouch with a drawstring mouth, which when opened was revealed to contain a handful of gold baubles, probably stolen: rings, earrings, brooches, and bracelets.

Other pocket litter included change in the amount of a half-dozen coins; a pill vial filled with capsules of many different sizes, shapes, and colors; a set of thumbscrews; a packet of chewing gum, a well-known American brand, the kind that claims to brighten your teeth while you chew; and a well-worn note-book, pocket sized, with a black leather cover and spiral binding. The pages were filled with hand-written notes and rows of number-and-letter combinations.

Kilroy indicated the notebook. "This looks promising. It's gibberish to me, but maybe the code breakers can make something out of it." He tucked it away in a sealed inside vest pocket for safekeeping.

Vang Bulo said, "What about the ambulance? Do we blow it up?" His head was down below ground level, out of the main airstream of the storm, but he still had to yell to be heard over howling winds.

"It'll keep," Kilroy said. "Why advertise our presence?" He unsnapped a pouch on his web belt, taking out a length of yellow plastic restraining tape.

Vang Bulo said, "Those things remind me of the alligator strips used to secure the tops of garbage bags."

"Yeah, they're good for securing garbage, all right," Kilroy said.

He took hold of one of Hassani's arms and rolled him over on his belly. Hassani groaned.

Vang Bulo said, "Is he coming around?"

"Not enough to matter," Kilroy said. He placed Hassani's hands behind his back, crossing the wrists. He looped the plastic strand around the wrists, fitting the tip through the catch and pulling it tight. The plastic restraints were thin but tough. Hassani would be unable to break free. Nothing less than a gorilla could snap that strand by force. It worked like handcuffs but weighed a lot less and was easier to carry.

Kilroy rose, giving an after-you-Alphonse type of gesture. "He's all yours."

Vang Bulo looked skeptical. "How come I get all the grunt work?"

Kilroy held his hands out in front of him, the backs of them turned up. A posture like a surgeon holding out his hands waiting for the nurse to snap on the rubber gloves.

"These are artist's hands. They've got to perform later tonight. We mustn't risk straining them with overwork or otherwise risking their delicate coordination," he said, with heavy sarcasm. But he meant it, too.

Vang Bulo said, "You're going to work that gag one too many times."

"It's no gag, it's the truth," Kilroy said, an innocent man unjustly accused.

Grumbling, Vang Bulo handed Kilroy his rifle to hold. He straddled Hassani, squatting down and bending forward, hooking his meaty hands under the other's bound arms. He straightened with a grunt, hefting Hassani off the ground and standing him upright, then turning him around and tossing him over one massive shoulder. He stood there holding the other man without sign of strain.

Kilroy slung Vang Bulo's rifle across his back and leveled his own, taking the fore. He moved out, Vang Bulo trotting after, with Hassani slung across his shoulder. They moved along at an easy, jogging gait. Easy for Kilroy, anyway, since he wasn't laden with Hassani's dead weight.

About twenty yards north of the bridge, they came to a place where the east side of the ditch was worn away. They paused. Kilroy said, "I'll take a look-see."

He clambered up the cleft in the ditch. He stuck his head up above the edge, cautiously. Nobody took a shot at it. Not that he was expecting that, but he wasn't not expecting it, either.

Sand particles and grit stung his exposed flesh and pattered against the plastic lenses of his goggles. He looked around, but there wasn't much to see.

A road ran from the east side of the bridge across the landscape, trailing off into a lazy S-curve in the near distance, disappearing into a gap between two low mounds. The scene was blurred by the sandstorm. He looked back, across the ditch toward the west. More of the same. No curiosity-seekers came from either direction to investigate the crash and shooting. Why should they? This was lonely country at the best of times. It was generally untenanted, except by smugglers, fugitives, and other border hoppers. And most of them were pinned down in their lairs, waiting out the storm.

That's why Hassani Akkad and his gang had been using this night for the trip to the farmhouse and back.

Kilroy scrambled up to the top of the bank, crouching low, scanning from left to right. It looked clear, and he motioned Vang Bulo to come up. The big man climbed the cleft as easily as if he were climbing stairs without a human burden thrown over his shoulder. His ascent was silent, barely dislodging more than a stone or two in his passage.

Kilroy listened to see if he was breathing hard. He wasn't. The man was in top physical condition.

They moved out, crossing an open space for about fifty feet before coming to a ridge. The ridge was about eight feet high. A stand of brush made a smoky gray patch against the ridge's darker mound. The bushes screened a notch in the ridge. On the other side lay a clearing where the SUV awaited.

Kilroy prowled the clearing, leading with his rifle barrel. The site was empty; they were alone. Vang Bulo stooped, letting Hassani slide off his shoulder and slinging him to the ground like a sack of potatoes. From a pocket he took out a device about the size of a stopwatch, square shaped and flat, but rounded at the edges.

The SUV was rigged with proximity motion detectors. The device held a gauge to monitor their readout. Vang Bulo checked it. All signs were negative, affirming that the vehicle was untouched and untampered with.

He pocketed the gauge, grabbed the collar at the back of Hassani's neck, and dragged him across the ground to the rear of the SUV. Hassani cursed him, shouting over the wind.

Kilroy joined them. The gang chief had wriggled himself partly upright and now sat with his back propped up against a rear tire and his legs stretched out in front of him on the ground.

Hassani's forehead, nose, and lips were mashed and bleeding. His chin and the left side of his jaw where Kilroy had kicked him were plum purple and swollen. He waggled his jaws experimentally, groaning. His stony gaze, hooded and sullen, grew hot. He glared at Kilroy. "I think you broke my jaw."

Kilroy said, "Not the way you're wagging it."

"You kicked me. An unforgivable insult. For that, you will die," Hassani Akkad said. "Wait—there is still a chance for you to save yourselves. Free me. Let me go, and you may live to see another day."

Kilroy smiled gently. "I can guess what would have happened if any of the victims you kidnapped had made such a demand of you."

The other blustered, "Kidnapping? This is a ridiculous charge! What victims?"

"You know, the ones you kept chained and blindfolded for weeks at a time. The ones you sold to radical terrorist groups, to be beheaded in time to make the evening news on al-Jazeera. You'd have taught them a lesson pretty fast.

"Listen up, Hassani Akkad. You pulled plenty of kidnappings. Now it's your turn," Kilroy said. "You've been bagged."

"You are mad. Still, I will play along with the game."

"You sure will," Kilroy said, chuckling humorlessly.

The clearing was ringed with mounds that sheltered it somewhat from the winds, but gusts reached down into the hollow where the SUV stood. Hassani squirmed, turning his head, craning, squinting against the sandstorm.

He said, "Where are the rest of your men?"

His captors made no reply.

"I see," Akkad said at last, a crafty expression stealing on to his face. "There are no others. Just the two of you. And why not? How many does it take to attack a defenseless noncombatant ambulance? Swine! Only a little Satan or two little Satans from the Great Satan USA would be so contemptuous of the laws of war and the common decency of all mankind as to launch a cowardly attack on an innocent medical vehicle!"

"He's sure got you pegged," Vang Bulo said to Kilroy.

"And you!" Kilroy replied.

Hassani was impatient. "Let us come to the point: How much? How much will it cost for me to ransom myself out of your infidel clutches?"

Kilroy said, "After all the trouble we went to to get you?"

"Every man has his price. What's yours?"

"Colonel Munghal," Kilroy said.

After a pause, Hassani, stiff faced, said, "I never heard of the man."

"That's why you flinched when I said his name."

"You are mistaken."

Kilroy shrugged. Vang Bulo moved in, grabbing a handful of Hassani's shirtfront and jerking him up off the ground to his feet.

Kilroy opened the back of the SUV. Inside, a couple of machines, an all-terrain vehicle, and a dirt bike were fastened in place on the floor. He said, "Throw him in the back and let's go."

Hassani cried, "Wait! Hear me out before you do anything rash!"

"I'm waiting," Kilroy said. "But make it quick. We've got a date with Colonel Munghal."

"You don't know what you are doing. If you proceed with your reckless course of action, you will succeed only in getting yourselves killed along with me," Hassani said.

"We'll take the chance."

"I can trade for my life!"

Kilroy was dubious. "What have you got to trade?"

"Someone far more valuable than I. Someone your masters would very much like to get hold of. They will reward you greatly."

"Who?"

"Do we have a deal?"

"Not until I know what you've got to trade with."

Hassani took a deep breath before making his pitch. "Does the name Ali al-Magid mean anything to you?"

"What does it mean to you?"

"He is a very important man."

"We've got you," Kilroy said. "I'll admit it's an unequal swap, but you know what they say about a bird in the hand."

Hassani Akkad snarled, his split lip making him wince. "Professor Ali al-Magid," he said venomously. "You had better check on that name with your superiors before you commit a blunder of historic proportions."

Kilroy said, "I know who al-Magid is: the one prize package that could tempt even a toad like Colonel Munghal out of his hole. Al-Magid will keep fine right where he is. That's where we want him. We'll keep you. I'm sure that the Colonel will want to tell you himself about what a great job you're doing."

Hassani Akkad realized the inevitable. His head bowed, downcast. An instant later he looked up, glaring. "Who betrayed me?" he demanded. "Someone must have sold me to you. Who? I have the right to know!"

"I don't guess it'll do any harm to let you know," Kilroy said. "It was Jafar. Your brother Jafar put the finger on you."

The other barely blinked. "I do not believe you."

"Okay, don't."

Hassani began blinking, more and more rapidly now. "Not that I give one grain of credence to your grotesque, absurd, and insulting accusation, but just for the sake of argument, what could possibly motivate my beloved brother Jafar to stain his hands—and his name, and that of all his posterity, if any—with such infamy?"

"It's simple," Kilroy said. "He wants your job. They don't call him The Whale for nothing. He wants to be the big fish."

Vang Bulo said, "A whale is a mammal, not a fish."

"I know, but I'm trying to make a point here."

"From the look on Hassani's face, I'd say you made it."

Hassani Akkad was in a state of rage. Veins swelled, standing out on the sides of his forehead and cording in his neck. His eyes bulged. He looked like he'd been bitten by an adder and was puffing up from the venom.

Before he could shout, Kilroy slapped a wide, flat strip of duct tape across the other's mouth. Two more strips laid across the first in an X seemed to effectually silence Hassani, more or less. Garbled, choking, guttural cries of fury were muffled by the duct tape, though not entirely cut off.

Hassani was loaded into the back of the SUV, and the hatch closed. Kilroy and Vang Bulo went around to the front and got in the cab. Vang Bulo got in the driver's seat.

Away went the vehicle, on a collision course with Colonel Munghal.

# Eight

The Rock of the Hawk marked the site of the coming showdown. The rock was the most prominent feature of a pass that connected Iraq with Iran. The pass was a gorge running east-west through the hills. Its eastern end lay on the Iranian highland, while its western end opened on a piece of Iraqi land occupied by the Akkad gang farmhouse.

Its winding course caused it to loop due north and due south in places before returning to its primary orientation. It was narrow in some places, and never too wide in most. At its narrowest, though, near the Iraqi terminus, it was still wide enough to allow the passage of a pickup truck, jeep, or similar-sized vehicle. It was too narrow for anything larger, like an armored vehicle, to proceed.

In some places, mostly on the Iranian side, it was a wide *wadi* flanked by low hills. Nearer to Iraq, it was bounded by rock cliffs.

The pass was a real smuggler's highway. Other, lesser branches wormed through the hills to the north and south, opening at various points along the route. Some were no more than clefts in rock, while others were slightly better than game trails.

In Iran near the border, on the north side of the gorge, stood the Rock of the Hawk. It was so named because of the fancied likeness a knobbed formation near the summit held to a hawk's head seen in profile. The rock was a landmark indicating the nearness of the opening into Iraq.

Below in the defile were three men: Kilroy, Vang Bulo, and Hassani Akkad. Kilroy was in a sniper's nest; Vang Bulo was spotting nearby; and Akkad was tethered to a dead tree limb in the center of the pass. More precisely, Kilroy was in position on the north side of the gorge, where a sloping fan of dirt and stones skirted the base of the cliff. The fan was studded with boulders and other, smaller rocks which had fallen from the heights above.

A pair of car-sized boulders stood about two-thirds of the way up the fan. They were shaped somewhat like a pair of eggs, each stuck in the ground at the wider end. They leaned against each other, forming a triangular-shaped space at their bases that opened on the pass below. Behind the twin boulders lay a hollow. That was where Kilroy was set up. It was a natural foxhole.

Vang Bulo was posted on the same side of the gorge several dozen yards farther west, in a jumble of rocks at the base of the scarp. Not far beyond him, the pass took an abrupt turn, creating a blind corner that hid the opening into Iraq. He stood on a flat-topped boulder eight feet high, holding a pair of night vision binoculars at his side. From where he stood, looking east, he could keep Akkad and the rest of the passage reaching into Iran in view.

Hassani Akkad was placed about two hundred feet or so east of Kilroy's sniper's nest. He sat on the ground facing east. His hands were tied behind his back, not with the plastic restraints that had been used earlier, but with a length of thin metal baling wire looped around his wrists, the ends of which had been spliced together with a pair of pliers. He would have needed a wire cutter to get free. The wire had been tied tightly, and his hands had long since lost much of their feeling through loss of circulation, becoming numbed blocks of meat dangling at the ends of his wrists.

That was the least of his worries.

A noose was fitted around his neck, one end of a five-foot length of the same thin, tough, unbreakable wire used to bind his hands. The other end was tied to an anchor of deadwood, part of a tree limb that had fallen to the base of the cliff. It weighed about seventy-five pounds and was shaped like an oversized wishbone.

Vang Bulo had found the tree limb earlier in a cleft at the foot of the north cliff face and had dragged it out into the middle of the pass's dirt floor. He'd handled the heavy work involving the baiting of the trap, moving the deadwood into place, and wiring Akkad to it. Kilroy had sat that one out, smug in the position that he couldn't risk damaging his hands or straining himself with a rough shoot upcoming. Muscular tensions might undo the precise work he would soon be called on to carry out. That it was true made it no less irksome to Vang Bulo.

Here was Hassani Akkad, and here he would stay.

The wire leash would see to that. The noose was rigged with a sliding loop that drew it tighter around Akkad's neck whenever he was so unwise and ill considered to strain or tug against it.

He'd already forgotten himself once or twice, tightening its constricting grip so that the wire loop pressed taut against the corded tendons and throbbing veins of his neck.

He was sitting on the ground now, legs extended in front of him, leaning back against the dead tree limb to which he was fastened. Adding to his woes was the fact that he'd been fitted with an explosive belt that was wrapped around his belly.

It was like a money belt, only instead of being strung with pouches for hiding cash, it was strung with pouches containing blocks of plastic explosives, all rigged with electronic detonators tuned to a handheld remote-control device in Vang Bulo's possession. It was also rigged so that any attempt to undo the belt without first disarming it would instantly set off all the explosives, unlikely though it was that Akkad could free his hands to even make the attempt to escape from the belt.

His jacket was zipped closed, hiding the belt beneath it. The duct tape strips fastened over his mouth gagged him, preventing his giving warning of his booby-trapped condition, stifling his choking outcries. Above the gag his nostrils flared, gaping; his eyes bulged.

The sand still flew, but the floor of the pass was protected from the storm, mostly. Some stray, wild winds still swooped down into the gorge, buffeting it. For the most part, though, it was gripped by an eerie stillness, counterpointed by the violence of the winds sweeping high above, over the clifftops.

The winds blew with a shivery, moaning sound. A lonesome sound, Kilroy thought. The sound was lonesome. He was not. Between Vang Bulo and Akkad and his sniper rifle, he had plenty of company.

He'd handled plenty of assignments working solo, often in hostile territory behind enemy lines. Generally, given his druthers, he preferred working alone. That way he didn't have to worry about anybody screwing up but himself, and if he did screw up it would be his own damned fault.

Most shooters work in two-man teams consisting of a shooter and a spotter. For this assignment, Kilroy was the shooter, and Vang Bulo was the spotter. But the Ugandan was more than just a spotter. He was Dog Team all the way, an action man. You could trust him to do his damned job and take care of himself and not do anything stupid. He was a pro.

Having a partner expanded the possibilities of what Kilroy could do, of what they both could do. He couldn't have worked this particular setup solo, couldn't have gotten Akkad out here all by his lonesome. An insurmountable logistical problem for a lone hand. With Vang Bulo, it was doable.

Kilroy's handler was also working the Azif region. The handler was a real deep cover shadow agent, working so deep that he was practically subterranean. He and Kilroy were working different ends of the same assignment.

Vang Bulo was unaware of the handler's identity. This was standard Dog Team procedure, indeed standard intelligence procedure everywhere, information being disseminated on a need-to-know basis. Kilroy was senior man in the partnership, and so he was the one to interface with the elusive operative. Should Kilroy be terminated or otherwise neutralized, the handler would pair with Vang Bulo to complete the mission.

Kilroy now half sat, half lay in the hollow behind the boulders. The bathtub-sized depression was thick with sharp pebbles and stone shards that jabbed him in the damnedest places.

He was armed with a sniper rifle, an AK-47, a LAW, a string of grenades, a snub-nosed .38 in a side pocket, and a knife sheathed to the inside of his boot. Plus some other goodies.

He had a pair of night-vision binoculars and a lightweight, miniaturized transceiver by which he could communicate with Vang Bulo. The headset consisted of an earpiece and a curved plastic arm no wider than a soda straw that ended in a tiny speaker bulb. The arm banded the lower half of the right side of his face while not touching it. The condensor microphones in the tip could pick up a whisper and transmit it with crisp clarity to a receiver.

The space at the base of the rocks formed an upward-pointing triangle that was about four feet high at the apex. It provided clear, unbroken sight-lines to the scene below. A clear, unimpeded line of fire, too. He had all his ducks in a row. Now if only Colonel Munghal would be so accommodating as to put himself in Kilroy's gunsights.

That was the loose end in the plan, a potential big one. There was no way to be absolutely sure that the

Colonel would actually take to the field to personally command the retrieval mission. The odds were good that he would. Jafar Akkad had said that Munghal would head the detachment tonight, and he'd gotten his information from Hassani, who was in a position to know. Hassani certainly believed that Munghal would manifest himself at the appointed hour.

Everything known about the man pointed to it. Munghal's profile showed that he preferred to lead from the front. He was not a desk man. He liked to be out in the field, where the action was.

So said the analysts, the Dog Team analysts. Kilroy had never met any such persons, not knowingly. If he had, they'd kept it to themselves. He had no idea where in the dizzying depths of the Dog Team's clandestine apparatus they might be located, nor did he ask.

Team players didn't ask questions outside the realm of their immediate operational interest. That was made clear from Day One of their training program. Snoopy types were dropped from the program. They disappeared, and you didn't see them any more. That didn't mean they were dead. The military was huge and the world was wide, and there were countless posts to which they could have been assigned where one would never see them again. Of course, it didn't mean they hadn't been liquidated, either. The Dog Team was serious business, and the secret of its power lay in its secrecy.

One thing was sure: the civilians at the Pentagon were out of the loop. This was Army business and damned sure not anyone else's. Let those blankety-blank political types ever get their hooks into something like the Dog Team, and they'd never let go. A clandestine Army elite killer unit? They'd put it to work for their own agendas. Only that would never happen, because the Dog Team would never let it happen. When you got right down to it, a secret assassination unit was bad medicine, bad to mess with. It was easier for the politicos to find some other outfit or operation to get fat off of. Safer, too.

Kilroy was unsure whether the Team was operated from somewhere deep within the labyrinth of the Pentagon or from a seemingly unconnected off-the-shelf civilian front company, or both. Or neither. The organization's infrastructure was a mystery to him. Like any covert operation, it was rigorously compartmentalized. More so, due to the international illegality built into its structure. Nobody involved wanted to turn up at the center of a congressional probe or World Court war crimes tribunal proceeding. They were determined not to. Team personnel up and down the chain of command were insulated behind false fronts and third-party cutouts to preserve anonymity.

Kilroy's handler gave him the assignments and the vital intelligence needed to carry them out. Kilroy preferred it that way. The less he knew about other Team players, the less they knew about him, and the less they could tell if ever taken by the foe.

No, Kilroy didn't know the analysts who'd concluded that, given all the available facts, it could be predicted to a reasonable certainty that Colonel Munghal would obligingly present himself for demolition. How well did they know Munghal?

It was now or never. If Munghal showed tonight, well and good. If not, then it was Game Over, the end of this op. The Top Dog and his planners would not dare risk al-Magid falling into the hands of the Iranians. They had dangled him way out at the end of the line, using him as bait to monkeywrench the siphoning of top Iraqi scientists through the pipeline into Iran.

Behind it all lay the sinister genius of Dr. Bharat Turan Razeem, who, along with A.Q. Khan, was one of the fathers of Pakistan's atomic bomb. While Khan's role in disseminating illicit A-arms technology to rogue states such as Libya and North Korea was exposed to the world, Razeem continued to labor in secret, finally perfecting a process that he'd been working on for years.

These steps culminated in the electron coupler, a relatively low-cost, high-yield device that served as a catalyst toward developing weapons-grade fissile material from the waste by-products of a nuclear reaction. If a country had a nuclear reactor, it could use the device to leapfrog over many exacting and expensive steps toward building nuclear weapons. Needless to say, it was of great interest to any number of states desirous of arming themselves with an atomic sword.

Such a one was Iran. Possession of a working electron coupler would circumvent the restrictions on importation of nuclear technology imposed by a U.S.-led blockade, an imperfect yet still effective ban. But Tehran lacked specialists in Razeem's discipline of nuclear physics, having concentrated its resources on more conventional modes of processing radioactive waste materials into ingredients for an A-bomb.

Iraq did not. Difficult circumstances and slim budgets after the 1991 Gulf War had caused Iraqi's nuclear weapons establishment to take a closer look at Razeem's process, then still a theory long from being established fact. Saddam's research facilities had managed to make considerable progress on their own in the field, and were close to a break-through on the eve of the war against the Coalition.

Iran's feared and fearsome secret service, the Pas-daran, learned of the Iraqi effort and reached out to collect the cream of the Razeem process initiates. Colonel Munghal was put in charge of the acquisi-tion operation.

Munghal used Captain Saq as a go-between to Iraqi crime boss Hassani Akkad. Akkad was already in the kidnapping game, so it was no big deal for him to target nuclear physicists along with foreign jour-nalists, volunteer aid workers, truck drivers, and the like. Munghal picked the top Iraqi scientists he wanted, and Akkad picked them up. The captives were moved by night to a series of safe houses in Azif and outlying districts, terminating at the farmhouse west of Rock of the Hawk pass. From there, they were handed over to Captain Saq and the Iranians.

After the first few disappearances, Army coun-terintelligence detected the pattern and the plot. Monitoring of the small circle of Iraqi Razeem process specialists narrowed the field of choices for next prospective victim down to a relative few.

The likeliest was Professor Ali al-Magid. He taught at a graduate school of the provincial university. One weekday at lunchtime, he stepped into an ele-vator. In it were two men, strangers to him. The doors closed, and the car began its descent. There was a faint hissing sound, as of air escaping a leaky tire. The professor felt a sharp medicinal or chemical taste tingling at the back of his throat. His face flushed. He felt very hot. His head seemed to swell from the inside out, blowing up like a balloon. He tugged at his collar to loosen it. His knees buckled. The next he knew, he lay on his back on the floor of the elevator car, looking up at the two other passengers. They seemed a great distance away and receded still more as he lost consciousness.

The two men were U.S. intelligence agents, spies. Operatives. They had exposed al-Magid to an invisible knockout gas released from a pen-sized canister wielded by one of the duo. They both wore nose filters.

The elevator went straight down, with no stops, to the basement. There one of the men produced a long, silvery tube like a tire air pressure indicator and stabbed al-Magid in the side of the buttocks with the pointed end. This object injected a pinhead-sized chip through his garments and into his gluteus maximus, burying it out of sight in his flesh.

A stimulant to hasten recovery from the short-lived effects of the gas was administered to the unconscious man via an aerosol nasal spray. The next thing al-Magid knew, he was lying on his back on a padded bench in the lobby of the science building. A knot of individuals clustered around him, looking down at him with a ring of faces whose expressions varied from concern to curiosity to indifference. None of these faces belonged to the two men who had ridden with him in the elevator.

The professor was informed that he'd fainted in the elevator and been brought to this bench in the lobby to recover. He was more confused than anything else. They told him that he must have been working too

hard and that he should go home and get some rest.
He did so. He had a splitting headache, and his hip
and rear were sore and bruised, probably from when
he'd fallen. So he told himself.

He was oblivious that he'd been hung out to dry
and left with his ass flapping in the breeze. His col-
leagues and other likely kidnap targets among the
Razeem process specialists all had their security details strengthened, while he was left unguarded. He
was bait.

Hassani Akkad rose to the bait. His gang closed in
on al-Magid, tightening the circle until there was no
way out. Then they made the swoop. The professor
was snatched in early morning, after he'd left his
apartment on the way to work. Akkad's goons had
hustled him into the backseat of a car that whisked
the professor away.

After that, it was a nightmare of fear, intimidation,
and deprivation as al-Magid was inserted into one
end of the kidnap pipeline. He was kept blindfolded or hooded for hours at a time, until he lost
track of whether it was day or night. He was occasionally struck or kicked, and randomly terrorized.
Actually, for an Akkad gang abductee, he was de-
cently treated. That's because the Iranians were
paying for him to be delivered intact and functioning. Other kidnap victims rarely fared so well.

Hassani's connection to Captain Saq had resulted
in a surplus of weapons being shipped across the
border into Iraq. By making the arms available at bargain prices to militia leader Waleed Tewfiq, Akkad
established an alliance with the Red Dome Mosque
cadre. This fact allowed him to operate safe houses
in the district. Coalition forces stayed out of Old

Town to avoid provoking a confrontation with the imam and his followers that might enflame Shiite sentiment against the American-sponsored Iraqi interim government.

Akkad kept al-Magid penned in a safe house within sight of the mosque's minaret towers for several days while finalizing the arrangements for his delivery to the Iranians. Complicating matters were the sudden, violent attacks on gunrunners and their customers in the borderlands. The massacre of Fadleel and company, the slaying of the scout car crew, and the disappearance of the vehicle itself had sent shockwaves up into the Iranian military intelligence apparatus.

Colonel Munghal sent word to Hassani Akkad that he was to spearhead the al-Magid acquistion himself to overawe by his fearsome presence the interloping marauders and bandits who were preying on the established marauders and bandits in the region.

Colonel Munghal had begun his career in Iran's security apparatus as a lowly noncom in the Shah's SAVAK secret police, where he'd proven himself an ace interrogator and torturer. He wasn't so high up that he couldn't reverse field and throw in with the ayatollahs during Khomeini's rise. He picked a good time to turn his coat, throwing in with the rebels when the outcome of the struggle still seemed in doubt. He had no doubt that the regime would be overthrown. Few were in as good a position as he to appreciate the extent of the weaknesses of the Peacock Throne.

He did for the Islamic Revolution what he'd been doing for the Shah; namely, rooting out rebels, subversives, dissidents, and other foes or potential foes. He flipped his old network of thugs, spies, and informants, turning them against the counterrevolutionaries for whom they'd once worked. He was ruthless, merciless toward those whom the mullahs of Qom set him against. When he targeted a loyalist or suspected loyalist—or someone felt to be hostile to the new regime—he targeted not only that unfortunate individual but also his or her spouse, children, family, and friends for imprisonment, brutality, torture, and sometimes, mass executions.

The period after the Shah's downfall, when the ayatollahs consolidated their reign, was a busy one for Munghal. Purges were conducted on a societal level, with Bahai'ists, communists, secularists, intellectuals, dissidents, and others liquidated by the tens of thousands. That's when wholesale murder demanded a military approach, and he began his rise through military intelligence ranks into the elite Pasdaran spy service.

Now, at the height of his power and prestige, Colonel Munghal was wanted dead by the intelligence services of a half-dozen Arab countries, Israel, and the U.S., not to mention his own homegrown competitors for power in Tehran's top ruling circles.

All that remained now was the waiting.

Waiting . . . Kilroy had no problem with waiting. Like Jesse James in the traditional folk ballad, Kilroy, too, "came from a solitary race." His was the infinite, terrible patience of the hunter. Besides, he couldn't afford to get excited. Excitement switched on all kinds of internal conflicts, including accelerated heart and respiration rates, which could make vital eye and hand coordination a hair less sure. He wanted to keep himself steady and make his shot.

Kilroy kept his mind busy by calculating the mechanics of the shot. A lot of negative factors were in play. The sandstorm was the greatest handicap to a successful shoot. The wind was not constant, but rose and fell in force. That could affect the ballistics of the shot, depending on the weight of the round and the type and amount of gunpowder in the cartridge. On the other hand, it was an asset in that he was counting on it to help confuse the enemy and facilitate his and Vang Bulo's getaway. They weren't in this game to seek martyrdom. That was the other side's hang-up. The Kilroy/Vang Bulo partnership was a going concern, and they meant to keep it that way.

The greatest variable was the final disposition of the target. There was no telling exactly where Colonel Munghal would be at the moment of truth. He might be close to the sniper's nest, or far to the east at the opposite end of the gorge. Kilroy was going to have to estimate where and when the window of opportunity would be at its widest. A tricky element, for if he held his fire waiting for the optimum shot, chance might intervene to deny him the target.

Kilroy checked his calculations, juggling them in his head, keeping them in flux. He wouldn't know which formula to use until he was actually lining up the shot. Every now and then he rose and stretched, shaking out his arms and legs, not wanting to tighten up. He didn't stray too far from the nest. The fan of dirt and rock surrounding him was too loose and unstable to stroll around on. The night was warm, hot, when the south wind blew hard. At least he didn't have to worry about keeping his hands warm and supple.

Vang Bulo perched on the flat-topped rock, using his night-vision binoculars to keep watch on the eastern stretch of the pass. Hassani Akkad remained where he'd been pegged, sitting on the ground with a wire sliding noose leash connecting him to the massive dead tree branch. Akkad had been dealt a hard hand to play out in this game, but Kilroy was untroubled by any twinges of compassion for the gang boss. He'd seen the videos of some of the kidnapped captives that Hassani had sold to radical terrorist groups: the victims, knowing their cause, the cause of saving their lives, was hopeless, but going through the motions anyhow, begging their respective governments to accede to their captors' impossible demands; the horror of their final agonies as they were butchered, heads grotesquely sawed off by the swords and knives of ski-masked, preening terrormongers.

Kilroy saved his compassion for the victims. Hassani could go to hell.

It was like hunting tigers. You hunt tigers by staking out a goat or pig or suchlike in the center of a clearing, climbing a tree overlooking the site, and waiting for a tiger to come prowling around, scenting fresh prey and hungry for a kill. Hassani in his day had left a plenitude of victims staked out for wild beasts to rend, maul and destroy: beasts that walked on two legs like men but were sunk far below the creatures of the wild, who killed only for food that they might live.

Now, Hassani Akkad was the goat.

# Nine

The sound of the wind was constant, sometimes rising in pitch to a high, thin wail; sometimes dropping to a low, sobbing moan; but mostly maintaining a kind of continuous, humming drone.

It reminded Kilroy of the sound of an *oud,* a traditional stringed instrument of Afghanistan. He'd heard it played around the campfires of tribal allies while on missions in that fractious land. Played with a bow, the *oud* produced an effect in him that went from irritating to, ultimately, near hypnotic—though still somewhat irritating.

A new note sounded in the mix of the wind's midnight moaning. Kilroy's ears tingled with it, and his pulse quickened.

Vang Bulo must have heard it too, for at the same moment he stiffened, standing motionless on the flat-topped rock. Something hard and intent showed in that stillness, an internal vibration like a hunting dog on point.

Kilroy spoke into the communicator. "Hear that?"

"It's them," Vang Bulo said, after a pause.

The newcomers could be heard before they could be seen. A signature sound of motorized vehicles preceded them. The sound was not uniform, for the engines did not operate at a steady rate. The noises rose and fell, depending on the difficulty of the terrain that the vehicles were traversing. This was rough, uneven country. Even the hard-packed brown clay of the gorge floor was textured like a washboard. Then, too, the twists and turns of the pass affected the motorized din. The vehicles' growling thunder echoed, booming, along open straightaways and was muffled by the limbs and shoulders of massive rock formations.

A trick of the landscape caused the oncoming din to fall off into near soundlessness just as the first set of headlight and searchlight beams thrust into the mouth of the corridor opening on the Rock of the Hawk.

The flat top on which Vang Bulo had kept his vigil was empty, untenanted, the big man having already taken cover. Firefly lights floated above the ground at the east end of the passage. They came on, resolving themselves not into a pair of headlights, but instead into three larger orbs and two lesser orbs. A puzzling configuration, until further nearness caused them to reveal their nature. Each was a single headlight mounted on the handlebars of a motorcycle. Three motorcycles in all, riding in advance of the other vehicles.

The bikes rode in triangular spearhead formation, with the lead bike being followed by a pair of two-rider jobs with sidecars. The sidecars were fitted with searchlights whose beams jutted out from them at varying angles. Headlight and searchlight beams both slashed across cliffside walls north and south of the pass.

Kilroy said, "I'm suspending communication now."

Vang Bulo rogered that.

Kilroy couldn't risk an untimely message interrupting his concentration while he lined up the shot. He unplugged the earpiece, eased the headset off his face, and switched off the comm unit. Its plastic armature folded down to something about the size of a cigarette, which he dropped into an inside breast pocket of his utility vest. Behind the three motorcyles came a jeep with four men in it. Behind that came a scout car of the type that Kilroy and Vang Bulo had stolen. It was followed with an eight-wheeled armored personnel carrier with a gun turret on top. Next came a two-and-a-half-ton truck with rail fence sides and no top, the carrier bed crammed with about eighteen armed troops. A jeep with a mounted machine gun brought up the rear.

Colonel Munghal's convoy.

Kilroy picked up his night-vision binoculars and held them to his eyes, studying the column. The light-gathering optics banished darkness, their special lenses reproducing the scene in dull, fuzzy green-and-white light. They turned the nightscape into a green the color of stagnant pond water seen on a sunless day, yet somehow shot through with white flashes and gleams.

The sidecars of both two-rider motorcycles were each equipped with swivel-mounted machine guns. The bikes were so close now that Kilroy could make out the riders with his night glasses. They wore helmets, goggles, short jackets, and driving gloves.

The column made no attempt at stealth. Quite the

reverse. Colonel Munghal was putting on a show of force to intimidate and deter what he thought were bandits and hijackers cutting in on the lucrative cross-border contraband trade, whose latest and most up-to-date commodity was trafficking in stolen Iraqi scientists.

The plan was for the column to advance to the western end of the pass, halting just this side of the Iraqi border. Akkad gang members from the farmhouse would meet them there to deliver Professor Ali al-Magid.

The column moved along at a steady, deliberate clip. Haste was dangerous in a landscape whose rugged terrain made the possibility of cracking a suspension or breaking an axle omnipresent. The motorcycles pushed forward, making their sputtering mosquito whine. On they came, nosing ahead of the column.

The lead bike's headlight beam fingered an obstruction in the middle of the gorge: Hassani Akkad. The vehicle halted, the two behind it following suit a few beats later. Searchlight beams, thinner and brighter than those of the headlights, pinned the unique roadblock. In the harsh glare of the lights, Akkad himself looked more animal than human, tethered to the dead tree limb. The wire leash around his neck was too short to allow him to straighten up. He got his legs underneath him, somehow managing to stand up on his knees—a difficult operation with his hands tied behind his back, and the wire loop cutting into the flesh of his neck.

Behind the motorcycles, the jeep braked to a halt, causing the scout car behind it to pull up short, setting off a chain reaction that caused all the vehicles in the column to come to a stop. There was confusion, especially toward the rear of the line, as to what exactly had caused the halt. Heavy engines idled roughly, spewing gray-white exhaust from stacks and pipes. Exhaust and dust clouds raised by the column were swept away by the wind.

Captain Saq was a passenger in the lead jeep. Behind it, the scout car's front passenger seat was occupied by Colonel Munghal. He was protected by a windshield of bulletproof, armored glass. No fool he, he'd stay behind that protective shield while his subordinates investigated the cause of the delay and how to remedy it.

Kilroy put down the night glasses and picked up his sniper rifle. It was a formidable instrument, a custom-made Swedish big-bore with a folding metal tube stock and was equipped with a night-vision scope. The bullets in the magazine were custom made, too.

Kilroy hefted the rifle and got into a prone shooting position in the nest. He'd be firing through the triangular gap at the base of the two egg-shaped boulders. He pointed the weapon east toward the stalled column.

Nearer, a lone motorcycle rider lowered his kickstand and dismounted, unslinging the light machine gun slung across his back and leveling it at the strange apparition framed in the lights.

The sidecar gunners shared his suspicions, training their swivel-mounted machine guns on Akkad. One thought to sweep his searchlight across the rocks at the base of the cliffs, searching for signs of ambush, scanning both sides of the gorge.

Kilroy put the motorcyle machine gunners out of

his mind. Vang Bulo had them covered and would handle them one way or another. Kilroy trusted him to cover his back. That freed him to concentrate on the job at hand.

Kilroy lined his sights up on Colonel Munghal, a balding, pear-shaped guy in a gold-braided commander's cap and military tunic. He had a black paintbrush mustache and a fussy little mouth and no chin. He didn't look like much, but then, neither had Himmler. No doubt he felt pretty safe behind that armored glass windscreen.

Munghal's face was angry, and his mouth was open and shouting. Kilroy centered the scope crosshairs in the middle of his face, between the eyes.

He squeezed the trigger.

Kilroy had always figured that when he finally got his shot at Munghal, the colonel would be sitting behind bulletproof glass in an armored vehicle. That was why he'd had special ammunition provided for the hit in advance.

Explosive-tipped bullets were no good here; they'd explode on contact with the armored glass, spending their force and possibly missing their target. His rounds were tipped with ultrahard, ultratough titanium alloys and hand loaded with a high-velocity propulsive powder mix.

The bulletproof armored glass was sufficient protection against most bullets, but not against specially constructed rounds like the ones Kilroy was using. The hard, high-velocity slug pierced the windshield, drilling a neat, round hole through several inches of armored glass.

Behind the glass lay Colonel Munghal. The bullet drilled him too, right between the eyes.

Kilroy fired a second and third shot in quick succession. The target placement was so precise that barely a fingernail clipping's width separated each of the three holes.

Munghal's head above the eyebrows disintegrated into mist.

Rifle reports were still echoing in the gorge when the lone motorcyclist fired his machine gun in the general direction from which the shots had come.

The sidecar machine gunners swiveled their weapons, bringing them up toward the twin boulders on the fan, sheltering the sniper's nest. That's when Vang Bulo used the remote to trigger Hassani Akkad's explosive belt. There was a flash of light, very bright. For an instant, Akkad's form was a black blur at the heart of a fireburst. Then it came apart, vaporizing.

The blast cut down the motorcycles and their riders, obliterating them. A wall of flame whooshed through the gorge, incinerating all trees, brush, and weeds before it. It licked out, engulfing the jeep before spending its force impotently against the scout car. But the jeep was an inferno, its passengers human torches.

One of them was Captain Saq. He half lunged, half fell out of the jeep, his clothes on fire. Bellowing, roaring, he charged blindly off to the side, toward the gorge's north wall. He got about a dozen yards or so before collapsing, tumbling to the ground. His clothes were on fire. So was his flesh. He rolled around in the dirt, trying to snuff out the flames. He succeeded, mostly. He shuddered, kicked, then lay still, his blackened form smoking. Half his face had been melted away.

Flaming debris rained down from the human bomb blast, scattering pieces of motorcycle scrap metal on the floor of the gorge. A burning tire bounced to the ground and rolled away, a wheel of fire. The inside of the jeep was a mass of flame. It burned with a sound like a high wind whipping banners and pennants, snapping them in the breeze. There was a lull that lasted several beats. Then the turret gun in the armored personnel carrier opened up with a series of jackhammer bursts, firing wildly and virtually at random. The gunner had no idea what he was shooting at. Rounds ripped into rock walls, ricocheting wildly, punching out rows of melon-sized craters and sprays of stone chips.

Kilroy went back to work. He didn't use the scope because the explosions and fireballs going off would bulldoze the sight's sensitive optics, causing the light-gathering lenses to white out. He aimed with the naked eye, pointing the rifle at what he wanted to hit, a method that usually worked for him.

He drew down on the scout car's forward compartment. The pulverizing of Colonel Munghal's cranium had sprayed the scout car driver with disintegrated matter. It stung and tore like a faceful of hornets, hitting him with such force that it stunned him. The actual physical impact had left him punchy. Kilroy shot him, the round drilling windshield and driver. The armored glass screen now had four neat little round holes punched through it. The driver fell, crashing back against the seat, then forward to sink out of sight.

The scout car wasn't going anyplace just yet, not until somebody else took the wheel. The column's forward motion was blocked, too. The Iranian troops knew that they were under attack, but they didn't know by whom or how many. The way they were getting hit, so hard and fast, made them think that they were under assault by an overwhelming force. They didn't know that Colonel Munghal was defunct, either. It wouldn't have made any difference to the final outcome if they had known.

The armored personnel carrier's turret gunner must have seen some muzzle flashes coming from Kilroy's weapon in the sniper's nest. The armored turret rotated, swinging the gun in line toward the fan and elevating it toward the twin boulders that sheltered the nest. The troops in the back of the truck were starting to react, grabbing up their weapons and blindly firing at the sides of the gorge. Some began hopping down to the ground.

A blast erupted that made the first look tame. Vang Bulo had delivered his knockout punch. Earlier, he'd sowed the sides of the eastern branch of the pass with a double line of claymore antipersonnel mines. The infernal devices consisted of bricks of plastic explosive lined with scores of steel ball bearings. Their detonators were all linked together so that the master key tripped them all simultaneously. Now, supersonic sheets of white-hot shrapnel scourged the column, ripping it broadside along its flanks. All those in its path were cut down. Shockwaves buffeted the sides of the convoy vehicles, rocking them in their tracks. The lead jeep toppled and rolled, bursting into flame.

The white intensity of the blastfire glare flashed lightning-like, fading quickly. Where ranks of troopers had been, the ground was littered with their bodies, sieved and smoking. The relative dimness vanished once more, eclipsed by a fireball that was the exploding gas tank of the troop truck. White-hot shrapnel from the claymores had peppered and pierced it, igniting the fuel load. It blew red, thrusting upward a pillar of fire that mushroomed at its crown, rolling in on itself.

The truck, what was left of it, was smoldering wreckage. The scout car had not moved since Kilroy shot Munghal and the driver. Its undercarriage was on fire, flames licking up the vehicle. A figure opened a side hatch and crawled out of it, dragging himself to the south side of the pass.

Only the armored personnel carrier still stood intact and battle ready. Firing resumed from the armored personnel carrier's turret gun. It fired at the sniper's nest, but the gun's elevation was too high, and the rounds passed harmlessly above the top of the rocks, pounding the cliff wall high overhead. Rocks rained down around Kilroy, each one as big as a cobblestone. None of them hit him. He lay cradled in the hollow behind the boulders, keeping his head down, eating dirt.

The firing paused. Kilroy reached for a LAW, or light antitank weapon, that lay beside him. It looked like a three-foot length of OD green plastic pipe. He shucked off the forward and rear protective lids at each end of the container, then unlimbered the underside pistol grip attachment and the topside sighting posts. Heavy enough to stop an APC, he hoped.

The APC was on the move, advancing, shouldering aside the crippled and abandoned scout car. It lurched deeper into the gorge. Some of the personnel it was carrying were still functioning. They began shooting out of the gun ports in the sides of the rear carrier box.

Vang Bulo popped up from behind a rock long enough to throw a grenade at the APC. It bounced off the armor plate hull and exploded. The blast rocked the vehicle but left it undamaged. A mechanized whine sounded as the turret rotated, swinging the gun barrel toward the rocks behind which Vang Bulo was taking cover.

Kilroy edged around the more eastward boulder, holding the LAW tube over his shoulder. He loosed a rocket at the APC. The missile generated a terrific backblast that trailed harmlessly behind the shooter. It arrowed toward the APC, striking it in front where the turret met the hull. The blast blew the turret off the machine, launching it into the air as easily as popping the cap off a bottle.

The APC shuddered, froze. The engine stalled. When the smoke cleared, a hole stood where the turret had been, rimmed by a collar of jagged, still-seething fused steel. Vang Bulo tossed a grenade into it. Smoke and fire jetted out of the hole.

The column was kaput, but that was only incidental to getting Colonel Munghal. Who'd been got.

# Ten

Time to withdraw. Exfiltrate.

No immediate threat showed from the wrecked remains of the column, but Kilroy was careful to shelter behind the rocks while stowing his weapon away. Swiftly, efficiently, with no wasted motion, working by touch, he broke down the sniper rifle to its components and fitted them into its protective carrying case. It was a precision instrument, one that he was used to and that had served him well and would continue to do so in the future. Provided he got away with a whole skin, of course.

He put the gun case in a carrying sack that he slung across his shoulders. He grabbed his AK-47, ready to move out. He didn't bother with the communicator. He chose to rely on a time-honored, low-tech option: a big mouth and lung power.

He shouted, "Cover me, Alpha!"

"You're covered, Bravo!" Vang Bulo shouted back.

It was the old Alpha/Bravo system. He was Alpha, the other was Bravo. One would shout for the other to cover him, then make his move while his partner laid down covering fire. Then he'd lay down covering fire while his partner moved out, alternating back and forth until they'd reached their objective, which in this case was a withdrawal from the area.

The burning convoy furnished a fair amount of light to see by. The wind carried the smoke and smell of burning eastward, away from the Dog Team duo.

Kilroy moved out of the sniper's nest in a half crouch, weapon cradled in his arms, keeping the boulders and then the limb of the fan itself between him and the burning remnant of the column. The foe looked all shot up, but it would only take one still-functioning soldier who could shoot to extinguish Kilroy. He hustled down the side of the fan, sliding in the loose dirt but managing to keep his balance. He ducked behind some rocks west of the fan, turning to cover Vang Bulo's retreat.

The big man flashed into the open, backlit for an instant by red firelight blazing in the east branch of the pass, outlining his solid, bulky form. He passed Kilroy, then ducked behind some rocks deeper west into the pass. An instant later he popped up, covering Kilroy's next run.

There was a lot of what seemed like shooting in the east branch of the pass, but it could have been caused by stores of ammunition being touched off by blazing vehicles. Masses of red and yellow firelight washed over the rocks, giving the gorge a hellish aspect.

The two men made their way west, hugging the north wall of the gorge. They rounded the limb directly below the Rock of the Hawk, circling a blind corner that took them out of the sight and firing lines of the corridor behind them. They weren't out of the pass yet. Another half mile or so of snake-like gorge lay between them and the western gap opening into Iraq. They jogged in that direction for another fifty yards or so before coming on a cleft in the cliff wall, the mouth of a side branch.

The side branch opened on the north wall, threading northwest. The two had to look smartly for the opening not to miss it. They'd actually passed the entrance, which was partly obscured by shoulder-high scrub brush. But the scrub brush served as a landmark by which to recognize it, especially at night.

They parted the brush and stepped between it, entering the side branch. The entrance here was so narrow that they had to proceed one at a time, in single file. Kilroy took the point, with Vang Bulo jogging several paces behind. The latter's shoulders brushed rocks walls on both sides.

After a dozen yards or so, the branch started to widen out, until it was about eight to ten feet wide. A thin strip of sky could be seen high above, the gap between the two cliffs through which the gully wormed its way. It was dark in the defile, but they didn't want to show a light, not yet.

Another hundred yards had to be traveled on foot. It seemed longer because of the darkness and the gully's twisty route. A wide place opened up, a long, lens-shaped clearing. Here, at the foot of the eastern cliff, a camouflage-pattern canvas tarp covered a bulky, waist-high mound.

Kilroy and Vang Bulo shucked off the tarp. Beneath it lay two vehicles—no, two and a half vehicles. One was a Kawasaki dirt bike, the other was a three-wheeled all-terrain vehicle. The half vehicle was a two-wheeled metal cart with a square hopper.

They had been and would continue to be integral to the success of the mission. They'd been carried in the back of the SUV earlier when the two men had blown the bridge and bagged Hassani Akkad.

The SUV had driven to the western terminus of the side branch. The side branch opened in the hills about a quarter of a mile north of where the Rock of the Hawk pass opened into Iraq. The west end of the pass opened on the Iraq side on land occupied by the Akkad gang farmhouse.

It would have been difficult to move the SUV stealthily past the farmhouse and its defenders to enter the pass into Iran, and far more difficult and dangerous to return the same way, since the fireworks in the foothills would stir up the whole neighborhood. The side branch was too narrow to be negotiated by the SUV, but not by the off-road vehicles carried in its rear compartment. The SUV was stashed, and the other vehicles unloaded.

Kilroy took the dirt bike, Vang Bulo the ATV. The two-wheeled hopper cart was fastened to a hitch on the rear of the ATV. Kilroy took the point, entering the side branch. Vang Bulo followed, his ATV towing the cart with Akkad.

It was a rough ride, but eventually they penetrated the side branch almost all the way to where it joined the Rock of the Hawk pass. This lens-shaped widening of the trail marked the limits of their motorized trek. The rest of the gully was too thin and rugged to allow passage by wheel.

They had to park and walk the rest of the way, which wasn't all that far, less than two hundred yards. First, though, the ambushers moved the vehicles off to the side, covering them with the concealing tarp.

Then they followed the rest of the side branch on foot, herding along Akkad, whose feet had been untied so he could walk to the pass on his own two legs. No man ever walked the last mile to the electric chair with less enthusiasm. And that was before they'd fitted him with the explosive belt and tethered him to a dead tree limb, staked out in the middle of the pass for Munghal and company to discover.

The getaway was simpler, since they were no longer laden down with Akkad. The duo would retrace their route through the side branch in reverse, emerging in on the Iraq side where the SUV was hidden.

Kilroy took hold of the two-wheeled cart's tongue pole and dragged it to the middle of the clearing. "If anybody follows us this way, they can break their necks on it," he said.

He and Vang Bulo walked their vehicles into the open, pointing them toward the northwest turning of the side branch.

Kilroy said, "You didn't ask about the colonel."

"I don't have to ask. I know," Vang Bulo said. "You didn't miss. You never miss."

"Shucks. It's true, but, well, shucks."

"Besides, if you had missed, we'd still be back in the pass, fighting for you to line yourself up another shot."

"But I didn't."

"What I said," Vang Bulo concluded. He straddled

the ATV. With him astride it, it looked like a little mini-tractor or a power lawnmower on steroids. It started up with a rude, blatting thunderclap, then quieted down somewhat.

Kilroy donned his goggles. He'd removed them to shoot the colonel and hadn't put them back on since. He'd need them for the ride ahead. Vang Bulo had had his on for the entire fight.

Kilroy kick-started the dirt bike. It was equipped with noise-baffling mufflers, but they could only do so much. The engine came alive with a sound like a string of firecrackers going off. The motor vibrated with power, a humming that Kilroy could feel clear up into his belly. The dirt bike shivered, like a racehorse trembling at the starting gate, eager to be off on the steeplechase.

The riders switched on their headlights. There was no making the run without them. The headlight's cyclops eye shone a beam into the depths of the narrow, craggy passage.

Kilroy glanced back over his shoulder. Vang Bulo was in motion behind him, giving him a thumb's-up sign. Kilroy's hands on the grips worked the clutch and throttle. The dirt bike surged forward, thick knobbed tires digging into sand and loose dirt. The ATV followed, its wide, fat tires churning.

They plunged headlong into the gully. Kilroy sometimes had to use one or the other of his booted feet to steady the bike on a tight turn. Boulders would loom in his path, and he'd swerve around them and continue on. Vang Bulo's was the steadier machine but less maneuverable, slowing on the turns.

Rock walls narrowed and widened, sometimes

curving northeast before returning to their primary northwest orientation. It was a wild ride, all
speed, sensation, and rushing movement. Fallen
rocks and projecting spurs made it even more of an
obstacle course. A half-buried rock, if taken wrong,
could flip a cycle or ATV.

Headlight beams scrolled along stone walls, throwing up flashing glimpses of gnarled dwarf trees and
bushes that grew sideways out of cracks in the cliffs.
The gully began following a northwest curve. A serpentine course suddenly burst free into the open.
They were on the far side of the hills, in Iraq.

They slowed, halting. They killed their lights.
Blackness hammered down, vaulted by the faintly lu-
minous rivers of sand and dirt streaming across the
sky. They were in a bowl-shaped depression ringed
by boulders and jagged rock outcroppings. It was
partly sheltered from the sandstorm, but not as
much as the side branch had been. They rode up the
basin's north inner wall, topping it and coming out
on a vast, sandy flat littered with boulders, spurs, and
rocky outcroppings. It had an alien, forbidding
quality to it, like a Martian landscape. There was the
hulking black bulk of the hillside to their east and
and the slightly less utter black of the sky, with its low-
scudding dust streams and burly winds.

Kilroy throttled down, cutting the engine off and
dismounting. He stood stiff and bowlegged. "Feels
like my tailbone's busted," he complained.

A nearby rocky spur concealed the SUV, which was
parked behind it, facing out. Vang Bulo climbed in
it and started it up. The machine rolled out from
behind the outcropping,

Kilroy went around to the back of the vehicle and

raised the hatch. He unfolded a sliding ramp, lowering one end to the ground. He drove the ATV up the ramp into the rear compartment. The dirt bike was far lighter than the ATV. He wheeled it up the ramp and into the rear of the SUV.

The off-road machines were secured upright in place by floor-bolted clamps. Kilroy hopped down from the back of the SUV, closing the rear hatch.

Shooting sounded in the distance, off to the southwest. Strings of faint popping noises that were shots were bottomed by occasional loud crumping sounds of grenades going off. They came from the direction of the Akkad gang farmhouse.

Kilroy stood in the open, the wind blowing sand in his face. He squinted through his goggles, still not able to see much. Blurred smudges of light filtered through the storm showed where the farmhouse was, though not the structure itself.

Something was burning out there, an outbuilding or vehicle, burning strongly enough so that the winds hadn't yet extinguished the blaze. Points of light that were muzzle flares stitched the blackness surrounding the site. Vang Bulo rolled down the driver's side window and stuck his head out of it with an ear cocked, listening to the gunfire.

"Our guys raiding the farmhouse," Kilroy said. "Mmm, sounds like a hot one." He went around to the front passenger side and got in. Vang Bulo put the SUV in drive and drove away. The SUV was dark, with only its parking lights for illumination. Here on this side of the border, the landscape was mostly all sprawling fields marked out by roads and cut by canals, some active, others dry.

Kilroy said, "Sneak up on the farmhouse, but not too close. I want to take a look-see."

Vang Bulo gave him a quick side-glance. "What's the matter? Haven't bagged your quota yet?"

"I'm always looking to up my stats."

The SUV angled toward the farmhouse, which was still a long way off. When it neared, Kilroy cautioned, "Not too close. We don't want to get shot at—by our own guys or anybody else."

Vang Bulo's mouth downturned at one of the corners. "You are the original backseat driver."

"Not too far away, either," Kilroy continued, ignoring the other's remark. "Let's see what's going down."

"For your information, we are now on overtime."

The machine crept up on the farmhouse, using a line of tall palm trees as a screen to hide them from view of those in and around the structure. The palms were about five hundred feet away from the farmhouse.

"Plenty of shooting going on over there," Kilroy said, rolling the words around his tongue like a mouthful of fine whiskey, savoring the taste.

Vang Bulo smirked. "Just itching to get into it, aren't you?"

Kilroy didn't deny it. "I'm a neighborly fellow. I like to pitch in and help out where I can, so long as it's not costing me any money."

"It's okay as long as you don't get shot. Or worse, get me shot."

"There's that too," Kilroy conceded. "Steer for that knoll there," he said, pointing. "That'll cover us."

The SUV made for the knoll, a low hillock topped by a bald, rocky knob. It was about a football field's length away from the farmhouse. Vang Bulo kept it between the SUV and the farmhouse. He pulled in behind it.

Kilroy got out of the SUV, taking his sniper rifle with him.

# Eleven

*I wanted action,* Steve Ireland said to himself, *and now I'm going to get it.*

The prospect was exciting but scary, scary in a good way, like in the opening pause before kickoff in a big game.

This was a big game, all right. High stakes. The highest, maybe. Nuclear. What could be higher than that? Except for the fact that he was risking life and limb, too. Oh, yeah. There was that, too.

He realized he was thinking too much and he silenced the voice in his head because it was a distraction, and being distracted was a good way to get yourself killed when you were minutes—seconds, maybe—from going into combat.

He was a member of ODA 586, an Army Special Forces unit poised to make a night raid on the Akkad gang farmhouse on the Iraq-Iran border. Their mission: to rescue a kidnap victim and terminate the farmhouse cell.

The borderland was a potential minefield for Coalition and Iraqi interim government interests.

The Coalition's prime mover was the U.S., and Washington put a high premium on preventing Iran from acquiring nuclear weapons. The Iraqi interim government wanted to avoid conflict with Iran. It was having a hard enough time securing internal Iraq and getting a permanent government up and running without becoming embroiled in a war. So there was a built-in tension between Washington's immediate goals in Iraq and its broader strategic goals in the region.

Iran had been smart enough not to put all its atomic eggs in one lead-lined basket. In addition to several atomic reactors that were up and running, Tehran had salted away possibly as many as two dozen secret nuclear weapons research labs in farflung locations throughout the land, many secreted underground in the midst of populous areas. It would be impossible for a combined U.S. aircraft and missile strike to get them all in one hit. The attempt would generate horrendous numbers of civilian casualties that would be a propaganda disaster for American interests.

The main vehicle of the atomic weapons program was the so-called Atoms for Peace project. Iran had already openly built several atomic reactors and had several more under construction. They were power plants designed to supply electricity to the Iranian grid. This could be argued to be more or less legitimate, apart from the subjective consideration that with its plentiful stocks of oil and natural gas, Iran already had more than enough power supply available without the additional atomic-generated stores.

But it was the by-product of these conventional reactors, the enriched uranium and other radioactive waste material, that was the key component needed to make atomic bombs. It was this element that had come under the microscope of a skeptical Western world suspicious of Tehran's motives.

Here was where the importance of the Razeem process came in. It was the element of distraction and diversion. While international arms inspectors and nuclear nonproliferation administrators fought to probe Tehran's handling and disposition of the fissile atomic waste, a crash secret program was underway to shortcircuit the entire multi-staged operation by building and operating a Razeem electron coupler.

Iran lacked experts in the process. Iraq had some. Iranian Pasdaran secret police had put Colonel Munghal in charge of the acquisition operation. Iraqi crime gangs abducted scientists with some expertise in the Razeem process and shopped them to the Iranians.

The latest victim in the quest to build the coupler was Iraqi Professor Ali al-Magid. He needed rescuing and the kidnap ring was slated for demolition. Tonight.

So Steve Ireland and the rest of the members of Special Forces unit ODA 586 had been told earlier this day, during a final briefing delivered by a liasion CIA operative: Albin Prester.

It was a joint CIA/Special Forces operation. This was the new shape of covert operations, black ops. The adminstration in Washington wanted CIA mostly out of the paramilitary business, apparently feeling that the Agency's spotty post–Cold War track record in the field was not a confidence builder. CIA defenders countered that they were being made the fall guys for a power grab by the administration's civilian appointees at the Pentagon. The agency didn't want to cede the power and prestige that came from running their own ops. Their paramilitary capacity hadn't been taken away from them, not officially, but their freedom to move had been cut way back.

Which suited army top brass just fine. They had never much trusted the CIA's ability to carry out paramilitary ops on its own. Its best use was as a cut out, a third force that could bury U.S. fingerprints on an overseas op, thus providing deniability. But the agency had personnel and resources not readily available to the military, providing the basis for an alliance of convenience.

The current mission was indicative of a new working relationship between certain mid- and upper-level CIA personnel in the clandestine Directorate of Operations and Army Special Forces intelligence officers.

So much Steve Ireland had been told, or deduced from various scraps and bits of related information he'd managed to pick up here and there. Some of it was probably true. But it was a sure bet that there was plenty he hadn't been told. There was a heavy intelligence component here and these intelligence deals were always like that: wheels within wheels.

The mission parameters were delicate. The border was a hot zone. The U.S. government followed a policy of exerting multiphased pressure on Iran to deter its nuclear weapons ambitions. These included not-so-subtle allusions and even threats of military action to be taken in the near future, to present-day clandestine black ops missions into Iran for reconnaissance and surveillance—and everything in between.

But Washington wanted to exert pressure when it wanted to exert pressure. Conducting a full-scale military operation so close to the border was a provocation Washington was not prepared to initiate at this time. The closing of the kidnap pipeline would be conducted solely in Iraq, with a minimum of fuss and a maximum of deniability.

That was the official line, at least as far as the CIA/Special Forces mission was concerned. It didn't take in the Dog Team's secret agenda, so carefully compartmentalized and insulated from discovery by outsiders and even Army insiders.

But of such things Steve Ireland was as yet happily unaware.

Tonight was the night, the op was a go. The Special Forces unit had been on standby at Border Base Foxtrot for the past few days, and it felt good to be given the green light to actually get out and go do something.

A line of three Humvees left the base at night, the sandstorm whipping up a mass of murky darkness. The storm, the wildness of it, had an intoxicating effect on Steve Ireland. Extremes always did.

The Humvees worked their way northeast toward the border. The storm slowed down their advance but masked their presence. They rode bunched up, maintaining visual contact. Visibility was poor.

The staging area was a *wadi* west of the farmhouse. The three vehicles halted there. Even without the concealment of the storm, the tops of the banks of the *wadis* would have hidden them from the view of any observers at the farmhouse. Several fitful hours followed.

Prester of CIA was there with the unit. He'd come along with them on the mission, at least as far as the jumping-off point. But he wouldn't be there for the kill. He was no trigger puller, he hadn't trained with ODA 586, and in a shooting situation he'd be lucky not to be a liability. His role was strictly advisory, observational, and auxiliary.

ODA 586 team leader Sgt. McBane—Bane, as he was known—was in command of the mission, the final authority on all operational details.

He'd been schooled by Prester in operating the handheld locator device linked to the transmitter implanted in al-Magid. McBane'd be carrying the locator device during the foray.

It was time to go. The unit formed up into two five-man squads. Another two men would stay behind to secure the vehicles and staging area. Prester would remain with them. All were fitted with headset transceivers allowing them to communicate.

As the squads formed up, Garza said, "Right here is where some cornball says, 'This is it.'" Nobody had anything to say about that.

They clambered up the east bank of the *wadi*. Storm winds tore at them, hot streaming blasts that sprayed them with a high-intensity stream of airborne sand, chaff, and dust.

They faced the farmhouse, several fields distant, a dimly lit structure with shrouded lights glowing amid a mountainous vortex of sand and storm. Too distant to make out any human figures who might have been patrolling the area.

The attack would be a pincer movement. One squad would circle around from the north, and the other would come up from the south. The squad coming from the south was First Squad. Bane headed it.

Bane gave the signal for both squads to move out.

"This is it," Garza said, gulping.

He was in Second Squad, Steve Ireland's squad, which would be coming in from the north.

The squads arrowed out, separating, crossing the fields in a crescent-shaped movement that would swing them seemingly out, away from the objective, only to send them curving back, to hook it on the tips of their horns.

It had been a long time since this farm had raised any other crop beside weeds. A dirt road ran east-west; the farmhouse sat north of it. Branches split off from the main road at right angles, dividing fields into lots. The lots were crisscrossed with irrigation ditches, now dry.

The farmhouse was a low, rambling rectangle of a building whose long sides ran north-south. Beyond, to the east, rose the foothills of Iran. Most of the farmhouse's nearby outbuildings were east and south of it, including a big, corrugated metal garage barn and a couple of equipment sheds.

Second Squad neared the farmhouse. The back of the farmhouse, since it fronted east. It was a flat-roofed building with thick, mustard-brown stucco walls. The upper half of the rear wall was lined with a row of deep casement windows with dark wooden shutters that were now closed. Pale light showed behind some, but not all, of them.

The structure's roof was bordered by a waist-high parapet. Sentries were posted on it, but the storm made them keep a low profile. The farmhouse gang didn't know that they'd been burned, that their locale was no longer a secret.

Their concern as regards security threats was focused eastward, toward Iran. There in the borderland hills was where the recent troubles were located, where Fadleel's gunrunners had been slaughtered and the scout car misappropriated. Where al-Magid would be handed over to Colonel Munghal at the western mouth of the pass of the Rock of the Hawk.

The Akkad gang apprehended no trouble from the west. Any such apprehensions they might have had were suppressed by the sandstorm, which discouraged doing anything much in the way of keeping watch on all quarters.

It was estimated that the farmhouse was guarded by anywhere from fifteen to twenty defenders. Steve Ireland had every confidence in the superiority of Special Forces fighting skills over less well-trained though numerically superior forces, but he couldn't help wondering if the mission wasn't somewhat undergunned.

Secrecy sometimes trumps security, and it looked like this was one of those times. It would have been one thing if the mission had just been to kill any and all of the enemy on site. It would have been easier.

A hostage rescue was a tricky thing, a complicating factor.

Hostage rescues weren't necessarily a Special Forces stock in trade; it was more of a Delta Force specialty. ODA 586 wasn't a hostage rescue team, but such a rescue was something they were trained to do.

That's what happens when the military gets involved in the spy world, Steve thought. Lines get blurred. Gray areas predominate. You had to keep watching for hidden motives and secret agendas, even among the guys on your own side. Especially the guys on your side. Where did common-sense caution end and paranoia begin?

It was a distraction and in combat, distractions were dangerous. But you've got to take your missions where you find them, and make them work. So Steve Ireland told himself.

Second Squad swung wide of the farmhouse. From where they were they could see some of the grounds east of the structure.

The farmhouse fronted a dirt yard. On the opposite side of the yard was a metal garage barn. Its face was turned to the farmhouse. It had a peaked roof and two bays. The walls were made of sheets of thin, corrugated metal. They were badly rusted. Walls and roof were dark with corrosion that had bitten deep. An electric light hung from the wall above the tops of the bays. More lights showed inside. The bay doors were closed against the storm.

A handful of men stood outside, keeping watch. They kept pretty close to the garage, on the lee side, sheltering against the sandstorm. They stood huddled together. Two of them separated from the others and went on patrol, making a quick circle around the garage and some nearby sheds.

A dog darted out from behind a couple of fifty-gallon drums standing against a shed wall. It rushed the two men on patrol, snapping and barking at them.

They both started, the man standing nearer the dog reacting more violently. He jumped to one side. The other started, too, but managed to recover some of his poise before his partner could notice his upset.

The dog stopped short, leaning on its front paws and yapping fiercely at the duo. The first man, the one who'd jumped, unslung the auto-rifle strapped across his shoulder and started to level it.

Quick as thought, the dog turned on a dime, running away. It rounded a corner of the shed, taking it out of the man's firing line before he could get a bead on it. The man raced around the corner, but by then the dog was well away into the distance and the man put down his weapon, mouthing obscenities in the dog's direction.

The two men cut short their rounds, returning to the garage and entering it by a side door. Light from inside slanted through the open doorway, laying a yellow oblong down on the ground. A number of men were in the garage, what looked like a half dozen or more, not counting the two who now entered, closing the door behind them. Three more remained outside, flattened against the north side of the garage.

There were more in the farmhouse, too, at least a half a dozen.

* * *

The time had come for Steve Ireland to separate himself from the rest of Second Squad. The mission required him to operate more or less solo.

The locator not only identified al-Magid as being in the farmhouse, it even showed where in the farmhouse he was being kept: the northern end. Steve was posted to the northwest corner of the building. Other squad members would approach the farmhouse from different angles.

He angled one way while the rest of Second Squad angled another. He felt a pang watching the squad move off. He was on his own now.

Time to get to it, then. He looked around. A dry drainage ditch would allow him to get close to the building while providing some cover. He stepped down into it and hunched down low, moving toward the farmhouse. He was linked to the others only by his comm unit headset. He moved forward in a crouch, M4 machine gun at the ready, leading with its blunt snout poking out.

Then came his encounter with a dog of war. A real one, not just a figure of speech. A mangy dog pack haunted the area around the farmhouse, searching for what scraps of food and garbage they could forage and harrying the site's inhabitants. Akkad gang members were of two minds about the dogs. When one of the beasts became too obnoxious or aggressive, they shot it. This was a windfall for the rest of the pack, who fell on the dead dog to rend it to bits and eat it.

And yet the dogs might still prove useful to the gang, if only according to the theory that they would serve as watchdogs, their barks and growls warning of the presence of strangers and intruders. But they weren't watchdogs; they were mangy, backbiting curs so unruly and disputatious that they were as liable to be snarling and ripping at each other or at nothing at all as they were to be howling down some unannounced newcomer.

So the gang members mostly ignored them. It was a case not of the boy who cried wolf, but of the dogs who cried wolf. Tonight's sandstorm further minimized the dogs' effectiveness, since the roaring chaos of the winds had already driven the beasts into a frenzy. Steve Ireland could hear them as he moved toward the farmhouse.

They ranged unseen on various parts of the grounds, ceaselessly playing out the rites of dominance and submission. The alpha males routinely harrassed and terrorized the rest of the pack, in between attempts to best each other. The top dog, the one who can defeat all comers, becomes leader of the pack.

Steve was a hunter, and back home he'd sometimes gone on night hunts where hunting dogs were used. Hearing the hounds baying in the moonlight during those hunts, he thought it a primordial sound like a fanfare of bugles that would send chills down his spine. A joyous sound.

But there was no joy in the snarlings and mutterings and shrill cries of pain coming from the farmhouse dog pack. They sounded like a machine slipping gears and tearing itself apart.

The dog that suddenly came on him now, in the ditch near the farmhouse, made no such warning noises, however, but came on him silently. It had sensed him long before he sensed it. It was not the same dog as the one that had startled the guards patrolling the outbuildings. This was another dog from the same pack. A mongrel, it was built somewhat along greyhound lines, the top of its head coming level with a man's waist. It was moon colored, with a boxy snout, pointed triangular ears, and moist reddish-brown eyes. And a mouth of ripping fangs. Like all the pack, it was half starved, its ribs showing.

It came on Steve Ireland from the south, padding toward him. At the last instant, some eager whine or bloodlust snarl escaped it. Stealth was discarded now, replaced by speed. It leaped ahead, its forward motion quick, intent. It charged head down, low to the ground.

Its panting breath, the sound of its claws tearing into the earth, alerted Steve and caused him to look in its direction. A glance was all he got as the beast coursed across the ground toward him. It seemed to have materialized like a phantom. One instant it wasn't there; the next it was charging at him, slavering for its fangs to be at his throat.

To shoot would prematurely betray his presence and endanger the whole operation. Given a slightly longer lead time, he'd have drawn his survival knife and used it to gut the animal. There was no time. The hound would be on him in a heartbeat. It was already almost upon him, gathering itself for a leap.

He had just enough time to swing up his weapon and deliver a slashing butt-stroke, bringing it up from way down low and jabbing it hard against the hound's snout and tender nose. The blow impacted with a most satisfying crunch. The devil dog's eyes crossed, its forward motion stunningly arrested. It did a kind of backward flip, somersaulting head over heels and crashing to the ground.

It shook its head, dazed, its eyes slowly unfogging. Talons scrabbled on dirt as it got its paws under it and managed to stand up shakily on all four legs, swaying. Yipping and whining, it ran away with its tail between its legs.

Once it started running, it seemed to steady itself on its feet and darted a swift straight course elsewhere, until it was out of sight. Steve watched it go with no small sense of satisfaction. *I showed him who's top dog,* he said to himself.

He closed on the farmhouse without further incident. Other squadmen were watching the roof and grounds. Should a sentry or patrol start toward Steve Ireland's locale, he'd be alerted by comm set.

He crouched opposite the windows in the west face of the building's north end. The windows all had dark wooden shutters that were closed. Light filtered through the spaces between the slats. The air was so hazy with fine-grained dust that it made the light cling to the window squares like glowing fog.

There were guards up on the roof. He could hear them, their voices, in the lulls when the wind fell. In the center of the roof stood a structure like a square-sided bandbox. One of its sides housed a door that accessed a stairwell leading down into the building. The guards hung around this structure because it provided shelter against the sandstorm.

They didn't like having their faces sandblasted every time they turned toward the direction from which the wind was blowing. They ducked out of the storm and into the protective kiosk and the stairwell below.

Steve rose out of the ditch, slipping noiselessly across the ground to the farmhouse. He flattened his back against the wall, glancing left and right. He saw no immediate threat. No one had seen him. He was alone behind the back of the farmhouse.

A shuttered window rose to his right. Thin sheets of pale, watery light slanted through the slats. Their downslanting angle hampered his view into the room. He couldn't hear much, either. From inside came sounds of motion, stirrings, murmuring voices. All vague, indistinct; nothing he could put a handle on.

Shadows fell across the window, the shadows of figures moving around in the room. Their movements made the shadows glide across the slatted shutters. By squatting down so that he looked up through the spaces between the slats, he was able to catch a partial glimpse of the inside of the window.

The shutters were secured from inside by a horizontal crossbar held in place by a pair of brackets affixed to their inner sides. The bar looked pretty solid. Beyond the shutters, the window consisted of square panes set in an iron grid. It was closed, all but a gap of six inches at the bottom, even though it was a warm night. The glass was so smeared and grimy that it was almost opaque.

By going through some contortions he was able to peer through the open space at the bottom of the window. He couldn't see much. His view of the room was by necessity circumscribed and narrow. The interior was dimly lit. He caught glimpses of parts of bodies moving back and forth in front of his slitted window opening. The bodies were intact; it was his view of them that was truncated. He couldn't see the hostage, but he was reasonably sure that al-Magid was not in a direct line with this window.

He reached into his pack and took out a stun grenade. It was similar in size and shape to a hockey puck. One face was covered with a film of thin gray plastic. He peeled it off. The face was now coated with sticky adhesive. He pressed the sticky side against the lower-left corner of the shutter frame.

The grenade was a concussion job, with little explosive power. It would deliver a blinding flash and shattering noise, both designed to shock and awe its victims so they would be paralyzed with ineffectiveness for several critical seconds—heartbeats that meant the difference between life and death.

The charge it carried was virtually nil, but it had enough oomph to blow the shutters off their hinges and clear the window frame. It would blow the glass, too, which was potentially hazardous to anyone in its path. That was why he'd checked to make sure as best he could that the captive was nowhere along its line of force.

He couldn't help but note the paradox of being so solicitous of al-Magid's welfare on the one hand, and having received orders to kill him if that was the only way to prevent the gang from carrying him into Iran.

Steve edged away from the window. He reported his current status over the comm set. The other members of Second Squad were in position. First Squad was not yet ready. They were still moving up toward the south end of the blockhouse and the outbuildings.

Steve figured that the Go would be given in no

more than five minutes. Before that happened, however, the unexpected occurred.

Shooting sounded. More shots followed, strings of popping noises. They came from somewhere off in the distance. It's harder than one might think to determine the source of sounds without a visual cue to direct the search.

East of the farmhouse, amid the hills of Iran, lights flashed. That's where the shots were coming from. Shots and blasts. The blasts looked like heat lightning and were followed by big booms.

Nobody at the farmhouse knew it yet, but it was the sound of the Dog Team's Kilroy and Vang Bulo taking apart Colonel Munghal's convoy.

It was a distraction, a diversion for the farmhouse gang. The bunch in the garage came out first to investigate. They stood facing east, watching a line of fire rise from somewhere in the pass of the Rock of the Hawk. The sentries on the farmhouse roof lined the east rail to see what was happening. A couple of men came out of the front door into the yard. Another stood in the doorway, looking out toward the hills. They were calling back and forth to the crew from the garage, trying to find out what was happening. No one had a clue.

The Special Forces unit took advantage of the opportunity to tighten their cordon around the target area. Niles in First Squad was crossing an open space between two sheds when one of the gang in the yard saw him. A burst of auto-fire ripped out as the gang member shot but missed.

The fat was in the fire now. Special Forces team leader McBane gave the GO signal. The two squads moved into action.

Steve Ireland armed and activated the stun bomb. He moved a half dozen paces to the right of it. He crouched down, covering. He counted off to himself, "One one thousand, two one thousand, three one thousand." He squeezed his eyes shut, covered his ears with his hands, and opened his mouth to equalize the coming pressure.

The stun bomb detonated, going off like a sonic boom, shaking the farmhouse on its frame. The concussion caused a cloud of dust to leap from the walls into the air. The blast was about equal to that of a quarter stick of dynamite. A bit more powerful than what Steve Ireland had been counting on. It not only blew the shutters off the window but blew the window in, too, glass, frame, and all. Smoke poured out of the blank oblong hole where the window had been.

Steve's ears rang and he felt more than a little bit stunned himself, but not so much that he froze instead of reacting. He stuck his machine gun muzzle in the lower-right-hand corner of the window frame, into the room. He wielded his weapon from a crouch, showing as little of himself as possible.

The room, what he could see of it, was square sided, starkly funtional. Visibility was poor due to all the smoke and dust in the air. Stone dust rained down from the concrete ceiling. Manlike shapes stumbled around inside, flailing and coughing.

An explosion went off on the east side of the farmhouse. Shots banged in the yard. Gunfire rattled, increasing in firepower and fury. There were shouts, screams. Some of the latter were drowned out by more gunfire and abruptly silenced. The guns remained vocal. It sounded like a pretty hot firefight.

A man loomed up at the window and stood there, swaying. He must have been standing directly in front of the window when it blew. His face and body bristled with glass shards that had penetrated his flesh. He was streaked from head to toe with ribbons of red stuff.

Steve Ireland fired a blast into the other's middle at point-blank range. He fell backward violently, toppling from sight.

Another man swam up in front of him. He wore a navy blue jogging suit with white racing stripes and a heavy-banded gold wristwatch, and carried an AK-47. Steve fired first.

The man in the jogging suit backpedaled, staggering rearward until he slammed into the opposite wall. He stood leaning against the wall, eyes bulging, mouth gaping, head lolling. He was still holding on to his weapon but it wasn't pointing at Steve anymore. His legs bent at the knees, and he slid down the wall, sitting down on the floor. A dark red vertical smear that could have been laid on with a stroke of a housepainter's brush marked the wall. He fell forward, and the weapon fell, clattering, from his hand to the floor.

Steve Ireland had already moved on to the next opponent. The key to clearing out multiple foes was to not freeze and hang on one target, but to stay loose and fluid and move on to the next and the next, knocking them down one after another until there were no more targets left.

Several men stood clustered diagonally across from him in a corner. One wore a dark turban and a bowling shirt. Another wore a T-shirt bearing the logo of a British soccer club. He was pulling a long-barreled

.44 out of a shoulder holster. The shoulder holster
reached from under his arm to the top of his belt. It
had a spring catch and flew open at the top to facilitate the shooter's draw.

A third wore a pale yellow button-down short-
sleeved shirt, brown baggy slacks, and sneakers. He
had wavy hair that fell in a curling lock over his
forehead; moist, wide, dark brown eyes; sharp features; and a thin wisp of a mustache. He looked no
more than eighteen years old. Hc was snatching up
a rifle from where it stood leaning against the wall.

Steve thrust the machine gun deeper into the
room, aligning it with the trio. He opened up,
squeezing off a series of bursts. The .44-toting gang
member was fast. The gun was in his hand, bucking,
pumping lead, the reports deafening. He missed.
One slug buried itself deep in the window frame and
the other sailed harmlessly through the window
and over Steve Ireland's head.

Steve didn't miss, placing a quick three-shot burst
in the middle of the gunman's face. The youth in the
short-sleeved shirt had his rifle in hand, but he was
still turning when Steve cut him down. The youth
spun, toppled, crashed. The man in the turban was
empty handed, but Steve cut him down anyway
before he could fill his hand with a firearm. The
room was clear of foes, as far as Steve could tell.
The room was thick with smoke and dust. He
couldn't see the captive.

There was a lull—at least, nobody else was shooting at him. For now. Steve used the opportunity to
clamber up to the window sill and hop down into the
room. He landed lightfooted, catlike. A thought

came to him, something about going from the frying pan into the fire, but he brushed it aside.

He was breathing heavily through his mouth. Gunsmoke choked him, making it hard to draw a breath. It stung his eyes, too. He got his back to a wall to one side of the window and looked around, scanning as much of the scene as he could. The stun bomb had blown out the ceiling lamp.

A couple of construction-style portable electric lamps in wire holders were hung from hooks and pegs on the walls. They provided some light to see by. At the southeast corner of the room, a doorway with no door opened into a hall where lights burned. Some of their glow shone through into the room.

Shooting sounded in the hall, and outside the farmhouse, too. Lots of it.

Steve still saw no sign of the captive. Bodies littered the stone floor. One was that of a hooded man bound to a chair that lay on its side on the floor.

Steve felt fairly sure in guessing that that was the captive. The captive was motionless. There were no wounds on him that Steve could see, but visibility in the room was spotty.

A figure darted from the hall into the doorway. He was a big man with dark hair and a thick mustache. He wore tinted glasses that veiled the tops of his eyes but that were clear at the bottom rims. He wore a light blue polyester leisure suit, a shirt with floppy airplane-wing collars, and a black leather belt several inches wide with an ornate and oversized square silver buckle. His shiny square-toed black boots had silver buckles on their uppers and three-inch heels. He held a machine gun.

He rushed in the room unaware of Steve's presence,

which took him by surprise. Not a happy surprise, either. His expression was outraged, as though amazed by the American's Yankee Doodle effrontery. He had even more reason for outrage an eyeblink later, as a burst from Steve's weapon cut him down. Steve stitched a diagonal line across the other's torso.

The gang member bounced around in the doorway, half turning, half falling into the hall. His finger tightened on the trigger of his machine gun. Lead sprayed, tagging the stone walls and floor. Concrete and rock shards flew upward. Steve shot him again, and the other dropped the machine gun, silencing it. He fell down and was dead.

Steve tried to look everywhere at once and cover everything with the muzzle of his M4. He panted for breath, as if he'd just finished running several miles. He was stifling inside his helmet, body armor, and fatigues. Sweat seemed to start from every pore. He realized he was grinding his teeth.

The room was a butcher shop, and Steve Ireland was the meat cutter. He felt slightly sick, the residue of the juices of fear and adrenaline.

A body on the floor twitched, and he fired a quick burst into it. Good thing it hadn't been the captive. The captive continued to be motionless.

Steve stepped through the doorway into the hall. A Special Forces trooper stood there: Garza. He and Steve saw each other at the same time. It was a good thing that neither of them fired by reflex.

The farmhouse's front door was open. Through it, Steve could see a couple of bodies of Akkad gang members sprawled in the yard.

Another Second Squad member entered, coming

in from the yard. Calhoun. Calhoun was a medical specialist.

Steve said, "Am I glad to see you! Come take a look at al-Magid."

Calhoun said, "How is he?"

"I don't know, that's why I want you to take a look at him."

The front door was to Steve's right. It opened on to a wide hall, where a stone staircase with wooden banisters and railings took a zigzag course upward to the roof.

A rattle sounded at the top of the stairs. Garza was facing in that direction. Steve and Calhoun had started for the north end room. Steve glanced at Garza. Garza did a double-take that was almost comical in its extremes. His eyes bulged, his jaw dropped. He took a deep breath to shout a warning.

Steve was already moving, pivoting toward the direction where Garza was standing, swinging the machine gun along with him.

A gang member crouched at the top of the stairs, just below the roof, where he'd been hiding. He fired his rifle. He was shooting downward at a sharp angle and missed all three Americans.

Steve pointed the machine gun at the top of the stairs and sprayed lead. The gang member was neatly pinned inside the stairwell, half crouching, half sitting on the stairs just below the wooden landing.

He cried out and fell, dropping his weapon. He tumbled down the first flight of stairs and across the landing, crashing into and through the wooden railing and banisters, and landing with a sound like wet laundry thumping to the floor.

Garza covered the stairs and front while Calhoun

followed Steve into the north room. The captive lay on his side, with his hands tied to the back of the overturned chair. Steve stood on one knee beside him. He checked for booby traps and other devices. Iraq was the home of the IED, or improvised explosive device, and he wanted to make sure that the Akkad gang hadn't been doing any improvising of diabolical mechanisms on the captive. He found none. While he was checking, he had to handle the captive. The other's flesh was warm and in his chest a heartbeat.

"He's alive," Steve said. He reached for the hood to unmask the man. Hand on the bottom of the hood, he paused. He said, "I just had a hell of a thought—what if it's not al-Magid under the hood? What if they switched him for a ringer? Then what do we do?"

Calhoun said dryly, "Keep on going straight into Iran."

Steve pulled the hood off. Calhoun pressed in, looking over his shoulder.

"Ali al-Magid," Calhoun said, a bit breathlessly.

Steve said, "All right."

Ali al-Magid was unconscious. His skin was sallow, his breathing labored. Clusters of half-healed cuts and bruises showed on his face. His mustache was straggly and drooping, he had an eight-day growth of beard. A string of saliva leaked from a corner of his mouth, leaving a wet, glistening patch of drool on his chin.

Steve said, "Is he knocked out?"

"Drugged, I think," Calhoun said. "Help me untie him."

Steve used his knife to cut the ropes binding al-

Magid to the chair. He and Calhoun eased the unconscious man to his back on the floor. It was as good a place as any. The room had been shot up pretty bad. There was a lot of blood on the floor on the other side of the room, where most of the bodies had fallen.

Calhoun hung up one of the wire-basket electric lamps nearby. He opened his doctor's bag and went to work.

Steve Ireland would only be in the way. He went out, into the front hall. Garza and Ervil, another squad member, were coming down from the roof, descending the stairs. Ervil had a long, narrow fish face and pale, watery eyes. Everything about his face was hard and bony, except for the eyes, which were like skinless green grapes.

"We cleared the roof," he said. "Nobody up there."

Steve indicated the view through the front door to the yard and outbuildings. He said, "Out there?"

Garza said, "A turkey shoot. The gang outside was obliging enough to bunch up when we caught 'em in a crossfire."

Niles appeared, coming out of the south wing of the building. He was a light-skinned black guy with pointed features and almond-shaped eyes. "All clear," he said. "Me and Creedy did a room-to-room search and didn't find anybody else. Not even a body. Most of the gang must've gathered outside to see what the shooting was all about."

Steve said feelingly, "What was it all about?"

Niles shrugged. "Damned if I know, but it sure was convenient. It flushed most of the bad guys out into the open."

Ervil said, "Some border dustup, most likely. More of these bastards double-crossing each other."

McBane reported in by his communicator that the site was secured. Steve Ireland went outside to see what there was to see and to determine what he could do, if anything. Even sandstorm murk felt refreshing after being penned in the farmhouse miasma of smoke, blood, and stink.

Several bodies of gang members lay strewn on the ground in front of the farmhouse in the angular contortions of violent death. More corpses lay scattered on the ground in front of the garage. The garage was on fire. A couple of cars and trucks that had been stored in there were now burning. Bullets had exploded the vehicles' gas tanks, and flaming gasoline had spread the blaze to the walls and roof of the structure.

Winds fanned the flames, whipping them up like a stream of oxygen fueling a blowtorch. They carried away the smoke, whipping it along in near-horizontal streamers that stretched toward the north. They carried away much of the heat, too.

The members of ODA 586 had escaped serious injury. Ernie Greco, "the Greek," had been tagged in his upper left shoulder. He said he was all right, but his eyes went in and out of focus and he was a little wobbly on his feet.

Calhoun sat him down and patched him up. He'd set up shop in the farmhouse's front hall. There were too many bodies in the north room. The Greek's wound had bled a lot, but the bullet had passed through the muscle without hitting any blood vessels or bones.

The unit had two medical specialists, Calhoun and Paulus. Paulus was examining al-Magid. Team leader McBane was looking over Paulus's shoulder, watching. Al-Magid lay on his back with a blanket covering him, still unconscious. Paulus thumbed back one of scientist's eyelids, lifting it, looking at the eye. Paulus said, "Drugged. I could give him more stimulant, but he just had one shot, and it might be a strain on the system to give him another too soon—"

McBane said, "Don't bother if he can get along without it. Just as long as he doesn't die on us."

"Not much danger of that. His heartbeat is slow but strong, steady. His condition is serious but not critical."

One of the first things McBane had ordered done was to detail a man or two to make sure that all the enemy bodies in the farmhouse were dead. They were. Outside, a couple of unit members carried out a similar task, making the rounds of the bodies sprawled in the yard.

One Special Forces troop, Creedy, had a face nearly as wide as it was long, a square-shaped torso, and thick limbs. He was eyeing a body that lay near one of the tool sheds southwest of the garage.

The body was of a sharp-featured, wiry young man in a dark thin windbreaker with white piping. He lay prone, with his head turned to one side and his arms raised.

Creedy thought he'd seen him twitch. He turned, started toward him. The young man jumped up and started running away. Creedy shot him in the back. The youth fell, motionless. Creedy went to him, toeing the body. It lay in a similar position to the one it had been in when the youth was shamming, except that now his eyes were open, and so was his mouth. A cup's worth of blood had spilled from his mouth, soaking into the ground.

Garza and Ervil were nearby. They started toward him, weapons at the ready. Garza said, "Trouble?"

"Not anymore," Creedy said. "This one was faking. Careful. There could be others."

"Not the ones we saw. They were all shot up, shot to shit."

"That don't mean nothing. Some of these babies are tough."

"Not tough enough to get around with half their brains leaking out."

"Why not? You seem to manage all right."

"Now listen, Creedy—"

Ervil said, "Cut the shit, both of you. We've doing a job here."

Garza said, "Creedy started it with the trash talking—"

Creedy groaned. "For Pete's sake, can't you take a joke?"

Ervil said, "Can it."

They all went back to work. ODA 586 had accomplished the first part of its mission, namely, securing the person of Ali al-Magid and neutralizing the farmhouse personnel. Now it remained for them to exfiltrate the safe zone of Border Base Foxtrot.

Tillotson, the comm specialist, had set up in the farmhouse. The winds were muffled, making it easier to hear, and there was less chance of windblown sand getting into the hardware and messing it up. The personal headset transceivers worked on a tight beam that was functional within the area of the farmhouse and its immediate surroundings but that tended to break up outside a radius of several hundred yards.

A radio was used to communicate with the men left behind at the *wadi* and at Border Base Foxtrot. Donnicker and Virgil had stayed behind with Prester and the radio at the vehicles. Virgil was radio man.

Tillotson was preparing to contact Foxtrot to initiate the withdrawal procedue when an emergency message came flashing in from Virgil at the *wadi*. Virgil said, "Company's coming!" He sounded excited. "A caravan of hostiles just went by here."

Tillotson said, "How many?"

"Six cars and trucks filled with armed men. They just crossed the bridge north of us and are heading toward the farmhouse road."

"What's your situation?"

"We're okay. Our vehicles were hidden around the bend so they didn't see them. Or if they did, they didn't stop. We didn't get too good a look at them, but I can tell you this: they're loaded for bear and they're moving in fast on your locale!"

Tillotson passed the warning to McBane. McBane said, "It's too late to withdraw, so we'll have to make a fight of it."

The farmhouse was the strongest point from which to make a stand. It would be the core of the resistance. The situation favored not a static, passive defense, but an active one. Teams of mobile, free-ranging defenders could take the fight to the enemy with every chance of inflicting serious damage. "Let's give them a little welcoming party," McBane said.

The farm road stood between the farmhouse and the *wadi* and ran north-south. Access roads met it at right angles. One access road lay south of the farmhouse, another north of it.

Two three-man teams were set up, each covering one of the access roads bracketing the farmhouse. The teams were positioned west of the farmhouse to intercept the hostiles well in advance of the stucture. Berger, Creedy, and Paulus covered the south road; Ervil, Niles, and Steve Ireland covered the north road.

McBane, Tillotson, Calhoun, and Garza occupied the farmhouse.

Virgil, Donnicker, and Prester would man a Humvee to take the invaders from the rear should the opportunity present itself. They were being held in reserve until the enemy had committed his forces.

In the south road team, Creedy manned a .50-caliber machine gun, seconded by Paulus, who would act as spotter, feeding the weapon the cartridge belt and keeping it unsnarled, while Berger was armed with a rocket-propelled grenade launcher.

In the north road team, Ervil worked another big .50 machine gun, Niles was the belt feeder, and Steve Ireland would handle a grenade launcher.

Both teams took cover behind roadside hillocks and mounds. ODA 586 had an element of surprise working for it. The enemy was in the dark as to what had happened at the farmhouse and the number and disposition of the forces arrayed against them.

On the other hand, it wasn't a complete surprise. They knew something; otherwise they wouldn't be speeding toward it with anywhere from two dozen to three dozen armed troops in half a dozen vehicles. And as they neared, they would see the light of the burning garage to further warn them.

Who they were was as yet unknown to the Special Forces unit. That the newcomers were unfriendly was certain. Americans had no friends in this part of the region. That the intruders were insurgents was also clear.

What they were was Akkad gang members and associates. When Hassani Akkad and his men in the ambulance had failed to return some time earlier or to answer the ever-more-urgent cell-phone queries directed at them from their fellows in Azif, the hardcore element in the gang had grabbed their guns, jumped in their vehicles, and headed out to the farmhouse.

Along the way, they'd discovered the ambulance in the ditch by the wrecked plank bridge, with all its occupants but Hassani murdered and him gone. They raced toward the farmhouse, in the course of which they'd been seen by the three men posted by the Humvees in the *wadi*, who'd given the alert to their fellows at the farmhouse. But this exact sequence would not be known to the Americans until some time later, the next day, after events had played themselves out. McBane and company could be fairly certain, however, that whoever was coming were friends of the gang and no friends of theirs.

In the farmhouse, Tillotson was trying to raise Foxtrot, but the base's radio signal was elusive. The sandstorm played hell with radio communication. Calhoun finished patching up Garza's wounds.

Garza was shirtless, and his left shoulder and upper arm were taped up. Garza picked up his rifle and took up a position at one of the west windows.

Al-Magid lay off to the side, covered with a blanket, breathing heavily but steadily. McBane told Calhoun, "Keep an eye on him. I don't want him jumping up and running off on his own."

"No worry about that. He's out like a light," Calhoun said. "Tillotson can keep an eye on him. I'll cover the roof." Calhoun picked up his weapon and climbed the stairs to the rooftop.

Tillotson labored over the radio, still trying to raise Foxtrot.

The caravan had taken the bridge north of where the Special Forces Humvees were stashed in the *wadi*. It was a simple plank bridge, like the one where the Red Crescent ambulance had been ambushed. The route from the bridge eastward cut the farm road at a place above the northern farm access road.

The lead vehicle turned right on the farm road, heading south, the other vehicles falling in line behind it. It and two vehicles directly behind it soon turned left, entering the farmhouse's north access road.

The three remaining vehicles continued onward, making south until they came to the intersection with the farmhouse's south access road. They entered it, splitting their forces.

Steve Ireland watched three vehicles rush toward him along the farmhouse's north access road. He was on the north side of it, and Ervil and Niles were on the south side. The sandstorm caused the outline of the vehicles' headlights to blur, as if seen through a canvas screen.

The lead vehicle was a dark Mercedes sedan. It was old and battered and needed a new paint job, but it was a Mercedes. The engine was in good shape, and the car moved. The windows were all rolled down, with guns sticking out of them, guns wielded by the occupants of the car.

The second vehicle was a light-colored compact car. It was somewhat smaller than the first, though the same number of gun barrels bristled out through the open windows. The group in the tan car were so crowded that they were practically sitting on each other's laps.

The third vehicle was a pickup truck. A machine gun was mounted across the cab roof, pointing at the road ahead. A gunner stood behind it, working it. The pickup bed was surrounded on three sides by a set of shoulder-high metal railings for the men in the back of the truck to hold on to while they were standing up.

The car-and-truck combo didn't wait for their compatriots in the other half of the caravan to get in position on the south road before attacking. They came on.

Ervil lay prone, gripping the machine gun handholds. He sighted the machine gun on the Mercedes, swinging the muzzle toward where the driver would be. He opened fire. The machine gun bucked, spitting lead. Sparks flew as rounds struck the car body and windshield posts, making spanging noises when they ricocheted. Niles held the underside of the belt loosely in both hands, maintaining an uninterrupted feed into the weapon.

Ervil kept firing into the car, aiming at the men and not the machine. Slay the men, and the machine would take care of itself. The windshield disintegrated. So, too, did the driver's head and upper body. The car swerved, fishtailing. It flashed toward the place where the Special Forces trio was set up. It drifted toward its left, riding up on the shoulder, closing fast on the mound behind which Steve Ireland lay. For an instant it was coming straight at him, and he had time to wonder if it would climb the mound and sail over him, or bulldoze it and him along with it. He never found out, because a vagary of the driver's dead hands on the steering wheel caused the Merc to swerve back to its right, removing him from its path. Momentum kept it coming more or less straight on down the road. It flashed past the mound and the rockpile on the other side of the road, where Ervil and Niles manned the machine gun nest.

The Merc rushed on for another twenty or thirty yards before it ran off the road into a ditch and rolled. Shouts and shrieks sounded from inside the vehicle, mixing with the crunch of collapsing metal. The outcries stopped well before the Merc stopped rolling.

The other two vehicles changed course, leaving the road. The light-colored compact car angled north, and the pickup truck angled south. The pickup's roof-mounted heavy machine gun fired in Ervil's and Paulus's direction. The gang gunner knew where the enemy machine gun was, having seen its muzzle flares when it was putting the blast on the Merc.

The gunner aimed at them, but he had a lot to overcome first. It was hard enough to hit anything from a moving platform such as the pickup truck. The vehicle had left the dirt road for the even more uneven and bumpy terrain of a field, all rutted and washboard irregular. The heavy machine gun's formidable rate of firepower was offset by the bouncy ride. The gunner couldn't hold a bead on his opponents in this duel of the machine guns. By the same token, the pickup's shaky, unpredictable course made it difficult for Ervil to tag it with his weapon.

The pickup hit a particularly rough bump, causing one of the riders in the rear to be thrown clear of the vehicle. He was catapulted into empty air, crying out as he followed a tight parabolic arc that finished in a crash landing on hard ground.

Steve Ireland readied himself for the onslaught of the compact car. It left the road and drove across the field north of the road. The guns sticking out the windows on its right-hand side fired in the direction of the rockpile behind which Ervil and Niles were set up. The bullets went high, sailing harmlessly overhead.

The car swerved farther north to avoid the mound behind which Steve sheltered. He led it slightly as he lined up the grenade launcher and fired it. It made a sound that went *puh-tock!*

It was a tough shot and he misjudged the range, causing the grenade to overshoot the car, although it exploded nearby. The car lurched, one of its lights blacking out. Shrapnel tagged some in the car, yielding cries of pain.

The shouting from inside the car stopped, but the car kept going, curving toward a stone wall bounding the field. It slowed, but not in time to keep from crashing into the stone wall. The other headlight went dark.

Before Steve could loft another grenade at it, machine-gun fire started tearing up the road around where he, Ervil, and Niles were planted. It came from the pickup's roof-mounted machine gun. The pickup had managed to reach a hillock in the middle of the field and was sheltering behind it, keeping the hillock between them and Ervil and Niles.

The hillock was a low one, and its highest point barely reached the pickup's roof. The gunner was able to shoot across the top of the mound at Niles and Ervil. The rest of the pickup was hidden behind the mound. The men who'd been riding in the back of the truck had all dismounted and taken cover.

The rockpile was highest where it faced the access road. It presented less cover toward the hillock where the pickup stood. Less cover, but some. Ervil and Niles flattened as the pickup gunner loosed a series of bursts at them. Steve Ireland was in the line of fire too on the other side of the road. He ate dirt while machine gun bullets tore up the ground around him. He could feel the vibrations of the rounds impacting the earth. The ground was torn up, sending dirt clods geysering.

Steve spotted a roadside ditch. He threw himself into it and flattened. The untimely attack had kept him from following up by launching a few more grenades at the compact car.

The pickup truck's machine-gun fire temporarily halted. Steve took advantage of the lull to peek over the top of the ditch at the compact car. There was motion in the car. The rear doors were forced open, and several men piled out. There were four in all, and they were armed.

Commotion and weak cries sounded in the front seat. The man in the front passenger seat was alive. He was trying to open the door, but it was jammed and he couldn't move it. He called for his comrades to help him.

Steve triggered the launcher to peg a grenade at the car. Again, it went puh-tock. The sound goosed the four gunmen into diving over the stone wall to the shelter of the far side. The man in the front seat cried for them not to leave him.

The grenade hit the car with a whoomping noise, followed immediately by a blast. The car was engulfed in an eruption of red glare. The gas tank blew, and the car became a fiery octopus, growing tentacles of flame that suddenly thrust out in all directions.

Ervil and Niles crawled around, moving the machine gun to the southern limb of the rockpile and pointing it at the hillock. The pickup truck gunner knew that something was up from the lack of fire coming from his foes. He poured more lead at them, making a fearful racket as the slugs streamed into the rockpile, sounding like jackhammers breaking up pavement.

The other half of the caravan consisted of a jeep and two Ford Explorer SUVs. The vehicles were all filled with armed men. The jeep was short and snouty, with fat, knobbed tires. The two Explorers were exactly alike, dark green with tinted glass. The tinted glass was something of a liability at night.

The Explorers drove more slowly than the jeep, which hurtled along at a breakneck pace. A gap opened between the jeep and its two followers as they plowed east along the farmhouse's south access road.

Berger tagged the jeep with a rocket-propelled grenade. The projectile hit the jeep head-on. It was like the jeep had hit a brick wall, only instead of bricks, the wall was made of an explosive blast. The front of the jeep got smeared, and the rest of the vehicle started coming apart at the seams, unable to contain the fire that was engulfing it. A couple of tires blew, and the jeep started slewing around, pinwheeling as it slid to a stop in the middle of the road and stood there, burning.

The Explorers came on, a gap now widening between them. The tail car was hanging back. Creedy fired the machine gun at the lead Explorer. A nasty surprise lay in wait. It was armored, with bulletproof glass. Creedy kept firing bursts into it. The bullets seemed to have about as much effect on it as hailstones. It flashed past, striking the wrecked jeep a sidelong blow and knocking it off the road.

The second Explorer, the tail car, abruptly left the road and drove across the field toward the farmhouse. Creedy gave it the treatment, firing across the field at it, raking its right side. It shuddered under the impact but kept going. He concentrated fire on the machine's underside. The tires were solid rubber, but he managed to shred the right front tire. The Explorer sagged, curving toward the right. The metal wheel dug a line in the dirt.

The driver fought it, wrestling it to the left, fighting to pull it out of a slide. Creedy's bullets savaged the right rear tire. The Explorer ground to a halt in the middle of the field, at a point southwest of the farmhouse and northwest of Creedy and Paulus. It was at a tilted angle that served as a natural barricade.

Doors opened on the driver's side of the Explorer and gunmen got out, sheltering behind the armored SUV. The first Explorer kept on going, leaving the road and curving north, circling back around the outbuildings.

Berger craned, looking for a shot with the rocket-propelled grenade, but the Explorer zipped around the corner of a shed and out of sight. The burning garage stood between the shed and the farmhouse. The blaze had lessened but was still going pretty good. Twisted, red-hot metal struts and walls collapsed, sending a shower of sparks skyward.

Some gunmen leaned around the rear corner of the second Explorer and started shooting at Creedy, Paulus, and Berger. A couple more darted toward the farmhouse. Gunfire blazed from the roof and some of the side windows of the farmhouse, felling the attackers who were moving toward it. They were cut down. The remaining gunmen behind the Explorer divided their fire between the men on the road and those in the farmhouse.

It was getting hot for Steve Ireland. The four men who'd escaped from the compact car were on the far side of the stone wall, shooting at him.

Steve used the launcher to pop a grenade over the wall. It burst on the far side. A shriek sounded, then choked off. The shooting stopped. After a pause, it started up again. Three guns only, now; the fourth had been stilled. The shooters dispersed, ranging themselves so there was plenty of space between each of them along the wall.

Steve also had to worry about the machine gunner on the pickup truck. He and Ervil and Niles were close to being caught in a crossfire. Ervil and the gunner on the pickup truck exchanged shots, to no great result on either side.

Steve set down the grenade launcher and picked up his M4 machine gun. Spearblades of light that were muzzle flashes flared and spiked in three places along the stone wall. Steve pointed his weapon at one of the spearpoints, squeezing out bursts at it. The light winked out.

Ervil and Niles were feeling the heat from the shooters behind the wall. They were pretty well covered from the pickup gunner but less so for the shooters to their rear. Niles took up his rifle and turned around, firing from a prone position at the two shooters remaining behind the wall. That gave Steve something of a breather.

It was a short-lived one, for he became aware of a vehicle moving up on his right. The first Explorer had circled north around the back of the burning garage and was now curving west, toward the farmhouse's north access road.

He reached for the grenade launcher. The shooters behind the wall started pinning him pretty good, forcing him to flatten in the low-sided ditch. He could hear the Explorer's engine winding out, the sound of its heavy underside bumping and scraping against the rocks and furrows of the fields. Niles saw the Explorer coming up and turned his rifle on it, raking the driver's side. Bullets bounced off its armored surface.

The Explorer was pointed north, its wheels edging to the left to begin the turn onto the north access road. Then it faltered. It started to go into a left-hand turn, but instead of completing the curve it kept on going, crossing the road at an angle and arcing toward the stone wall. A bullet hole pierced the windshield directly opposite the driver's head. A similar hole pierced the driver's forehead, an angry third eye. He was dead—shot by Kilroy.

Kilroy had finally gotten into position on the half-buried rock knob at the northeast corner of the fields. With his night-vision glasses he'd scanned the scene, following the developing clash. He recognized the attackers as Akkad gang members. He'd seen the lead Explorer run the gauntlet of heavy machine-gun fire directed at it by Creedy, and knew that it was armored. He still had some titanium alloy bullets left. He knew what to do with them. He'd put the crosshairs of his sniper rifle's scope on the Explorer's driver and squeezed the trigger.

The rest was a matter of skill and ballistics, and Kilroy had both working for him. The high-velocity had drilled the bulletproof windshield and driver alike. The man in the front passenger seat lunged for the steering wheel, trying to wrestle it from the hand of the driver. Before he could, the Explorer crashed into the stone wall. The two shooters behind the wall scrambled for cover.

Steve Ireland stuck his head up. The crashed Explorer was a sitting target. Motion and noise came from inside. Some of the passengers still lived.

It was like shooting fish in a barrel. Steve Ireland's

launcher lofted a grenade right on the Explorer. It came down with a soft plop, like an egg dropping into a kettle of boiling water. Then it blew.

The Explorer was armored, but the plating on the roof was less thick than that on the sides and undercarriage. The explosion gutted the roof, sieving it and streaking down on those inside. Making a real mess of them.

A fuel line was severed, and a fire started burning somewhere under the machine. It made a crackling noise, like dry twigs snapping and corn popping. Tendrils of smoke, thick and slow and serpentine, curled up from beneath the undercarriage. The flames touched off a line of leaking fuel with a whoosh. Fire crawled back up the line, into the fuel tank itself, touching it off. The blast was big.

The pickup truck gunner must have paused to watch or been otherwise distracted, because he stayed in one place for a beat too long, and Ervil nailed him. The gunner folded at the knees and dropped into the truck bed, minus a head.

The handful of gang members sheltering behind the hillock suddenly broke into the open, rushing the farmhouse. They ran headlong into a blistering fusillade from the house being laid down by McBane and Garza. That stopped their rush, pinning them in the open. Then Ervil swung the machine gun muzzle their way before they could retreat to the shelter of the hillock. He fired—and that was that.

* * *

Steve Ireland and Niles continued exchanging potshots with the two shooters behind the wall. Nobody scored.

Storm winds whipped the flames of the blazing Explorer into long orange-red streamers streaking north. Patches of blazing gas provided fitful, unbalanced illumination.

The last real pocket of resistance was the bunch at the second Explorer, southwest of the farmhouse. That group sheltered behind the vehicle, firing at the farmhouse and at Creedy, Paulus, and Berger. It was something of a stalemate until Virgil, Donnicker, and Prester came up from the *wadi* and across the fields in a Humvee. Virgil drove and Donnicker manned the turret machine gun. Prester rode shotgun.

They rolled up behind the gang members sheltering behind the Explorer. Donnicker at the machine gun made quick work of them.

The two shooters behind the wall stopped shooting. After a while, Steve Ireland and Niles took notice of the lull. It might have been a trick to lure them out in the open, so they stayed put. More time passed, though, without further sign of the two shooters. Steve and Niles worked their way toward the wall, alternating between advancing and covering each other's advance. No shots were fired at them.

When they reached the wall, they found that the shooters were gone. The missing shooters could barely be seen, thanks to the light of the burning Explorer. The two had made their way north and were just disappearing behind the screen of a line of palm trees.

Steve said, "Too far away. They're not worth wasting a bullet on."

Niles said, "What happened?"

"I guess they had enough."

They stood watching the palm trees for a bit, but the shooters failed to show themselves. Steve and Niles turned, starting back toward the farmhouse. They'd gone no more than two paces when they heard a pair of shots ring out. The shots came from the north, beyond the palm trees. Two shots, no more. They had a ring of finality to them. Silence fell on that quarter.

Steve and Niles glanced at each other. Niles shrugged. They went to rejoin the others.


Kilroy saw the two shooters abandon their posts at the stone wall and flee north toward the palm trees. He was waiting for them when they emerged from the other side.

No costly titanium-alloy rounds for them. Ordinary bullets from his AK-47 would suffice.

And did.


Later, when the members of ODA 586 had a chance to compare notes, nobody could explain why the first Explorer had crashed into the wall.

The best explanation (and that was a weak one) was that a round from Creedy's machine gun had somehow gotten through the armor plating during the Explorer's headlong charge, and that it or a piece of shrapnel dislodged by it had wounded the driver, not killing him immediately, but having a delayed effect that allowed him to circle around to the north access road before he expired.

That tied it up in a neat package, satisfactory to the recordkeepers.

The explosion had blown out the Explorer's windshield, destroying the evidence of the neat bullet hole penetrating armored glass. Nobody bothered to examine the machine's burned-out hulk or the charred remains of its passengers. Which spared them from finding the titanium bullet penetrating the driver's skull, and opening up a lot of questions into matters best ignored.

# Twelve

Much happened in the next twenty-four hours following the night of Colonel Munghal's death and the farmhouse raid. ODA 586 successfully returned to Border Base Foxtrot. Ali al-Magid was operated on in the base hospital, where a surgeon who'd been sworn to secrecy operated on him, removing the microtransmitter implanted in the side of one of his ample buttocks. The implant was taken possession of by Albin Prester, who was present in the operating room, clad in an antiseptic surgical mask and rubber gloves.

Al-Magid was airlifted to the Green Zone in Baghdad, to a secure hospital at an American military base. After eighteen hours of sleep, he returned to consciousness, dazed and confused but on the road to recovery. Along that road he would encounter many American military intelligence agents who would debrief him extensively on his experience in captivity and, no less important, on his knowledge of the breadth and depth of the mastery of the Razeem process to be found among Iraqi scientists.

His debriefing would take a considerable length of time. When they were done squeezing him of every vital particle of intelligence, they might hand him over to Iraqi government authorities, provided that the government and authorities in question were not inimical to the vital national security interests of the United States. Which was by no means a sure bet, due to the fitful leaps and odd morphings that the new Iraqi state was creating.

In Iran, the assassination of Colonel Munghal was cause for consternation. The high-ranking Pasdaran secret police official had had his hand in so many different dirty businesses, foreign and domestic, that there was no telling who'd had him killed, and for what reason. The author of the plot might well be Iranian. Munghal had many enemies. Perhaps a faction in the Pasdaran itself feared him and needed his removal to further some internal intrigue. Or perhaps he'd fallen out with the holy city of Qom, and the mullahs had issued a secret fatwa ordering his destruction.

Tehran was not overly fond of its erstwhile Iraqi allies. There was a suspicion that the Azif militiamen were the source of their troubles. Hassani Akkad had been a great thief. If militia leader Waleed Tewfiq suspected that Akkad was cheating him, he might have moved against the gang boss and his Iranian allies. Had Tehran been certain, it would have struck against Waleed. But there was no way to be sure. Whatever hand had pressed the button on Colonel Munghal to make him go away, that hand was hidden. Best not to take strong action until the culprit was known.

Besides, Munghal had headed the Iraqi brain-drain pipeline. That could well be cause for war, if properly exploited. If the Americans could prove an Iranian kidnap plot to hasten the development of atomic weapons, they would take it before the rest of the world and rub their faces in it. The bellicose Westerners might well platform it into an armed military onslaught. It wouldn't be the first time. Tehran's policy was that this scenario was to be avoided at the present time if at all possible.

That kept Tehran from making a fuss about the destruction of the colonel and his column. It didn't want to call attention to the event. It didn't want it known that Munghal was in the area at the time, or even officially confirm his death, for that matter. Too many questions would be raised.

The Pasdaran seethed, aching to lash out but handcuffed by uncertainty and the need for secrecy. Tempers were not improved by the fact that the electron coupler project had come to a crashing halt.

In Iraq, certain interested parties were no less soured. Imam Hamdi had previously reviled and loathed the Shiite Iranians due to religious differences, but he'd have been willing to make a deal with the Devil himself to expand the power of his sect— and himself. Now, he had no deal.

Waleed Tewfiq was equally unhappy. The scientists-for-arms pipeline had been a good thing for him. Now it was closed. He was unsure of what exactly had happened on the night of the raid, but he suspected that one faction of the Akkad gang had double-crossed the other, and that both had been virtually wiped out in the mutual slaughter.

He'd have liked to get his hands on a couple of

gang members to put them through the wringer and find out what they knew. But there didn't seem to be any in Azif. Those few who'd escaped the carnage had gone into hiding, among them Jafar Akkad.

As for the Iranians, Waleed was cynical. Only they knew what had really happened on their side of the border. Waleed had known Captain Saq personally. The captain was a snake. Now he was said to be dead. Colonel Munghal was known to Waleed by reputation only. His reptilian nature was such that he made Saq seem like a warm-blooded, friendly fellow. Munghal, too, was reported dead.

Reported by whom? Iranians. Waleed Tewfiq would believe Munghal and Saq were dead only when he personally saw their dead bodies. Until then, he would have his doubts.

He felt the time had come for him to extend his power in Azif and beyond. For some time now, the militiamen had exerted control over the civil government established in the administrative complex of the town. Many officials were secretly pledged to the cause, the mosque, the imam—and him. Those who were not were mostly soft fools to be cowed or cuffed into obedience. Without the Coalition forces to protect them, they were nothing. It was time that he forced an official understanding and acknowledgment that the mosque was the supreme religious and secular authority in Azif, that the civic government existed solely on the Red Dome's sufferance.

This would be accomplished in two ways: the open and the hidden. The open would be a series of marches and protests staged against the administrative complex. Thousands of believers would surround the government buildings, paralyzing their workings. The business of Azif would be at a standstill.

The hidden way was where the real work was done. The Americans could not protect the hundreds of Iraqi men and women employed in some capacity by the Coalition. When darkness fell, the Americans retreated to their fortified Greentown compound and their military bases. Their hirelings remained in Azif, where their homes and families were. These innocent masses were the ultimate soft targets. Kill enough, and the rest would all bow down.

Waleed Tewfiq began gathering the militiamen for a mass meeting.

# Thirteen

It was the night after the raid, the night of the big mass meeting at the Red Dome Mosque. The tumult in Azif seemed far away from a junkyard on the flat between the town itself and the Graveyard of Martyrs to the south.

The sandstorm was long gone, and the night sky was clear. Not many lights were now burning in Azif. The hour was late, and even most of the militia patrols and other nightriders were already straggling home to their beds.

The junkyard was a tract of land heaped with the twisted metal carcasses of vehicles that had been burned or bombed out or both on the streets and highways of Azif. They'd been towed out here by a civilian contracting company based in Greentown. That had been early on. Safety considerations soon made it impractical to devote time and energy to clearing the Azif cityscape of wrecks, especially since insurgents sniped at and bombed the tow trucks and wreckers sent out to secure the hulks, thus making more wrecks. But in the time they'd been operating, they'd managed to create quite a junkyard on the flat.

A handful of outcasts, pariahs, and crazies lived in the warrens of the yard. They were a mangy crew, all men, living scarecrows wrapped in rags. They were filthy, unshaven, covered with caked layers of grime. They had brown broomstick limbs; some faces showed open sores, broken teeth, an empty eye socket. Slumped at the bases of towers of charred wrecks, they looked like a clutch of living mummies.

They didn't need a fire because it was a warm night. Had the night been colder, they might or might not have lit a fire. They didn't like to call attention to themselves. The human scarecrows occasionally stirred, creeping along, not showing themselves much.

But they moved fast when they heard something coming from the Graveyard of Martyrs. Silence routinely reigned in that quarter. Nothing happened there. The graveyard was thick with unexploded artillery shells. Beyond lay marshy wasteland.

Noises sounded from the direction of the graveyard mound. Vehicle noises. They came up from south of the graveyard, circling around it to the east. The scarecrow folk flitted to their hiding places. They skulked around in the junkyard maze, peeking through cracks and crevices and around corners.

The vehicle rounded the curve of the graveyard knoll, emerging into view on the flat. It was an armored scout car, the one stolen from the Iranians by Kilroy and Vang Bulo. It bulled ahead, lurching into the open and rolling north past the junkyard and onward toward town.

It looked like it meant business.

* * *

Azif was restless. The slums of Old Town teemed with life, ceaseless, pulsating, agitating. The epicenter of the activity was the Red Dome Mosque. Here were comings and goings at all hours of the night.

The police were afraid to go to Old Town after dark (nor were they keen to do so during daylight hours). The only police or Iraqi National Guard soldiers who ventured into the district at night were those allied to Imam Hamdi or Waleed Tewfiq's militia, or both. That encompassed a number of individuals, since the sect had managed to place its adherents throughout the official government infrastructure.

Adding to the danger were local street gangs and other entrepreneurs who set up checkpoints at various squares and junctions to extort and rob passersby who couldn't keep them from doing it. The Red Dome followers were immune to their importunities, since the small fish inevitably scattered to their holes when these big fish ventured out among them.

A big fish that was most emphatically not of the militia stirred abroad in the streets of Old Town this night. An armored scout car.

After the incident of the farmhouse raid, Kilroy and Vang Bulo went to the secret underground bunker built into the side of a hill. They stayed there through the day into the following night. Then they moved out in the scout car. A round-about route through lonely places avoided observation and brought them up out of the marshlands to the graveyard and Azif beyond.

Old Town was an intricate maze of narrow streets

and alleys, with many abrupt sharp turns. The local unemployed young toughs who congregated around Tanners Square had gone into business for themselves. In this time and place, business meant forming a street gang, neighborhood defense unit, or militia. What it was, was young males in packs with guns. Everybody in the district had guns, but the gangs had organization.

The Tanners Square gang existed because it was easier for the militia to let the local gangs squeeze the crazy quilt of streets and squares that made up their turf, and then squeeze them, than it was to devote the resources to directly controlling the numberless petty fiefdoms that comprised the district.

In a country where no self-respecting household was without a Kalash or two, the Tanners Square gang, like others of its ilk, was equipped with standard equipment, mostly assault rifles with some handguns, a few grenades, and some swords, knives and axes.

The street gangs mostly copped their style from Jihadi rap groups they'd seen beamed in on satellite TV or on smuggled or bootlegged CDs and DVDs sold in bins in local market stalls. Military, gangster, and radical terrorist–style elements all made themselves felt in the mix.

The Tanners Square gang numbered several dozen members in all, all from the neighborhood tenement block. The late hour had thinned out their numbers, with only a dozen or so armed members manning the roadblock that they maintained to control access into and out of the square.

The roadblock was a half-assed barricade of a few burned-out car skeletons, some empty fifty-gallon drums, piles of concrete blocks, and bales of rusted wire fencing. The barricade was of necessity impromptu. It had to be able to be removed quickly, in case any mobile militia units should happen to be passing through.

The big guns wouldn't take kindly to having their progress interfered with by the small fry. Should the street gang present a bar to the militia, even unintentionally, they would have to be punished.

The militia militants tolerated such gangs as long as they cooperated, since they formed a kind of internal checkpoint and monitoring system. Anyone moving around in the district was likely to cross paths with several such checkpoints. The street gangs kept the militants apprised of who was moving among the streets by day and night, and for what reasons.

When the gangs stopped strangers who had no pull with the militants or other power brokers, they would usually beat and rob them. That was one of perks of the system.

Once, long ago, there had actually been several tanneries on the street. In Muslim folkways, tanneries are unclean, a taint that affects those who work in them. Tanners are held in low esteem by the majority in much the same way that the untouchables of the Hindu caste system are regarded by those who consider themselves their superiors.

The tanneries had gone out of business and existence several decades earlier, but the taint seemed to hang over the square. Its neighbors viewed it as an undesirable location and were similarly disdainful of its occupants.

There was a restlessness in the air. The mass

meeting at the mosque had stirred up tension. Old Town was working itself up to the boiling point. It hadn't reached it yet, but soon would, within another day or two. No more.

The Tanners Square street gang didn't bother to set out scouts, not tonight or any other. They weren't that organized. They were a band of mostly cocky local punks with too much firepower. But then, there's firepower and there's firepower.

The scout car came out of the night, closing on the square.


The barricade was lit by some flickering kerosene lanterns stolen from a long-shuttered construction site. They burned with a grimy yellow light, highlighting the dinginess of the surroundings. Most of the street gang members present were huddled in dugouts, sleeping. The one or two sentries posted were napping in place.

The first thing the street gang knew of the scout car was its engine noise. They awoke, rousing quickly. The sound of an approaching vehicle could mean opportunity—even loot, plunder. They grabbed their guns and hurried to the barricade.

The engine noise was loud, industrial strength. It blatted along the dark corridor of the street opening on the square.

The intruder could be seen now, a dim hulking shape rolling jauntily up the street. Ambling. There was something insolent about its easy, unhesitating advance. Something sure to irk the haughty pride of a gang of arrogant young toughs used to cowing their less well-armed neighbors.

Angry shouts sounded among the masters of the square. Eyes narrowed. Rifle bolts were thrown back, safeties disengaged. A dozen-plus street gang rowdies lined the inner side of the barricade, facing the oncoming vehicle. They were itching for trouble. That's when they thought it was a civilian car or truck.

When they saw it was a military vehicle, their belligerency melted away. So did they. They vacated the barricade, peeling off to the left and right, diving for cover.

The scout car came on, not slowing, but not hurrying either, steadily advancing. It speared the barrier at midpoint, bulling through it. The barricade came undone.

The scout car continued onward, wheels milling up clouds of dirt and debris. and dust. It crossed the square and entered a street on the far side of it. The passage led deeper into Old Town, toward the Red Dome Mosque.

# Fourteen

The Red Dome Mosque lay in the heart of Old Town, in a square from which streets and alleys radiated in a starburst pattern. The building fronted east. It was a large structure, with grounds to match. The square was a vast open space, an oasis of light and air in the midst of an extensive and crowded slum district.

Many of the blocks of buildings were hundreds of years old—and looked it. The illusion of having traveled back in time to the days of the Ottoman Empire was spoiled by the clusters of television satellite dish receivers on the antique rooftops. Sandwiched within the ancient cityscape were blocks of apartment and tenement housing that had been built during Saddam Hussein's reign. Saddam had been big on construction schemes.

The new blocks had the same physical plant as most mass housing built in urban-renewal projects in the second half of the twentieth century. They featured lots of steel, glass, stone, and poured concrete—especially lots of poured concrete. Some of Saddam's

kinsmen and fellow tribalists were heavily represented
in the poured-concrete business. Azif was a dusty,
gritty location. Buildings that had been built there
within the last three decades looked as old and weath-
ered as the ones that had been standing there for cen-
turies.

Most of the mosque's surrounding neighborhoods
were antique, squalid near-ruins. Builders were discouraged from raising new buildings in the district.
Residents and imams alike feared that if the slums
were torn down as a prelude to urban renewal, the
new buildings would never be built, or if built,
would be parceled out to newcomers more loyal to
the national regime than to the mosque's power brokers, thus taking the first, fatal steps toward lessen-
ing the imams' powers by disassembling the hordes
of seething poor people who made up its base.

The mosque's broad, flat liver-colored brick dome
was topped by a black iron cupola, a hexagonal
structure that was topped in turn by a peaked roof
and bordered at the base by a square iron platform.
Tonight wind buffeted it, rattling the cupola and
making the rigging that wired it in place sing.

The building had three slim minaret towers, positioned at the northwest, northeast, and southeast
corners. There was no southwest tower; it had toppled in 1847 and had never been rebuilt. The northeast tower was weak and decrepit, unsafe and likely
to collapse. It was sealed off, and no one had entered
it to climb its winding stone staircase for years, if not
decades.

The muezzin made the five-times-daily call to
prayer from the top of the southeast minaret.
Clumps of horn-shaped speakers were attached

to the underside of the circular black-iron observation platform ringing the tower room. They ensured that the call was heard throughout the district, as well as throughout much of the rest of the city.

The square wasn't as open and airy as it used to be. Not lately. A good part of it was taken up by the parked cars and trucks of militiamen. The vehicles did double duty by serving as an outer barrier against car and truck bombers.

The square was usually the scene of a fair amount of activity until late into the night. Squads of militiamen came and went during the hours of darkness, going out on errands of violence, intimidation, and destruction in Azif and outlying areas and returning. The imam's followers did some of their best work at night.

The militants were mostly town dwellers, products of the slums and outlying districts. They were Sunnis and Saddam Hussein loyalists. Former loyalists. Even the most fanatical Saddamites realized the chances of their leader making a comeback were virtually nil. This realization had caused many former members of the dictator's Ba'ath party to declare their new allegiance to Imam Hamdi's fiery brand of Islamic fundamentalism.

The mosque was the spiritual center of the insurgency in Azif, but Imam Hamdi was too canny to overplay his hand. Coalition forces were leery of moving against religious personalities. Mosques were the third rail of Iraqi society, not to be touched by the infidel on pain of receiving a potentially lethal shock.

Should things get too out of hand, the Americans

would get their Iraqi government partners to pressure radical mosques and even search them should need be, but the Iraqis themselves were skittish about tangling with the powerful clerics.

The Red Dome Mosque had been built during the age of armed sieges, its thick stone walls designed to resist the artillery of several hundred years ago. Many times in its history, it had served as an arsenal and military strongpoint.

Coalition investigators had charged that it was being used for that purpose again, as a storehouse to maintain a ready supply of guns, ammo, and bombs for the militiamen. A spokesman for Imam Hamdi had recently condescended to issue a statement to the Arab news media indignantly denying the charge that the mosque had been turned into a fort by militia militants.

"This is a false, base, lying canard," he had said, "not only against a pious religious teacher, our revered Imam Hamdi, but also as a vicious slur on all Believers. The slander serves a more sinister purpose, providing a pretext for the occupiers to invade, overthrow, and defile the holy sanctuary of the mosque." The Coalition suspected otherwise, but so far had lacked the will to force an investigation or search, or even to send the imam a stiff note of protest.

Imam Hamdi maintained a cadre of anywhere from seventy-five to a hundred hardcore militiamen as a permanent party established on the mosque grounds. This group served him as an effective combination of bodyguards and palace guards. He had no fear of Coalition troops coming for him. A word from him would fetch hundreds of armed supporters and thousands of men, women, and children from the district rallying to defend the mosque, and quickly.

The northwest minaret's tower room held a heavily armed guardhouse. It had served as the launching platform for the rockets that had been fired at the U.S. helicopter gunship several days earlier. Militia leader Waleed Tewfiq liked to lob a rocket into one or another quarter of the city every so often, just to remind everyone that he was there.

The southeast minaret, used for the muezzin's call to prayer, also doubled as a weapons platform.

It was late now, midway between midnight and dawn. Inside the building, several score of militiamen slept on blankets and bedrolls on the mosque's stone floor under the central dome. Their weapons were stacked beside them. They were veteran fighters, and the first alarm would rouse them into action.

Lights were low beneath the dome. The interior space was dark and gloomy even in broad daylight. There was some small amount of electric lighting, not much, used mostly to indicate doors or corridor entrances or stairwells.

Most of the militiamen inside were sleeping, but not all. Some insomniacs and restless types lay awake on their bunks, staring into space or reading prayerbooks or talking to each other in low, hushed tones. Voices tended to sound muted in the booming cavernous space of the mosque.

Not Imam Hamdi's, though. The leather-lunged

cleric knew how to use the space's echo chamber to great effect when he was preaching a sermon.

But for now it was mostly quiet, though never still. There was the slow deep breathing of ranked rows of massed sleepers. Occasionally someone would groan or cry out in his sleep. There were motion sounds, the sound of the mosque itself settling on its foundation, its looming structure shot through with phantom groanings and creakings.

Sentries were posted in the northwest and southeast tower rooms. Spotlights and searchlights, their lens disks diamond hard and bright, shone from the two towers. A couple of banks of floodlights clung to the upper corners of the mosque's eastern face, shining down and lighting up the front of the structure and the broad, shallow stone stairs descending from it to the stones of the square. Other, lesser lights were placed along the perimeter of the square.

The south side of the square was perhaps less well lit than other areas. The street opening out from it ran between the backs of two separate blocks of buildings. It was narrow, ill kept, and little used, being generally deserted. In this district, the wise traveler kept to the broad, well-lighted avenues and shunned the dark places, the haunts of derelicts and thieves.

Guards were posted along the perimeter. One of the guards during the midnight-to-dawn shift was one Bashir, whose head was shaped like a keg of nails and whose torso was barrel shaped. He was making the rounds with a squad of a half-dozen men when he froze, tilting his head toward the square's south border. There was something canine about the gesture, like a dog cocking an ear to pin down a vagrant sound. He motioned to the others. "Quiet! I hear something."

The rest of the squad fell silent. They and he stood motionless for a moment, listening. One, impatient, began, "I don't hear anything—"

"Shh!" said Bashir.

Abruptly he stalked off, one hand gripping the top of the sling that held a rifle strapped across his shoulder. He strode heavy footed to the south end of the square, the others following. He halted at the square's edge, facing the mouth of the dim, shadowy street.

Frowning, he leaned forward, peering down the street. Machine noises emanated from the darkness somewhere deeper into it. Suddenly, a shape moved into view, rolling towards him.

It was the scout car. The armored vehicle had followed a twisty path through the mazelike alleys and byways of the south side with its weedy lots, concrete block buildings, and whitewashed stone walls. Now it came on toward mosque square.

The militia had no armored scout cars. Of that, Bashir was sure. The vehicle now approaching could only belong to someone else: an enemy. It surely intended hostile action, coming as it did stealthily and with its lights dark.

Its origin was puzzling, though. Bashir knew all the vehicles of the Coalition and the Iraqi interim government, and this was none that he recognized. He wondered what devil's spawn had sent it.

Not letting his questions interfere with direct action, Bashir unslung his weapon and opened fire. He had only to point his rifle and shoot without aiming to hit the machine. That's how close it already was. Slugs spanged off the machine's armored front. The rest of the squad opened fire at it, too. Gunfire roused the mosque's defenders, sounding the alert.

Vang Bulo drove the scout car, and Kilroy manned the turret guns. Kilroy pointed a heavy machine gun at Bashir and his squad and squeezed off several bursts, pulping them.

The guards in the southeast tower room were quick to react. They spilled out onto the observation platform, crowding the curved waist-high guardrail. They aimed their weapons down at the scout car and opened fire.

It was a tough shoot, an extreme downward angle. None of them had the range yet. Their bullets streamed overhead, passing harmlessly above the vehicle and tearing up the pavement around it. Not too close around it, either.

Kilroy wasn't waiting for them to wrestle any rocket launchers into position and get the scout car in their sights. He wrestled the heavy machine gun around, uptilting and elevating it to get a bead on the tower room. It was a sharp angle, and he had to hunch down into the armored turret well to properly sight the machine gun on the target.

The long, lofty spire with its round tower room reminded him of a lighthouse. The tower room was alive with lights and figures in blurred, frantic motion. Kilroy pointed the machine gun at the top of the tower and fired. The weapon produced an impressive industrial clamor, like a factory milling or stamping machine. It milled out streams of high-velocity slugs, hammering the tower like a pavement breaker. Kilroy stitched a line up the side of the spire until he reached the observation platform and tower room. He battened on them, pouring lead up into them like a fireman working a high-pressure water hose on a burning building. But he was there not to put out fires, but to start them.

Rounds sieved the black iron platform and those standing on top of it. Metal framework tore like paper, coming apart in scalloped ruffles, spilling screaming men off it to hurl them to the hard pavement a hundred feet below. They hit with a splat that was as much felt as heard, a nasty sound.

Kilroy poured another stream of lead at the tower room. Curved glass viewport panels disintegrated. He streamed the slugs into the round room. Lights flashed, crashed, sparked and went out. The tower room went dark.

At the northwest tower, the guards were desperate to get into action. They could see the guard post being shot out of the tower opposite them, but there was nothing they could do about it. The bulk of the dome and mosque screened them from seeing the attackers on the south side of the square. What they could not see, they could not shoot. The southeast tower guard now extinguished, the scout car once more resumed motion.

Vang Bulo didn't try to break through the barrier into the square. He made a right turn, heading east along the south side of the square until he came to the end, then turning left and rolling up to the north side.

The vehicle came abreast of the mosque's front entrance and halted. Some guards charged the scout car, shooting as they came. Kilroy pointed the machine gun at them and fired, turning them into bursting blood bags.

The mosque was a hornet's nest. The palace guard was up and rushing to battle stations. Streams of militiamen scrambled across the stones of the square, making for the scout car. Many shot as they ran. That doesn't make for much accuracy, so most of their bullets flew wild of the target, peppering the row of buildings across the street. Hits bounced harmlessly off armor plate.

The mosque's grand entrance was a pointed arch twenty feet high, inset with a pair of double doors. The doors were made of thick, iron-banded wooden timbers, blackened with age.

Now, they were opened from the inside, swinging open and out as they were flung back on their hinges. Through the high, vaulting doorway poured a mob of angry, well-armed militiamen, streaming down the stone front stairs.

Kilroy pointed the machine gun at them and opened up, mowing them down. They fell in rows. He swung the machine gun barrel from left to right and back again, raking lead across the ranks. The machine gun stuttered, firing not continuously but in bursts. Falling bodies tumbled down the stairs, sprawling on the stones of the square.

The advance checked, hung fire for a few beats, then broke. Some militiamen peeled off to the sides, seeking cover. Those already on the sides, outside the kill zone, stayed out of it. They flattened, took cover, or retreated.

Militiamen stopped pouring out of the front entrance into the meat grinder of the machine gun.

Light from the front-mounted floodlights fell on them. One man wore a yellow turban. It was unmistakable. Kilroy could make it out clear from the opposite end of the square. In this bunch, one man held the exclusive franchise on wearing a yellow turban, and that was Waleed Tewfiq. It was more than a signature trademark, it was a kind of badge of office, signifying his exalted status as militia leader.

That was one head Kilroy wanted for his trophy room. He worked to bring the machine gun to bear on Waleed Tewfiq, but he was too late. Waleed had already ducked back inside the mosque, sheltering behind the foot-thick stone wall beside the archway.

Others were falling back, too, withdrawing into the mosque. Some of those in the front ranks grabbed the oversized iron rings that served as door handles and began hauling and tugging the doors closed. They shut with a thud.

Kilroy fired into the doors. Rounds chewed at the door panels, churning up a spray of splinters and wood chips and a cloud of sawdust. The doors were full of holes but held.

Kilroy's focus had been on the front of the mosque. Those on its flanks had not been idle. They'd taken advantage of their respite from being targets to move up in groups of twos of threes, stealthily advancing on the scout car.

Kilroy switched from the machine gun to the minicannon. He worked the controls, adjusting them to bring the big gun into line with the front doors. They were in his sights.

He fired, the cannon bucking, spewing out a shrieking shell that streaked across the square to the double doors. The shell detonated in a massive explosion that obliterated the doors and much of the surrounding stonework of the doorway and façade.

Groans and cries of outrage and dismay sounded from some of the militiamen in the square. Smoke poured out of the archway. Kilroy fired again. The shell zoomed into the mosque and exploded. It triggered an even more massive response, a series of booming blasts that followed one after the other.

All remaining doors and windows in the structure were instantly blown out. The interior of the building filled with cascading fireballs. Monster tentacles of flame thrust out of empty window and door frames, unfurling across the square.

A pillar of fire leaped up to pierce the vent in the center of the dome. It blew the iron cupola skyward, up and up, like a cork tossed by a fountain. Blew it sky high.

A fireball vomited out of the front archway, trailing mountains of oily black smoke. The heat was awesome. Heat waves distorted the air, so that it rippled like running water.

Kilroy could feel the heat sucking all the moisture out of him. The cold sweat beaded on his flesh dried up in a breath. He felt as parched as a lizard on a rock in Death Valley at high noon. For an instant, he feared that the fireball would reach all the way across the square to engulf the scout car. It did not, its horizontal motion arrested as its leading edge curled in on itself and up, blossoming into a pillar of fire that enveloped the mosque.

That was the main blast. There were lots of little blasts, too, as a storehouse of explosives went off— grenades, mines, rockets, and crates of bullets.

By now the structure had become partially disassembled. Blasts were taking it apart from the inside. Rockets arched skyward in a spectacular fireworks display that lit up the night sky over Azif.

Kilroy said, "I guess they were using it as an ammo dump after all."

Something fell out of the sky, landing in the street in front of the scout car. A yellow turban.

The scout car started forward, rolling over the turban as it made its way toward the northeast corner of the square, where it entered a street and drove away. The sky was red over Old Town.

The next day, a wrecked scout car was found on the outskirts of town. It appeared to have struck a land mine, blown up, and burned. No other mines were found in the area where the wreck lay.

Inside the wreck were two bodies, so badly burned and charred that they were just barely recognizable as human.

The scout car had been badly burned, too, but certain portions had escaped the damage, most notably those that featured flag stencils, serial numbers, and other nomenclature testifying to the machine's Iranian origins.

# Fifteen

Two days passed. Azif was in a state of unrest. The mosque itself was a still-smoldering ruin. The dome that had given the mosque its name had completely collapsed. Many had died in its fall, not the least being Waleed Tewfiq, leader of the Red Dome militiamen.

Imam Hamdi had escaped destruction, however. He'd managed to get out by a side exit before the building had come down. His loyalists were already hailing it as a miracle. He had not escaped unharmed, having several broken bones. Also, most of the hair on his body, including his eyebrows and beard, had been singed off by a blast wave. He had gone into seclusion for an indefinite period of time. He gave no reason for the withdrawal, though popular opinion held that he wanted to give thanks for his miraculous escape with an extended session of prayer and meditation. The real reason was that he refused to show himself in public until his beard had grown back, to avoid making himself a figure of fun.

Old Town was wracked with grief and near-hysterical outbursts of mourning. Thousands attended a mass funeral for several score militiamen. Streets were thronged with a sea of black-clad mourners.

The funeral procession triggered a near riot, causing scores to be trampled underfoot. Seeing the results, Imam Hamdi was thoroughly glad that he'd avoided having to preside over the funerary rites.

Azif opinion ran hot and high against the local Shiite minority. The Coalition posted a large force of combat troops to guard the Shiite neighborhood.


On the morning of the third day after the raid on the mosque massacre—what U.S. tabloids were calling the "Mosque-acre"—ODA 586 left Border Base Foxtrot on a joint CIA/Special Forces mission.

With them were Albin Prester and Debbie Lynn Hawley. Prester had been their CIA liasion for the farmhouse operation. Debbie Lynn Hawley was introduced to the unit as the Weapons of Mass Destruction expert that she was. Prester never identified her as CIA. The Special Forces members could think what they liked. All they needed to know was that her expertise was vital to one component of their mission.

Intelligence sources had received a tip that the radical fundamentalists in the Shiite town of Quusaah were planning to send arms and fighters to assist their coreligionists in Azif's minority Shiite community.

It was said that the Shiite militias had established

their own pipeline, one that funneled men and material back and forth between Azif and Quusaah, and from Quusaah into Iran.

Radioactive material, looted from Iraqi hospitals during the war, was alleged to have recently been shipped east along the Shiite corridor into Iran. Such material was prime stock to make a dirty bomb, one that would use conventional explosives to scatter a cloud of toxic radium dust, any particle of which could be potentially lethal.

Prester and the Special Forces unit would investigate a site identified as a way station on the Shiite corridor, while Debbie Lynn Hawley would scan it for any traces of radioactive contaminants. It was typical of the unorthodox assignments that the pairing of Army trigger-pullers and CIA spies had resulted in.

The men of ODA 586 did not object. The spy gal was easy on the eyes. Debbie Lynn had that girl-next-door quality, except that she was here. All the other girls next door had stayed back home.

The group left Border Base Foxtrot in predawn darkness to get the jump on early-bird snipers and car bombers working the region. All of ODA 586 was present but Ernie Greco, The Greek, as he was known, was still recovering from the wound he'd received during the farmhouse venture. He said he was ready for action, but the medics wanted him to take it easy for a couple of days yet.

The unit traveled in a three-Humvee convoy that went to an abandoned pumping station northeast of Azif. The site was on a flat-topped hill north of a watercourse that ran roughly from east to west, a tributary to the Tigris.

There had once been a canal here when the river had been high and wide enough to serve as a highway for boats and barges. The pumping station had supplied water to irrigate a farm belt running between Quusaah and Azif. During the war with Iran, Saddam Hussein had diverted the river at its head, channeling it into another watercourse to serve his grand strategic design.

The war was long over, Saddam was defunct, but the river was no more. With no river, the pumphouse could not function and so was abandoned. The farms it had supplied dried up and blew away for lack of water with which to irrigate their crops. The whole area had an abandoned, dismal air to it.

The channel was enough of a natural watercourse to support a modest stream that ran through it year-round. The oncoming rainy season had quickened it, but it still was a long way from even rivulet status.

The north bank of the channel was ten to twelve feet high, its edge abruptly sheered off like a cliff. The channel bed below was covered with extensive mud flats, along whose center ran a lazy thread of stream water.

The pumping station was a big, warehouse-sized concrete building. Its long axis ran east-west, parallel to the edge of the north bank where it was sited.

On the inland side of the building, the ground sloped easily into a wide, saucer-shaped hollow ringed by low, broken ridges and lines of trees. The three Humvees were ranged in the hollow along the base of the hill.

It was early in the morning, so early that the hollow was a bowl of shade as yet untouched by the sun's direct rays. The day was already warm, though. Debbie Lynn wore a flat-crowned straw planter's hat with a flowered hatband to protect against the sun. It looked cute and sassy, as did she. Prester wore an olive drab duckbilled baseball cap. On him, not so cute.

They stayed with the vehicles while the Special Forces team went uphill and cleared the site. The unit had already cleared the hollow and the area around it, making sure that no ambushers lurked. All seemed quiet and unthreatening.

Lookouts were posted on the hilltop to keep watch on the surrounding countryside. The landscape was empty of all other traffic or signs of human life. The troubles in Azif and on the border had suppressed routine transportation movement in the region. Few dared to venture out on the roads for fear of becoming a target.

Next, the site had to be cleared in a somewhat different way. Radiologically.

Debbie Lynn Hawley was outfitted with something that looked like a camera case. It hung by a shoulder strap around her neck. She opened the lid and took out an object about the size and shape of a brick. It was a piece of sophisticated hardware whose upper face was covered with gauges and dials. Buttons and switches for manipulating it lay inset on the long, narrow sides.

She explained, "This is a rad detector. It's like an old-fashioned Geiger counter, only a thousand times more sensitive, and it doesn't rely on clicking noises to alert the operator to the presence of radioactive material. The data feed shows on the readout gauges. It'll sing out if I get a positive reading."

She climbed the hill to the pumping station. She was light on her feet, alert. Steve Ireland watched her go. So did every other male in the outfit. Steve thought she was cute as a button. Sexy in a sweet, wholesome way.

The pumping station building was a shell, with not a door left standing or a pane of glass left intact. The walls were high, like those of an airplane hangar. Several skylights pierced the roof, letting in light.

The structure was one huge, unbroken space. It had not been partitioned into rooms and halls. The floor was dotted with tanks and pools that had once been integral to the operation of the pumphouse. There were drum-shaped tanks, and tanks that looked like giant hot-water heaters, all wrapped in a web of sampling pipes and conduits worming through rusted metal scaffolding. The tanks were empty now, except for where several inches of rainwater and runoff had collected in the bottom of the containers.

Debbie Lynn walked the site, prowling both the inside and the outside. Wherever she went, her rad detector went with her. Steve Ireland was pleased to note that it remained blissfully silent. McBane asked, "Find anything?"

"No, it all comes up clean," Debbie Lynn said.

"Too bad you had to come all the way out here for nothing."

She shrugged prettily. "That's all right. There's no such thing as wasted effort in a search like this. Even a negative read is useful. It tells us that no radioactive waste has passed this way.

"Some radioactive material went missing during the early days of the war. We're not talking about any of Saddam's atomic projects, although we can't rule that out, either. I'm talking about radioactive material used in hospitals and labs and industry. It could be used to make dirty bombs. It wouldn't explode in a nuclear reaction, but a conventional explosive could send radioactive dust in the air and contaminate a large part of a city and make in uninhabitable.

"So, it's a relief to be able to find another site clear. If there were traces of radioactivity, we'd really have something to worry about."

Debbie Lynn's part of the mission was over. ODA 586's was just beginning. The unit would occupy the pumphouse and its surroundings, laying in wait for any Shiite insurgents who might want to use it as a way station en route to Azif. The tip was that insurgents would pass this way tonight.

McBane didn't want the woman present in case there should be a firefight later with hostile elements. He didn't want Prester around, either. Soldiers were soldiers and spies were spies, and it could be dangerous to both to let the rules blur. Prester could take care of himself, McBane knew. And he suspected that Debbie Lynn Hawley could, too. The agency didn't field incapables in this hot zone. But they weren't Special Forces. McBane knew by experience that he could trust his life to any of the members of his unit. The spies were an unknown quantity. But Prester was in. It was his operation, his informants who'd furnished the tip.

Earlier, back at the base, he'd told McBane, "Azif is boiling. We've learned that a Shiite terror cell plans to use the canal to infiltrate into Azif and help out the Shia there. They're supposed to be coming through tonight after dark. They might send out scouts earlier on, so we want to be fully established before they arrive."

McBane told himself that at least he wouldn't have to worry about the woman for too much longer. Now that her job here was done, she could return to base. Presently, he'd send a couple of men in one of the Humvees to drive her to a spot where she could be airlifted out by helicopter to Foxtrot.

The RZ site was far enough away from here to avoid having any Coalition helicopters overflying the pumphouse zone and so alerting insurgents that they were entering an area of interest.

McBane decided that he'd better send a couple of married men to escort Debbie Lynn. They could protect her and keep an eye on each other.

Later Debbie Lynn Hawley and Prester walked downhill to where the Humvees were parked. Steve Ireland paused to watch her, admiring the way her shapely rear filled out the seat of her khaki pants. He was so distracted that he failed to notice McBane coming up behind him.

McBane thumped his palm against the top of Steve's helmet. "Hey! Wake up, Irish. Make yourself useful, and go keep watch on the south."

Steve circled around to the south side of the pumping station. A cracked concrete apron extended about twenty feet beyond the wall. Knee-high weeds grew in the cracks in the walkway. Where the pavement ended lay another two dozen or so feet of flat ground. Mostly rocks and dirt grew there, along with a scattering of stunted shrubs.

Beyond that, the hilltop just ended, fronting on empty air. Steve went out toward the edge. The earthen bank ended here, just dropping off. It wasn't much of a drop, only about ten feet or so. Still, he kept from going too close to the edge for fear that it would give way under him. He tested the ground with his weight, feeling around with his feet. It felt solid enough, but why take chances? He halted about five feet from the rim.

The sky was gray with a yellow band at the south horizon. Below, after that ten-foot drop, the ground was flat, stretching unbroken to the south as far as the eye could see.

Starting from the north bank's base, a muddy expanse stretched out for a hundred yards or so. The mud was mustard brown. It stank, too, a pungent smell of decaying organic matter and mucky ooze. A stream crept through the center of the mud flats. Broad and shallow, the putty-colored waters unrolled sluggishly through swampy lowlands.

A desolate scene. A wasteland: no single human structure rose to break the monotony of the flat. It was marshland, and nothing would be built on its boggy, oozing soil. Clumps of reeds and cattails grew along the water's edge. There were a lot of birds flying back and forth across the flat.

Steve Ireland looked around for a place to set up a vantage point. He ran the risk of being skylined if he stood too near to the edge. He wanted to keep the pumphouse behind him to minimize his outline.

He glanced back at the station. Through empty

windows and doors and bays in the south wall, he could see inside. Special Forces team members moved purposefully about the site. Shadows fell on those in the building, preventing Steve from making out their faces. The pumphouse and hilltop were thick with troops. It looked like the whole unit was up here.

Two shots sounded, then after a pause, a third. Then a whole bunch of shots, popping away. They sounded distant, but not too distant.

Steve said to himself, *That can't be good.* Somebody on the hill shouted something indistinguishable. A flash showed inside the pumphouse, filling it with light. White-hot light that obliterated all else within.

The pumphouse came undone, fragmenting into a million pieces. The glare expanded, engulfing the entire hilltop in the space of an eyeblink. The hilltop came undone, picking up Steve Ireland and flinging him bodily outward into space.

A few minutes earlier, Debbie Lynn Hawley and Prester had gone to the bottom of the hill, in a place at the rim of the hollow, under some shady trees. The figures moving around on the hilltop were antlike blurs.

Debbie Lynn went around to the far side of one of the Humvees, so that it stood between her and the hill. Prester followed, trotting several paces behind. Debbie Lynn stopped short and turned suddenly, facing him. Smiling. Prester remembered that he'd always thought she had a lovely smile.

She held something in each hand. In the

right, a gun. It was pointing at him. In the left, a device that looked something like a cell phone. Her eyes were clear, her expression serene. There was no malice there, no gloating. Prester would have sworn to that. A great wave of body terror seized him, filling him with mortal fear. He recoiled, shouting, throwing up his hands in front of him. "No! Don't!"

At the same time, he was throwing himself to the side, trying to get behind the rear of the vehicle before she opened fire, knowing it was too late.

She fired twice at him, at point-blank range. Both shots scored, tagging him high in the chest and torso. The impact was wrenching, unmanning. His sideways lunge became a fall. He hit the dirt.

The men on the hill would have heard the shots. Somebody up there shouted something indistinguishable, the cry hanging in midair. Debbie Lynn knew she must act very quickly now. She started to come around the rear of the Humvee to finish off Prester. He lay sprawled on the ground but there was a gun in his hand, a flat, thin silvery palm-sized automatic. It looked like a toy, like a trick cigarette lighter disguised to look like a gun.

He snapped a shot at her from close to the ground and hit her in the leg. She fell down, crying out. She wriggled along on the ground, trying to get away from him, out of the line of fire. He was shooting again, but the Humvee's left rear tire stood between her and the bullets, and it caught them instead of her.

She reached under the car without looking and

fired some shots where she thought he must be. She heard bullets thudding into his flesh. He grunted, then groaned. The exchange had all taken place in a few seconds. All the while, she'd kept hold of the object that looked like a cell phone in her left hand. It was a remote-controlled detonator. She now pressed the red button, triggering the firing mechanism.

An imperceptible pause, and then the hilltop blew its top. Literally. It erupted like a volcano, a ferocious blast that obliterated the pumphouse and geysered tons of debris and dirt skyward.

Debbie Lynn could feel the shockwaves battering her. The sky darkened. Then came the rain of dirt and debris, a hailstorm of rocks pounding the earth, followed by dust and smoke clouds.

Debbie Lynn lay prone, hugging the ground. She would have crawled under one of the Humvees for cover, but she didn't know where they were. She was disoriented. She curled on her side in a fetal position, using her arms to protect her head from falling rocks.

Stones pelted, then pounded the earth. Some of them were as big as cannon balls. The chaos tapered off, subsiding. Debbie Lynn took stock. She still had her gun. She'd been shot in the right leg, below the knee. She didn't know how badly she was hit. The leg felt numb. She knew better than to risk putting weight on it at this time.

Prester—was he dead or alive? Alive, he was a threat. He could hurt her. Hurt her worse than he already had.

She knew that her shots had scored. But that was small comfort. He wore a flak jacket, as did she.

But her gun was filled with armor-piercing teflon bullets, able to pierce such protective vests.

She crawled around the rear of the vehicle, into the open. Clouds of brown dust and gray-black smoke wafted past her, obscuring the scene. A rent in the smoke allowed her to glimpse the hilltop. It was a smoldering mass, with crooked fingers of masonry marking where the pumphouse had stood. The structure was destroyed, a smoking crater, with spidery strands of fused metal beams and pipes wriggling from the top. Nothing lived, could have have lived, on that hill. Not a team member in sight. All had been obliterated.

Gone. So was Prester. Not gone dead but just plain gone, vanished. He was nowhere around the Humvees. There were blood drops on the ground, but when she tried to see where they led, a cloud of chemical-laced smoke rolled over her, making her eyes burn and tear so that she could hardly see anything at all.

Debbie Lynn tried to stand. Agony went through her, her wounded leg buckled, and she fell down. She had enough left to not fall down on the wounded leg, but that was about it for a while. If Prester had come upon her then, he'd have had her.

When the worst of the pain had passed, she eyed the wound. A bullet had penetrated her calf muscle. It looked like it had pierced the flesh and come out the other side. An ugly wound, one that had torn flesh and muscle and drawn blood. But it had missed the bones and key blood vessels, and was by no means mortal.

It bled, weakening her. She crawled to the far

side of the vehicle and sat with her back propped up against the rear tire and began tearing and cutting strips of cloth from her blouse to bind up the wound. A difficult task, made twice as hard by her unwillingness to let go of her gun. But she managed.

# Sixteen

Steve Ireland looked like hell. He felt worse. He couldn't hear much out of one ear, and the other was afflicted with a constant ringing. He felt like he'd been worked over with a baseball bat. His bones ached. His joints ached. His teeth ached. His eyes ached. He was stunned and numb. He had trouble keeping his eyes in focus. The scene faded in and out.

He shook his head to clear it and it felt like he was blowing his stack, just as the hilltop had done. His clothes were in tatters. Scorched tatters. He'd thought he'd smelled something burning. Now he knew what it was. Him.

At that, he wasn't too bad off. There didn't seem to be any bones broken. His ribs ached. Maybe a couple were cracked.

He'd survived a bomb blast. He knew that much, just from looking at what was left of the hilltop. It smoked like Vesuvius in one of its active phases. Vesuvius Lite, the vestpocket edition. Big enough to have almost done for him.

That must've been one hell of an IED, he told himself. He wondered if any of the others had gotten out alive. He didn't see any. No signs of life on that conetopped hill and its surroundings.

He still had two eyes and the normal complement of limbs that he'd started out with. That was something. Still, there could be internal injuries. He didn't know. His think machine wasn't working too good.

The blast had swatted him off the ledge as casually as a giant hand flicking away a mosquito. By doing so, it had saved his life, hurling him away from the bomb site. He'd been flung far out over the marshland, but the mud and boggy ground had cushioned his fall. He was coated with the stuff: sticky, pastelike mud. It smelled bad. It stank. He hoped it was mud.

He rose, standing on two feet, legs widespread for balance. He hoped he could stay there. He faced the north bank and started for it. The muck underfoot was thick and and claylike, reaching above his boot tops. It didn't want to let him go. He had to fight to take every step. The mud released him with a wet, sucking sound.

He looked around. The birds had quit the marshes. There had been hundreds of them among the tangled brush and thorn thickets. Thousands. But the bomb blast had scared them all off. Above, in the heights, flocks of birds could be seen wheeling around in great, shifting funnels.

Steve Ireland was more than halfway to the north bank when he realized that he didn't have his rifle. That was bad. That was a hell of a thing. His brains must have really gotten scrambled, not to realize a loss like that before now. If he ever needed a rifle, now was the time.

The bomb meant enemy action. Those who'd triggered the blast might come around looking for survivors. He was a nice fat target, standing out her all alone in the mud. He might as well be wearing a sign that said SHOOT ME.

He half turned, looking back. He saw his footprints stamped into the mud in a trail that led back to the place where he'd landed. He saw no sign of his rifle. No doubt the mud had swallowed it up. His communicator was missing, too, probably in the same place.

He'd be a lot better off taking cover than staying out here in the open, looking for a weapon he wasn't going to find. Fear gave him a fresh focus, lending energy and urgency to his steps. Time for him to start using his head. He scanned the wall of the embankment, looking for cover and the easiest way to the top. Maybe he could find a weapon up there.

Maybe he had one on him. Remembering his knife, he reached for it, experiencing a rush of emotion when he found it in its usual place, strapped to the sheath on his side. It was a feeling like when you thought you'd lost your wallet, only to find it safely tucked in your pocket after all. Only better.

Remarkable that the blast hadn't stripped it from him when it had torn away so many other clothes and objects from his person. That was just the breaks; a blast was a fluke thing. Today sure was his day for luck. Surviving the blast and finding the knife. If I get any luckier, I'll kill myself, he said to himself. If somebody else doesn't beat me to it.

He had to fight the urge to unfasten the safety snap, draw out the knife, and fill his hand with it. Caution took over. He was still plenty shaky and he didn't trust himself not to drop the blade and lose it in the mud. No, he'd keep it where it was until he needed it. He hoped he wouldn't need it.

He noticed a cut in the bank to the left of him. It seemed to access the top of the shelf. He changed course in the mud, angling toward it. Nearing it, he saw that the cut had been caused by a partial collapse of the bank, opening up a seam shaped like an upside-down V.

He reached the base of the bank and climbed inside the seam, fingers clawing at hardpacked dirt, scrabbling for a grip, grabbing bunches of exposed pale roots where they seemed strong enough to serve as handholds, and hoisting himself up. Nearing the top, he remembered he was in enemy territory and played it cagey, peeking over the edge to see if the coast was clear before pulling himself up.

What met his eyes was a scene of megadestruction. The pumphouse had been well seeded with explosives. Plastic explosives, most likely, and plenty of them. The building was gone, virtually leveled. It had been blown to bits and the bits scattered to the four winds. A crater marked the place where it had been.

This was no casual blow. This was a death trap. ODA 586 had been lured into it and blown into oblivion. The site was bare of all other life but himself, as far as he could see. The team had been wiped out, and only he remained. It was hard to process, but true all the same.

McBane, Ervil, Niles, Donnicker, Virgil, Creedy, Tillotson, Calhoun, Paulus, Garza—all gone. All that energy, vitality, personality, life experience, all erased in an eyeblink.

It was like losing an arm or a leg. One instant you're whole, the next you're not. They say that amputees can often sense the presence of the absent body part, like it's still part of them. There was an even a name for it: phantom-limb syndrome. Steve Ireland could appreciate the sensation. That's what he felt like. Only not the victim who'd lost a limb, but the limb itself. Does an amputated limb feel anything after it's cut off? He'd been cut off from the others. He felt like a phantom, a living ghost. Eerie, unreal.

Maybe he was getting ahead of himself. He'd survived. Maybe others had, too. He looked around. He didn't see anybody else. Didn't hear anyone, either. No calls, cries, shouts, shots, machine noises, nothing.

The landscape was brown, gray and tan, with gold and bronze accents that were dry weeds and brush. The sky was gray-white except for a band in the southwest quadrant above the horizon. It was clear and a soft, milky sky blue.

He watched and waited for a while. It was good not to move. He needed the rest. He was dog tired. Then he roused himself, pulling himself up to the top of the embankment and standing there in a half crouch. He didn't want to show himself, and hid behind a pile of masonry that was part of a collapsed wall.

A bird flew past. Steve's nerves were so strained that the sound of the its wings beating the air made him jump.

He started forward, skirting the crater where the pumphouse had been, picking his way through the rubble toward the far side of the hilltop. A section of stone wall jutted from the earth at an angle, blocking his way. He detoured around it. He came face to face with Albin Prester.

Prester was about twelve feet away, sitting on the ground with his back propped up against a tilted slab of stone wall the size of a pool table. He had a gun in his hand, and it was pointing at Steve.

"Maybe it's not my day for luck after all," Steve said.

Prester said, "Remains to be seen."

That was the first that Steve realized that he'd spoken the statement aloud and not just thought it.

Prester was hurt. His face was white, bloodless. It was easy to see where much of the blood had gone. His shirt front was soaked with it. Agony carved deep lines into his face. He sat with his right hand, his gun hand, resting on top of his thigh. He had enough left to point it at Steve Ireland. He held it steady, unwavering.

Steve calculated his chances. Prester was too far away for him to rush. He thought of the knife on his hip. A knife wasn't so hot against a gun, unless you were throwing it. His knife was flat bladed and balanced for throwing, but even so, a thrown knife is a gamble. Even if you can hit the target ninety-nine times out of a hundred, there's always that hundredth time when it comes up short. Besides, Prester could put a bullet in him long before Steve could draw and throw the knife.

Prester was badly wounded, perhaps even mortally wounded, but he was nobody's fool. His narrow-eyed gaze didn't didn't miss much. Prester wiggled the gun barrel, motioning Steve forward. "Come here," he rasped, his voice breathy and throaty. Bloody froth bubbled in the corner of his mouth.

Steve obeyed, advancing, his steps clumsy and halting. When he was a body length away, Prester motioned for him to halt. "That's close enough," Prester said.

Steve said, "What happened? Get caught in your own trap?"

"We're all caught in our own traps, but never mind the philosophy. Not now." Prester's words were clipped, as if he was biting them off. He said, "You think I'm responsible for this?" His free hand, the one not holding the gun, indicated the blasted surroundings.

"It wasn't any of my guys that did it," Steve said.

"In that case, I'll have to get rid of you, too, won't I? To make a clean sweep," said Prester.

Steve had nothing to say to that.

Prester eyed him up and down. "Christ, you look like you fell through the outhouse floor. You smell that way, too. What a fragrant bouquet for me to go out on."

He chuckled. The chuckling turned into a cough that threatened to have serious repercussions. Prester's face turned green around the edges, and fresh drops of cold sweat beaded on his forehead. He choked the cough off fast, stifling it before it could tear up whatever he had left that was keeping him going. The fit subsided. Prester looked scornful. "I felt so bad about setting your team up that I shot myself four times. Is that what you think happened? Use your head."

Steve shrugged. "Maybe your little blond accomplice crossed you. Or is she dead, too?"

"Hardly," he said dryly. "Unfortunately," he added, a beat later.

Prester released his grip on the pistol, turning it around and offering it to Steve Ireland butt first. He said, "Here. Take it."

Steve was mentally thrown. Whatever he'd been expecting, this wasn't it.

"Go on, take it," Prester urged. "What're you afraid of? If I wanted to shoot you, I would've done it by now."

Steve took the gun, weighing it in his hand.

Prester said, "Feel better?"

Steve unconsciously nodded. He did feel better. The feeling piqued his suspicions. What if Prester, for whatever devious reasons of his own, had passed him an unloaded gun?

He checked the gun to make sure it was loaded. There was a round was in the chamber and more in the clip.

"It's loaded," Prester said.

Steve said offhandedly, "Just making sure."

"You're not as dumb as you look. There may be hope for you yet."

"Thanks," Steve said. He pointed the gun at Prester.

The other's smile was thin, wintry. "You can't kill me. I'm already dead and just marking time until the Reaper comes. You're the one who needs the gun. You'll need it for Debbie Lynn—my 'little blond accomplice' as you called her."

"Why?"

"She's a killer. If you see her first, shoot. Don't be fooled by that perky, all-American demeanor. Shoot her down like you'd shoot a rattlesnake."

Steve was skeptical. "She set the bomb? I don't believe it."

"She didn't set it, but she set it off. The bomb was planted here by others. But she's the active agent of the conspiracy," Prester said. "She sold out. She's a traitor."

Steve demanded, "Who'd she sell out to?"

Prester shook his head. "Don't talk. Listen. There's a lot to tell, and not much time to tell it in. You're supposed to be dead, with the rest of your unit. But you're not. She couldn't have reckoned on that. It's the unexpected, the X factor. We can make it work for us. There's still a chance that something can be saved out of all this.

"Not me, though. I'm done. The flak jacket slowed her bullets but didn't stop them. It kept them from killing me right off, though. That and you're being alive could mean a second chance."

Steve was frustrated, confused. "Talk sense, mister."

"I'll talk," Prester said. It was a promise. "The things I'm going to tell you are things you need to know. Somebody's got to get the message through."

"What message? To who?"

"Shut up. I don't have the strength or the time to answer a lot of fool questions. But you must know this. You've got to contact Kilroy. Joe Kilroy, from Mercury Transit Systems. Kilroy, or Vang Bulo, his buddy, a big black guy."

Steve said, "I know who they are. I've seen them around."

Prester's closed-lip smile was quirked at the corners. "You only think you know who they are. Remember, Kilroy or Vang Bulo. They're okay. You can trust them. Nobody else. Tell them that Debbie Lynn Hawley is the traitor. They'll know what to do. But you've got to tell them. Nothing is more important than that. It's high priority. Higher than you know. The highest. Think you can handle that, hotshot?"

Steve said, "Yes."

Prester raised himself up on an elbow, leaning forward. "And remember—if you see Debbie Lynn, shoot. Shoot first and shoot to kill, if you value your life."

Steve suddenly started to walk off.

"Wait!" Prester said, throwing out a hand. "Where are you going?"

"You've got me so spooked about Debbie Lynn that I want to make sure she's not sneaking up on us," Steve said.

"Don't take too long. My time is short."

Steve crossed to where a gap opened in freshly churned mounds of earth. The explosion had dug deep and the heaps of black soil had a rich, loamy smell. He hunkered down, peeking through through the gap at the landscape below. He could see down the slope into the hollow at the base of the hill. It was empty of human figures. No Debbie Lynn. No nobody.

Three Humvees were parked off to one side, in the shade. A tempting proposition. Any or all might hold weapons or radios or both. And they offered escape from this gallows hilltop. But they were a fair piece away. Prester could die in the time it took for Steve to go down there and return.

The Humvees could be a kind of trap, too. Someone like, say, Debbie Lynn, could be thinking the same thoughts, waiting for any survivors to show themselves by trying to reach the vehicles. He scanned the brush behind the Humvees at the rim of the hollow, the logical place for an ambusher to lurk. He saw nothing out of the ordinary there, but still . . .

Prester, restless, was stirring. Steve went to him. "No sign of her," he said.

Prester said, "I didn't think there would be. She's tricky."

"She's not here now. Have your say. I'm listening."

Prester focused his pale-eyed gaze on Steve. "Ever heard of the Dog Team?"

Steve said, "I've heard the legend."

"It's no legend, it's true."

Steve nodded, a gesture indicating that Prester should go on with what he was saying, not that Steve was buying into it yet. If ever.

"I know it's true," Prester said, "because I'm a part of it."

Steve's face must have shown his disbelief.

Prester said, "I'm not raving, dammit! This is not the delirium of a dying man. I'm dying, but I'm not delirious."

"I believe you." That much of it was true. Steve did believe him, when he said he was not delirious. Prester was clear, lucid, in possession of his wits.

That didn't mean the rest of his story was true, though.

Prester said, "I told you I don't have much time

left. Maybe not even enough to get it all in. Which would be too bad for you. You need to know this if you want to live."

Steve said, "Go ahead. I'm listening."

# Seventeen

The Dog Team was deactivated around 1965, even before the Vietnam War had really gotten rolling. It had been in existence for close to twenty years. There may have been other outfits of a similar nature in existence in the past, maybe even all the way back to the Civil War, maybe even dating back to the founding of the Republic. Indeed, it seemed likely that given the nature of the American experience, and human nature, the Dog Team or something like it must have extant since Colonial days and the Revolutionary War.

But the Dog Team in its midtwentieth-century incarnation had begun in the post–World War II era. By 1965, the Dog Team had become too hot to handle.

The Dogs did assassinations in all kinds of places, including friendly and allied countries and neutral ones. Needful work, those liquidations, but it would have created an international scandal and a super propaganda defeat if it could be proven that an arm of the U.S. military had been carrying out

killings in other countries, no matter how much
those who got shot needed killing to promote vital
national security interests.

There was more, and worse, from a public-relations
standpoint. The Dogs carried out certain domestic
ops as well. Military hitters terminated men—and
sometimes women—on U.S. soil. They were nicely
motivated, those executions, but try telling that to
headline-hunting media and political types.

The Dogs were the last resort in certain ultrasen-
sitive spy cases, cases that couldn't be officially pros-
ecuted without risking the exposure of vital
information, such as the identities of double agents;
deep-cover penetration agents; contacts in foreign
embassies; or consular, diplomatic, or foreign military sources. Better that such cases never came to
trial.

But malefactors and traitors could not be allowed
to continue their subversive work, could not be allowed to go unpunished. That ultimate sanction of
termination was reserved only for U.S. citizens or na-
tionals who had turned traitor. Foreign spies were
different. There was a protocol worked out between
the professionals, a balance of terror. Kill foreign
spies in your country, and the offended sponsoring
nation kills your spies in its country. Bodies start
piling up fast. It's wasteful and bad for morale. After
all, despite the business of "if you're caught, the government will deny all knowledge of your activities"
notwithstanding, spies expect to be imprisoned if
captured for eventual exchange with the captured
spies of other nations.

But your own traitors, you have a right to kill. A duty,
some might argue. The Dog Team's domestic assas-

sinations were a potential political land mine in the context of the escalation of the Vietnam War and the corresponding rise of domestic antiwar protest groups. The coalition between business, government, and the military that had been spawned by World War II was starting to come undone in the Sixties.

There are secrets, and then there are secrets. The Dog Team's existence was a real secret closely held within the ranks of the Army and jealously guarded from other branches of the service. Not that there wasn't some overlap. Informal alliances between Army and Air Force elements allowed the Dog Team to carry out occasional assignments for the USAF. Similarly, the Navy had an apparatus similar to the Dogs, in their case staffed mostly by Marine Corps action operatives.

Army top brass broke up the Dogs, hid their traces as best they could, and hoped like hell that nobody would blab to Congress and the media. But even while the Army's premier assassination arm was being put down, the Vietnam War underlined the need for just such a clandestine assassination capacity.

Elements and concepts from the original Dog Team were put into practice during the Army/CIA counterinsurgency Phoenix Program, part of which included targeted assassinations of suspected members, enablers, and sympahtizers of the Viet Cong infrastructure. The killings were often the product of CIA and Army Special Forces teams working together in conjunction with members of the government of South Vietnam. Phoenix was carried out and nobody ever went before a congressional investigating committee or went to jail because of it.

Its existence was an open secret for those who knew where to look.

The Dog Team apparatus lay in limbo for over sixteen years, from 1965 to 1981, though the Army had never lacked the ability to carry out targeted assassinations of deserving individuals. The capacity was always there, under different names and places. But it lacked the well-organized, efficient, smoothly relentless efficiency of the original Dogs.

The present-day Dog Team was first reactivated by secret order of President Ronald Reagan during his first term, prompted by the terrorist group Hezbollah's bombing of the Marines barracks in Beirut, Lebanon, and the kidnapping of that city's CIA station chief and his subsequent torture, brainwashing, and execution.

The organizational infrastructure of the new apparat was conceived by CIA Director William Casey and a cadre of clandestine ops Army Intelligence officers. The secret was closely held by Casey and a handful of trusted associates who insulated the project from the rest of the CIA. The eccentric but canny Casey well knew that the agency had been penetrated and compromised during the years of post-Watergate drift and official sanctimoniousness.

Onetime OSS operative Casey used the big-business expertise that had earned him a fortune on Wall Street to establish a Dog Team entity that was an off-the-shelf, privately funded, self-sustaining enterprise.

Casey worked with several like-minded patriotic plutocrats to endow a private foundation that existed solely to provide continuing funding for the new Dog Team's ongoing operational expenses. A proprietary company was set up: the Mercury Transport

System. It, in turn, was controlled by a holding company that was chartered via a Cayman Islands offshore-banking-type deal.

Casey had compartmentalized and insulated the Dog Team apparatus in a way that would drive potential investigators crazy, should any such appear. Tracing the Dog Team through its different financial and corporate entities would be like peeling an onion, revealing layers within layers.

Mercury Transport Systems held some contracts with ultrasecret military and civilian intelligence agencies and departments. It had a platinum-level security clearance. Its cloudy no-bid military and intelligence business contracts enveloped it in secrecy, fending off casual investigation. It was so entangled in hush-hush trappings that those few key legislators who were aware of its existence were too hampered by security conditions or clearances to probe it. Congressional investigating committees and their permanent staffs and high-maintenance solons would have to hunt for publicity somewhere else.

Besides, for the really investigation minded, for those few who couldn't be diverted by appeals to their patriotism or self-interest or both, probing Dog Team doings could be unhealthy, if not downright fatal.

The Dog Team had been in operation ever since. Personality profiles of all Army recruits and personnel were scrutinized and computer analyzed for qualified candidates. An informal but extensive network of active-duty and officially retired Army personnel existed throughout the land, its members keeping an eye out for the rare personalities who would make first-rate Dog Team assassins.

That's how Joe Kilroy had made the team. Born Sam Chambers, he was the bastard son of Terry Kovak, the top assassin of the original Dogs. Heredity alone argued that he was a candidate to watch. The youth took to Army life like a duck to water, and took to the Dog Team track even better.

Dog work took a special breed, even among the highly motivated achievers who volunteer for Rangers, Delta Force, Special Forces, and suchlike elite military outfits. Psychologically, snipers came the closest to the Dog Team optimum personality profile. Candidates must be self-starters and be self-directed, able to work alone behind enemy lines for long periods of time.

But a Dog's tasks could be more hands on than those of the sniper. Sometimes the target was taken out at a distance by a high-powered scoped rifle, all clean and clinical, but other times, the action got a whole lot wetter. A Dog might have to shoot his man (or woman) at point-blank range, run them over with a car, stab them with an ice pick, throw a victim off a roof or out a window or in front of a speeding train, or dispatch them in any one of a number of lethal ways. These skills were needed now more than ever as the curtain rose on the War on Terror, a show that was destined to be a long running one.

All this was ancient history to Steve Ireland, Prester knew, and he disposed of it in a few sentences to bring him up to speed. The Dog Team was real, it was a clandestine Army assassination unit, and it was up and running today, in Iraq and elsewhere. That was all Steve needed to know for now. If he lived, he'd find out the details, the nuts and bolts of the organization.

Now, Prester told where he came in. "I'm Army," he said. "Always have been. I was officially separated from the service twenty years ago, but that was part of my cover for when I joined the CIA. I was part of a Dog Team intelligence component running a long-term penetration project. Our mission was to penetrate rival intelligence agencies, domestic intelligence agencies. We targeted the CIA, FBI, NSA, and the like. Not naval intelligence, though. Those Navy SOBs were too smart to let anyone Army establish more than a liaison role with their outfit. Nobody from the Army could get anywhere in the Navy, and vice versa. They're two separate breeds, like dogs and cats.

"Sorry. I'm rambling."

Steve Ireland wanted to make sure he was getting it right. "You were spying on the CIA?"

Again that thin smile from Prester, thin as a paper cut. "Not I—we. We, the Army. Which includes you. You're Army, too."

"I know it. I know what I am. What you are is what puzzles me."

"It was a natural progression," Prester said. "First, you spy on the spy agencies of hostile nations. Then neutrals, and finally, your own allies. How else are you going to know what they're up to? A nation has to guard itself against its friends as well as its enemies.

"From there, it was only logical to spy on the rival agencies of your own country, even if only as an act of institutional self-defense. The national budget is only so big. It's not the Chinese military or the Pakistani ISI or the Russian army that is in competition for funding with the Department of the Army; it's the CIA, ONI, NSA, and all the other alphabet outfits."

Steve nodded. It wasn't the first time such a thing had happened. When the Office of Strategic Services, or OSS, was formed in World War II, a number of veteran FBI agents quit the Bureau to join up with the new civilian spy outfit. When the war ended and OSS morphed into the Central Intelligence Agency, they moved over to top positions there. But some of them were plants. Their ultimate loyalty lay with legendary Bureau chief J. Edgar Hoover, and as the years turned into decades, they continued to faithfully report to him on Agency doings. That was something Steve Ireland could understand.

"Politics," he said, saying it like it was a dirty word.

Prester was unflinching. "Maybe so, in part. But the project I was in was about more than politics. Bill Casey was worried by what was going on in the CIA. A clique had established itself in the hierarchy, a self-appointed conspiratorial elite whose policies weren't necessarily those reflecting vital national security interests. A secret inner circle.

"Some of it dates back to Vietnam. We know that much. There was a lot of funny business there with Golden Triangle opium warlords flying their product to heroin refiners on CIA-owned airplanes. The Agency's end was used to finance the mountain tribes' war against the Viet Cong. A vital cause paid for by dirty means. With all that drug money flying around, some of it was bound to stick to CIA fingers or wind up in numbered Swiss bank accounts.

"The pattern repeated again during the eighties in Central America. Planes would fly weapons to the Contras and return with their holds loaded with drugs. The trade paid for the weapons but helped fuel the crack epidemic that hit U.S. cities. The war in El Salvador ended, but the trade went on and continues to this day. Those profits were too good to pass up.

"The conspiracy is still going on, stronger than ever. The Clique, that's what we call it. A secret elite group, planted deep in the heart of the agency, complete with its own aims and ambitions that don't include the rest of us.

"There's nothing glamorous about it despite the James Bond trappings. It's like a ring of crooked cops planted in a big-city police department. It's a good place to be to generate real money and covert power."

Steve said, "The same bunch has been around for the last thirty years; they must be getting old or dying out."

"Don't you believe it," Prester said. "The Clique doesn't sit still. They're constantly recruiting new members to replace the old. Senior members may officially retire from CIA, but not from The Clique."

He paused, resting, catching his breath. His head sagged, with his chin resting on his chest. His eyes closed. A wisp of pink froth hung down from the corner of his mouth. Steve Ireland began to fear that Prester had passed out. Or, worse, died. That would be a hell of a note, for him to expire before delivering the punchline.

Steve started to reach out for the other to take hold of his shoulder and gently shake it to see if that would bring him around. Prester's eyes opened, as if he'd sensed the motion. "Drifting . . . sorry," he said. "May not be much time left. What I've told you is the result of two decades of work—mine, and a lot of other people, some of whom were murdered by The Clique along the way.

"Here's where the modern era comes in. Iraq now is where the action is—where the money is. Billions of dollars are being pumped into the country to handle every aspect of rebuilding and reconstruction. For everything to supplying the troops with privately contracted mess halls and PXs, to massive construction projects, to training and equipping the newly created Iraqi police and national guard units.

"It's a big job, with a price tag to match. All those billions floating around, and not much accountability—hell, the now-defunct Coalition Provisional Authority has roughly ten billion in expenses that can't be accounted for—The Clique's going to be here. There are all kinds of opportunities to make money, including dealing with insurgents and foreign fighters.

"Counterintelligence is a two-way street. While we were trying to penetrate The Clique, they were trying to penetrate us. They're particularly interested in the Dog Team. Not only is it a potential lethal threat to them, it's also an opportunity. They're itching to get their hooks into the Dogs, to get some kind of leverage over them, and by extension over the Army."

Steve said, "What is this Clique? A global dope ring with pretensions, or one of those New World Order things?"

"Maybe both or neither. I don't know. I wish I did," Prester said feelingly. "It's too late for me to find out. Maybe you will. But I can tell you what they were doing here in Azif. They were doing deals with the

Iranians. Debbie Lynn Hawley was the spotter. She's the expert on the Razeem process, and which Iraqi scientists have the know-how to deliver on the electron coupler. She put the finger on the scientists for Akkad's kidnap gang. Her access to intelligence records allowed her to detail the location, routine, and security precautions of each victim to Akkad.

"She's good. She was a suspect, but never a serious one. I didn't know it was her until she shot me. Now I'm able to put it all together. Debbie Lynn Hawley is the traitor. Kill her if you can. Get word to Kilroy or Vang Bulo."

Steve said, "Why me?"

"It has to be you. You're the last man standing. I can't do it. I'm dead," Prester said. Then he was. Dead, that is. It was like the clockwork mechanism keeping him going had finally run down. He just stopped. He was motionless, eyes open.

Steve reached out, touching the other's neck, feeling for a pulse, knowing it was futile. There was no pulse. Prester had withdrawn from the field. Steve sighed, letting out the breath he'd been holding. He closed Prester's eyes.

Practical considerations of a survival-related nature returned almost immediately, shattering the somber mood. There was a job to be done. Steve would do what it took to get that job done. He began searching Prester's pockets, seeking he knew not what. Anything he could use: weapons, ammo, a communicator, ID, documents. Whatever.

A voice from behind him said, "Freeze."

# Eighteen

Debbie Lynn Hawley said, "Toss the gun. Not drop—toss. Toss it away from you, and do it now. Do it!"

Steve Ireland did it, slinging the pistol away from him. It fell on its side in a dirt pile. Debbie Lynn had the drop on him, and he couldn't beat that. Obedience would buy him a little more time.

"Okay, you can turn around now. Slowly, and with your hands held away from your sides," she said. "And no tricks."

He rose from where he'd been kneeling beside Prester, turning to face her. Debbie Lynn Hawley stood facing him about fifteen feet away, holding a gun leveled at him. Her weapon was a 9-mm Beretta semiautomatic pistol.

Some of the shine had rubbed off her. She'd been shot in the calf muscle of her right leg. She'd taken off her top and shredded it into strips that she'd used as makeshift bandages, binding up the wounded area of her leg. The wrappings were bloodstained.

She was naked from the waist up, under a flak

jacket. Even under the circumstances, Steve couldn't help but check her out. He had to admit she looked pretty good, even after the mussing up she'd taken. You would never figure her for a traitor and mass murderer. More proof, as if any were needed, that appearances can be deceiving.

She'd pressed a dead tree branch into service as a kind of a crutch. It had a Y-shaped yoke and a long, thick shaft. The yoke was wedged under her right arm, propping her up, supporting her on her right side. Her wounded leg was bent at the knee and she was favoring it, using the crutch to try and keep as much weight off it as she could. She held the gun in her left hand, holding it close to her, with her elbow at her side. Debbie Lynn was dirty and disheveled. She was hurting. Her fine-boned, elfin face showed the effects of the pain; she looked ten years older. Her teeth were clenched. Her hand on the gun was steady enough, though.

She shook her head in disbelief and said, "Man, you're hard to kill. I didn't think any of you soldier boys had survived the blast." She gestured toward Prester. "He was hard to kill, too. It was all that alcohol swilling and that lounge lizard act he put on. It was all a pose, but it fooled me. When the showdown came, he moved a lot faster than I'd expected."

"Why tell me?" asked Steve.

"Maybe I like a chance to gloat and show off how smart I am," she said. "Usually I have to hide my light under a bushel."

"Where'd you hide the bomb?"

She laughed, showing fine white teeth. They looked especially bright against her begrimed face.

"I didn't hide it at all," she said. "The Pasdaran did. That's the Iranian secret service to you, G.I."

"Where do they come in?"

"Your team hit the farmhouse and closed down the brain-drain pipeline. That's reason enough for them to want revenge. And Prester and a couple of his associates put a big hurting on Tehran when they whacked Colonel Munghal."

"Tough."

"Times are hard all over," she said brightly. "Pasdaran agents rigged the site last night, planting a shit-load of explosives all over the place. What with the tanks and pools and whatnot, there were so many places to hide a bomb that nobody could find them all.

"You didn't," she added, laughing. Her laughter was thin and trilling, like a fragment of warbling bird song.

Steve didn't kid himself. His chances looked bad—in fact, virtually nil. There was his knife, but she'd gun him before he drew it from the sheath. He wondered if he could catch a couple of slugs and still tag her with a thrown knife. Maybe, if he didn't catch one in the head.

He said, "Tell me one thing. Why do you do it? Is it the money?"

"It helps," she admitted. "But that's not the real reason."

"Which is?"

"You might say I'm in with the in crowd."

"That's not how I'd say it, but let it pass. Who are they?"

"Idealists," said Debbie Lynn Hawley.

Steve Ireland laughed out loud.

She didn't like being laughed at. Her face flushed and her eyes hardened. "Peasants always laugh at what they don't understand," she said.

He said, "I'm willing to give it a try."

"You just want to stay alive a little longer."

"Sure."

"See if you can wrap your caveman brain around this. The age of the nation-state is over."

Steve tried to keep from smirking. "That'll come as a big surprise to a lot of people."

"So did Nine Eleven," she countered. "Patriotism is obsolete. It's an outmoded concept. Capital knows no boundaries and floats freely around the globe to seek its own level. The new lords are those who've absorbed this simple fact and act upon it."

Steve scoffed. "Sounds like some of that New World Order doubletalk to me."

"Never mind the labels," Debbie Lynn said. "It's all about the Golden Rule. He who has the gold, rules. You flag-waving, nationalistic nitwits are obsolete. You're dinosaurs. And you know what happened to the dinosaurs, don't you, soldier boy?"

Her face was set in hard lines, and her eyes were glittering slits. She liked to talk. Steve Ireland had traded on that to eke out a few more precious moments of life. But one thing was clear. As much as she liked to talk, Debbie Lynn liked to kill even better.

"The dinosaurs are extinct," she said, answering her own question. She raised the gun, pointing it at his face. "So are you," she said.

A shot was fired, but not from Debbie Lynn's gun.

It cut her homemade crutch in two. She'd been leaning on it heavily, putting plenty of weight on it.

Now, with that support cut out from her, she folded up and dropped.

Her face showed surprise, eyebrows arching and mouth compressed to a tight wondering O. That lasted until she hit the ground, reinjuring her wounded leg. She shrieked, a keening puma cry.

Throughout she'd kept hold of her gun. She flopped on the ground and started shooting. Pain sent a wash of tears flooding her eyes, obscuring her vision. She was firing blind, pumping slugs in the direction where she had last seen Steve.

He wasn't there, having already thrown himself to one side. Debbie Lynn rose, standing on her knees, still shooting. Steve had hit the ground and came up rolling, drawing the knife from its sheath and throwing it at her. A glinting pinwheel, it came to rest point-first deep in the middle of her throat. If she'd been a man, it would have split her Adam's apple.

Debbie Lynn stopped shooting. She held herself very stiffly. Her head bowed, dipping, only it couldn't sink too low because the underside of her chin bumped up against the knife. Her lips parted, blood spilling from her mouth and splashing her chin. She fell forward, face down. Her weight pushed the blade deeper into her throat, so that the point of it came out the back of her neck. Not so much as a twitch or a tremor from her. She was gone.

Steve Ireland looked at his hands. He was surprised that he'd managed to hit the target, they were shaking so. He still managed to scoop up Prester's pistol with them.

A figure showed in the middle ground of the battered hillside. Kilroy. He stood holding a rifle, an AK-47 with a wisp of smoke curling from the barrel. He nodded companionably at Steve and started toward him.

He went to where Debbie Lynn Hawley lay face down. He glanced at the knife point sticking out of the back of her neck, favoring it with a little, appreciative nod, as if to say, Well done!

"Nice blade work. Like I said, you've got talent," said Kilroy.

"Thanks," Steve said. "I couldn't have done it without you."

"That you couldn't, son, and I'm glad you've got sense enough to realize it. You owe me big."

"I'm sure you won't be shy about collecting on it."

"I surely won't, and that's a fact."

Steve said, "Too bad you didn't get here sooner."

"Not necessarily. Then I might've got blowed up, too," Kilroy said. "Prester had me checking out a couple of leads for him. The tip about the pumphouse seemed too pat and he wanted me to crosscheck some of the informants. Never did get anything definite nailed down either way."

He looked around. "Well, we know now."

Kilroy turned his attention to Prester. His smile faded, his face becoming stiff and inexpressive. His gaze was not untouched by regret, even sorrow. "He always said that Debbie Lynn would be the death of him. He was joking then, or so I thought. Otherwise, why would he have married her?"

Steve was taken aback. "They were husband and wife?"

"That's right," Kilroy said. "What's more natural than for a middle-aged man to fall for a young cupcake? Oldest story in the world. Only this one had a twist. The marriage was all in the line of duty, of course. For him and her. They got married because that way it was easier for each of them to keep an eye on the other. They were both CIA. She kept her maiden name for professional purposes. It suited the agency to have a married couple who could be single when they had to be."

Steve sighed. "A deep game. And a dirty one."

"Like the man said, You ain't seen nothing yet."

"I'd prefer not to."

"Amen to that, brother."

A thought struck Steve Ireland, lighting fires behind his hooded gaze. He stroked his square chin thoughtfully. He said, "That was some shot you made, shooting her crutch out from under her."

Kilroy shrugged with affected modesty. "Shucks."

Steve seethed. "Don't country boy me! If you hit the crutch, you damned well could have hit her. If you didn't, it's because you didn't want to. You didn't want to kill her. You wanted me to kill her."

Kilroy's bland assurance was untouched. "What're you kicking about? She needed killing."

Steve said, "She could have killed me! If that knife missed—"

"But it didn't. Anyhow, I had the whole thing covered. If you were unable to handle her, I'd have finished her off. I just wanted to see what you had, if you had a little something extra on the ball. Which you did. 'Nuff said."

"You bastard!"

"How true." Kilroy's smile was lopsided. "Well, that's enough backchat. Let's get back to work."

"Doing what?" Steve demanded.

"Putting on the finishing touches."

"Such as?"

"Your knife is stuck in the throat of a high-ranking CIA operative," Kilroy pointed out in a conversational tone. "You just might want to get it out of there, especially since it's got your fingerprints on it. I know she had it coming, and you know she had it coming, but Langley might not see it like that."

Steve Ireland went to the body. He stood there looking down at her, not moving.

Kilroy's smile was gentle, mocking. "Squeamish?"

The other's jaw muscles flexed. He crouched down beside the body, flipped it over and pulled out his knife. "You're playing a deep game, Kilroy."

"You, too."

Steve shook his head. "I'm just a soldier trying to do his duty."

"Me, too. And him," he said, indicating Prester.

"We'll take Prester out of here. It'll confuse the opposition if they don't know what really happened to him, if he's dead or alive, and if he's alive, if he was captured by the insurgents, defected to the Iranians, fled to parts unknown, or what," said Kilroy.

Steve looked at him from the corner of his eye. "Like the old joke says, What do you mean 'we,' kemo sabe?"

Kilroy said, "You're Army, ain't you?"

"I am, yes. But what are you?"

"I'm Army, too. And as a matter of fact, I outrank you."

Steve grimaced. "Pulling rank is the one thing you could have done to convince me that you are Army."

"A big strong young fellow like you should be able to haul Prester out of here without any trouble."

"That an order?"

"Well, yes, if you want to get technical about it," Kilroy said.

Steve hefted Prester's body in a fireman's carry, slinging it across his back. The body was still warm, which he found somewhat unnerving. It was heavy, too. The weight began to oppress him as he stood in the morning sun, waiting for Kilroy to finish searching Debbie Lynn's body.

"Nothing," Kilroy announced, straightening up. "I didn't expect to find anything incriminating. She was too slick for that. We'll take her credentials and ID for future reference, though."

Steve asked, "What about her?"

Kilroy said, "What do you mean, what about her?"

"What're we going to do about the body?"

"Not a damned thing. Leave it for the birds. If they'll have her."

They started downhill, skirting the areas torn up by the bomb. Kilroy said, "A tough fight, but we won."

"Who won? The Army or the Dog Team?" Steve was breathing hard from the exertion and the macabre sensation of toting a corpse.

Kilroy cut him a sidelong glance. "Prester did some talking before he died. How much do you know?"

Steve said, "Plenty. What're you going to do, kill me to keep from talking?"

"You won't talk."

"What makes you think so?"

"Hey, cousin, you killed Debbie Lynn. What do you think those CIA black-ops guys would do to you if they found out? They don't know she was a traitor, and there's no hard evidence that proves she was."

"I'm not worried," Steve said. "You won't talk, either."

Kilroy beamed. "See? We understand each other already."

"How far am I going to have to carry the body?" asked Steve.

"Not far," Kilroy said. "Just to the bottom of the hill. My buddy is waiting there with our ride."

A tan SUV sat in the hollow, Vang Bulo standing beside it, watching them descend the slope. Kilroy said, "You're a lucky man, Irish."

"How do you figure?"

"What else can happen to you? You're already dead."

Steve eyed him suspiciously, wondering what he was getting at. "In case you hadn't noticed, Kilroy, I'm still here, and very much alive. Sorry if that upsets your plans."

"It might upset your plans more. You see, you died up there on that hill with the rest of ODA 586. That's how the record will read. You'll be marked down as killed in action in the files. Steve Ireland ends here."

Steve stopped in his tracks. "What're you trying to pull?"

"Don't worry, you'll be fixed up with a new identity," Kilroy said. "Didn't you ever want a job that took you to faraway places to meet exotic people—to kill them?"

Steve said, "I have that job—Special Forces."

Kilroy waved his hand, as if brushing away the

other's objections. "Never mind about that. You just graduated to the big time."

"Meaning the Dog Team?"

"I'd say you have every qualification."

Steve would have shaken his head if Prester's body hadn't been in the way. Hard jawed, he said, "Don't mistake luck for skill. It was just blind chance that kept me from getting caught in the blast with the others. Luck of the draw. It could have been anyone on the team, it just happened to be me."

"You know what Napoleon said: 'Find me the generals that are lucky,'" Kilroy reminded him.

"I'm no general," Steve said.

"No, and you're not going to be. Guys like us don't make general. We're field men—specialists— and you don't make the top rank that way."

"I'm not like you, Kilroy."

"Nobody's perfect. But like I said, you've got talent."

"I can see how the Dog Team got its name, if the others are anything like you," Steve Ireland said, "because mister, in my book you're a real, gold-plated son of a—"

"Don't say it." Kilroy wagged a finger in the other's face. "That'd be insubordination."

Steve resumed the descent, muttering under his breath. The sooner he was rid of his burden, the better. The burden of Prester's corpse, that is. The burden of Kilroy's influence, he suspected, would not be so easily shed.

The slope leveled out into the bowl. They crossed to Vang Bulo and the SUV. The Ugandan reached out with a terrible gentleness, helping to load Prester's body into the back of the vehicle. Up front, the radio was on. It was a scanner designed to carry military and police wavebands. The speaker squawked noisily, detailing an armed clash that had broken out in Azif when a Sunni mob had tried to cross the Coalition's protective cordon around the Shiite quarter of the town.

Steve Ireland said, "Sounds like a hot one. It could break out into a local civil and religious war at any moment."

Kilroy nodded. "That's one thing about being in the Dog Team—you never lack for work." His eyes got a faraway look.

So many foes, so few bullets . . . The Dog Team will return!

# THE CODE NAME SERIES BY
# WILLIAM W. JOHNSTONE

### *Available Wherever Books Are Sold!*

Visit our website at **www.kensingtonbooks.com**

# BOOK YOUR PLACE ON OUR WEBSITE AND MAKE THE READING CONNECTION!

We've created a customized website just for our very special readers, where you can get the inside scoop on everything that's going on with Zebra, Pinnacle and Kensington books.

When you come online, you'll have the exciting opportunity to:

- View covers of upcoming books
- Read sample chapters
- Learn about our future publishing schedule (listed by publication month *and author*)
- Find out when your favorite authors will be visiting a city near you
- Search for and order backlist books from our online catalog
- Check out author bios and background information
- Send e-mail to your favorite authors
- Meet the Kensington staff online
- Join us in weekly chats with authors, readers and other guests
- Get writing guidelines
- AND MUCH MORE!

**Visit our website at
http://www.kensingtonbooks.com**